FIRE

A. M. ROSE

Fire© by A. M. Rose

All rights reserved.
No part of this book may be used or reproduced in any manner without written permission, except in the case
of brief quotations embodied in critical articles or reviews.

This book is a work of fiction.
Names, characters, businesses, organizations, places, events, and incidents
are either the product of the authors' imagination or are used fictitiously.
Any resemblance to actual persons, living or dead, events or locales is
entirely coincidental.

Editing done by LesCourt© services

Proofreading done by Kate Wood Proofreading©

Cover designed by BCJ Art & Design©
*"This work by BCJ Art & Design is licensed under a Creative Commons
Attribution-NonCommercial-NoDerivatives 4.0 International License."*

BLURB

Fire is a racing prodigy. Well on his way to stand shoulder to shoulder with the best ones in history. His expectations of the new season were to train, race and win, not to nosedive into the ground and injure his wing.

Forced to miss the rest of the season, he's sent to schmooze with the rich and famous to stay in the limelight and keep the attention on himself. So he schmoozes. And wishes he could be literally anywhere else.

Until he walks in.

Nose in the air, disdain on his face, and secrets wrapped around him like an expensive suit.

Just figures Fire's mate would be the most pompous little brat ever.

On the plus side, riling him up should be fun, right?

Rio is a priority. He's the main character. It's what he's used to and he will settle for nothing less than red carpets softening his every step.

He lives for the attention and drama, dreaming of a mate who will understand that Rio's taste is impeccable and he just knows best.

Enter his mate.

Who disagrees with Rio every step of the way, makes him question everything he thought he knew about himself, but most of all, makes all the skeletons from his past resurface

So why doesn't Rio mind it as much as he probably should?

CONTENTS

1. Fire — 1
2. Rio — 7
3. Fire — 18
4. Rio — 29
5. Fire — 38
6. Rio — 51
7. Rio — 59
8. Fire — 71
9. Rio — 81
10. Fire — 95
11. Fire — 106
12. Rio — 113
13. Fire — 128
14. Rio — 140
15. Fire — 152
16. Fire — 166
17. Rio — 179
18. Fire — 194
19. Rio — 209
20. Fire — 220
21. Rio — 236

Epilogue	247
Bond	253
Also By A. M. Rose	262

CHAPTER ONE

FIRE

Well, this was boring.

Fire looked around the room, the stiff suit they'd wrapped him up in pinching in all the wrong places. He was at a charity event of some sort, having been forced into it by his managing company stating "it'd be good for him" to show up places while his wing healed enough to get back to racing.

It was an event to raise money for a school in a remote area, and while it was all geared toward helping children, Fire saw zero children around the richly decorated room. He was good with kids. He had siblings with children of their own, and he liked spending time with them.

What he wasn't good at? Schmoozing with the rich and powerful, ass-kissing, and fake-smiling until they realized they didn't actually need the third country house and could donate the money to a good cause.

Sadly for him, the room was filled with those people. Expensive suits, bejeweled wings, and itty-bitty little finger foods that just yearned for a trip to a burger joint outside his building once he was done for the evening.

"Not your idea of a good time?" An amused voice came from his right.

He turned, finding himself face to face with a mountain of a man. He had long hair and russet wings with leather detailing on a few feathers.

"Is it anyone's?" Fire asked, and the man laughed, free and loud.

"Not sure about everyone else, but I'm with you," the man said. "Duty calls, though."

"You working?" Fire asked.

The man nodded, pointing into the thick of the crowd, where the esteemed Council Leader, Kiran Castillo, was chatting with some equally important-looking people.

"Security." He extended his hand to Fire. "Arne. Miller."

"Fire," he said, shaking his hand.

"Oh, I know," Arne said, smiling. Fire's hackles rose just a bit before Arne spoke again. "My mate is a huge fan but was too shy to come say hi, so I said I'd talk to you first and call him over if you weren't a dick."

Fire snorted at that, relieved Arne wasn't there to talk about his injury or ask for an exclusive.

"I'd say I'm averagely dick-ish but able to tone it down as needed," Fire said with a smile. "You can call him over. Promise I won't bite or anything."

Arne stretched up and waved over people's heads. Fire watched as a gorgeous blond made his way over to them, dark green suit hugging his lithe body and mesmerizing watercolor wings spread behind him in a swoop of fluffy feathers.

"Um…"

"His wings get that reaction a lot," Arne said just as his mate approached them and cuddled up against his chest. "Hi, angel."

"Hi," a soft voice greeted him. Fire smiled at the way he was staring at him—awestruck, but too shy to say anything.

"Hey." Fire extended his hand toward him. "I'm Fire, and I just met your mate here."

The blond took his fingers gently and gave them a squeeze before pulling his hand back, a blush high on his cheeks.

"Levi," he said. "I'm a huge fan of yours."

"I'm very glad to hear that," Fire said, reaching behind himself to set his empty glass down. "Sorry about missing all the races this season."

"Oh, no," Levi said, shaking his head. "Just focus on getting better. There's always next season, and pushing yourself only makes it worse. Wing injuries are no joke."

Fire looked at his unique wings and upon further inspection found a few bald spots where there were no feathers. It didn't make them any less beautiful, but they spoke of a past injury. Levi brought his wings closer to his body, and Fire averted his eyes from them to avoid making him uncomfortable.

"No, they're not," he said with a shrug. "But they are in the job description, sadly."

"So how did you get roped into snooze-fest extravaganza?" Arne asked, and Levi smacked his chest, looking up at him with a cute frown on his face.

"Arne!" he hissed. "Someone is gonna hear."

"Yeah, well, that's the idea, angel," Arne said. "Someone might hear, and they might actually do something about it."

"I think they're doing it on purpose," Fire said. "They make it so boring that you pay just to get out of here."

Arne grinned at him, squeezing Levi's waist teasingly. "See! He agrees with me. It's boring."

"I never said it wasn't," Levi whispered through clenched teeth and a fake-looking smile. "Just that you shouldn't say it out loud."

That got a chuckle out of Fire, and he waved the bartender down, ordering another drink.

"Do you two want anything?" he asked, and Arne shook his head.

"Can't really drink on the clock," he said, nudging Levi. "You want another cherry liqueur, angel?"

Levi's eyes lit up, disgruntlement forgotten. "Yes, please."

Fire ordered one for him and his own whiskey. The bartender placed his drink on a small coaster in front of him and the cherry liqueur in an ornate-looking shot glass that made Levi gasp.

"Pretty," he murmured as he lifted it up and downed the sip of drink in it, cradling the glass to him and looking up at Arne.

"I don't think you can keep that, love," Arne said with a laugh.

"But I really like it," Levi said, almost on the verge of pouting.

Fire laughed with Arne, pulling a marker from the inside of his suit jacket and reaching for the glass. "Hand it over."

Levi gave it to him, and Fire turned the glass around, scribbling his messy signature on the flat underside of it. He waved the bartender over and showed him the glass.

"Do you mind, man?" he asked. "I have nothing else to sign for a fan."

"Go crazy, mate," the bartender said, shrugging. "We have more than enough."

He walked away, and Fire handed the glass back to Levi.

"There, you can keep that now," he said, and Levi beamed at Arne, feathers preening and fluffing up in his excitement. He looked like an extremely pretty toilet brush.

Levi wiggled his way out of Arne's arms. "Gonna show Jude."

Arne watched after him like a hawk as he made his way through the crowd to stand next to the Council Leader's human mate, Jude Hayes.

"He's sweet," Fire said, and Arne scowled at him, half-jokingly, but half looking like he'd be willing to tear his limbs off. "In a completely platonic, not-trying-to-make-a-move-on-your-mate way. Promise."

"Good," Arne said, more like a grunt. "I like you. I'd hate to have to do bad things to you."

"I mean..." Fire drawled with a silly smile. "You're a hot dude, and bad things can be fun."

Arne threw his head back and laughed. "I doubt your mate would like it."

"Not mated yet." Fire shrugged. "But looking forward to it. You and Levi seem really happy."

"We are," Arne said, looking toward his mate with a smile on his face that felt warm and intimate in a way few things ever did. "Took some work, but it was more than worth it. I'm sure yours will appear soon."

Arne clapped his shoulder just as a commotion picked up toward the entrance, and the guard straightened up, looking toward his charge.

"Break is over," Arne said, all signs of humor disappearing. "Good luck with your recovery, man. And thank you for the autograph and the glass. You made his night."

"My pleasure," Fire said. "See you around."

He watched Arne make his way to the Council Leader, several guards standing alert around him and his mate as the ruckus at the entrance gained more traction.

Fire saw cameras flashing in that direction and people gathering to watch as the doors to the large ballroom slid open and a figure flanked by several guards from a different security company waltzed in.

The figure was lithe and tall. He had a straight-tipped nose that was haughtily thrust in the air and arched cheekbones that begged for exploration along the ridges. His lips were the softest part of his face, a perfect cupid's bow topping them like a present for whoever was lucky enough to taste them. Dark brown hair had been slicked and brushed to the side over his head. Not a strand was out of place, and while it looked stylish, Fire doubted it was comfortable to have it that gelled down.

The man was dressed in a salmon-colored blazer with black lapels and buttons, a neckerchief secured around his neck in place of a formal tie. His long legs were encased in tight black slacks, and his loafers were shined to perfection.

The most stunning thing about him, though, was his wings. Dark pink and almost gauzy-looking, swooping high above his head. A cascade of black-and-pink pearls fell down to his waist and gleamed in the light, reflecting the shimmers of his feathers.

He smiled to the gathered crowd, offering an elegant hand for the people to shake before walking away, gliding on the marble floors like a shadow.

Fire had never seen anyone so beautiful. And so out of touch with everyone and everything around him. It felt like he wasn't even the same species as the rest of the attendees.

Fire felt his heart thundering in his chest, and the heat in the room amped up until he was convinced he'd suffocate in his suit. Something was pulling at his insides, making him yearn to go over and push everyone else to the side.

He wanted to march over to the beautiful stranger, take that hand in his, and never let go. He wanted to sequester him away from prying eyes and take that suit off his body. He wanted to see him covered in just those black-and-pink pearls as he lay bare beneath him. He wanted to hear him moan and beg, and he wanted that hair messed up from his fingers running through it.

Fire wanted to ruin him.

And as the man swept the room to make sure everyone was looking at him, Fire caught eyes with beautiful chocolate-colored ones for a single second and knew...

The poshest, most pompous, most beautiful man he had ever come across...was his damn mate.

Figured.

CHAPTER TWO

RIO

He loved a good entrance. He relished adoring looks and gasps of admiration thrown his way, and he enjoyed knowing every person in the room wished they were him. Well, except the ones who wanted to do him, but that was a completely separate category he didn't have the time or the will to get into. It helped that Kalie, his best friend, wasn't present too. Much as he missed her company, he liked not splitting attention with her even more. Sue him. He loved the spotlight.

His dress heels clicked on the marble floor, and he lowered his lashes, lip curling and a breath escaping as he realized there was no red carpet. He found that unacceptable for an event of that caliber and his acceptance of their invitation. He didn't attend a lot of these galas, so he reasoned whoever was organizing it should have adequately prepared for his arrival.

An email of complaint was already forming in his mind, one he'd sign with his black signature and zero sparkles in the design. He felt like that conveyed how serious he was and how much whoever received the email had messed up. His pink signature was for praise, and this did not earn it in the slightest.

"Mr. Charmichael!" someone called from his left, and he turned around to find one of his grandmother's friends stuffed into a red dress so tight, he swore he could hear the seams screaming with the effort to keep it on her body. Funny how her sense of fashion reared its ugly head only when it came to *his* choices of outfits.

Her puffy, bottle-orange hair was styled in a dated-looking hive on her head, and the makeup made her look about fifteen years older than she was. And she was already ancient as it was.

He forced his best fake smile to stretch his lips and nodded at the woman, extending his hand to her.

"Mrs. Avery, lovely to see you," he said, voice dripping with sweetness he absolutely didn't feel. She pushed her hand up, still clutching his, almost forcing him to kiss the top of her hand.

"Are you here by yourself, love?" she asked, the pet name doing nothing to disguise the contention in her voice. She was as fake as the diamonds dangling from her ears.

"Yes," he said politely. "My evening schedule cleared unexpectedly, so I decided to join the party for a while."

"Lovely of you," she said, peering around him, scowling at the sight of his wings. "My, that must be heavy to wear."

He smiled and fluffed up his feathers a little bit, the cascade of pearls he was wearing tinkling sweetly.

"I'm used to it," he said. "Expensive jewelry is always heavy and uncomfortable, but so worth it in my opinion. Wouldn't you say?"

She clutched a hand over her cheap necklace.

"Absolutely," she was quick to say.

"I thought you'd agree," he said with a smirk. "It's so easy to tell when it's a knockoff. I never miss it."

She sputtered for a second, and he used that moment to slink away, throwing smiles and haughty stares at people who tripped over themselves to greet him as if they had any interest in him other than his wallet. Which he was willing to open for an event like this, but he was also willing to help make others several thousands lighter before the night was done.

He walked over to a cluster of people gathered around the most prominent Kriila of their time. Council Leader Kiran Castillo.

The man never failed to make a stir, which Rio appreciated. The scandal of his mating to a human was the talk of their social circles and then the fall of the Landon family that followed was almost too outrageous to believe. Apparently, psychosis was a gene that could be passed down. The apple did not fall far from the tree.

The positive outcome of the whole debacle was the emergence of more human and Kriila couples. Finally comfortable enough to step out of the shadows and stand firm. Rio was glad of it even though his own family disapproved vocally. Archaic views would never fully disappear, but Kiran was breaking down a lot of walls, and Rio wanted to support him in the small ways he could.

"Council Leader," Rio greeted politely, turning to the man at his side with a genuine smile. "Mr. Hayes."

"Mr. Charmichael." Kiran grinned, shaking his hand and letting his mate do the same. They'd met at similar events before and exchanged a few words. Enough to be friendly in a setting like that.

"How's the evening going?" he asked, and Kiran shrugged.

"People seem to be more interested in eating and drinking than donating," Kiran said.

"You have to pick your targets right, Council Leader," Rio said with a small smirk, eyeing the room. "Just because someone glitters doesn't mean they're rich. Allow me to help…"

Several names dropped and several checks written, he excused himself from Kiran's company. He exchanged a few words with some people he'd consider friends, dodged a few he'd consider plagues on the world, and then made his way toward the bar. He deemed his socializing sufficient for one evening.

Halfway to the bar, he felt eyes on him.

Not the usual curious, simpering, admiring eyes he was used to, though. No. This felt heavier.

He looked over his shoulder and found nothing of importance. Nobody he hadn't seen already. And yet the feeling persisted. It tickled the back of his neck and made his wings flutter.

It made him want to take off a layer of clothing because it was too stifling. Too much somehow.

He took a few more steps and reached his hand to brace it against the cool surface of the bar, flagging down the waiter and ordering a flute of champagne.

His fingers felt cold enough from the marble, and he lifted them to place them gently over his neck. It felt nice, but it wasn't nearly enough. He took a deep breath through his nose and let it out through his pursed lips. Both his therapist and his yoga instructor would have been proud, had they seen him.

Not that it was helping, but he still drew in another breath.

"Feeling okay?" someone next to him asked just as he was about to exhale, and he turned his head around, forcing the gasp that threatened to tumble out to stay behind his pressed lips. He didn't want to give himself away.

He didn't want to be seen shaken or weak, but this man…

Oh, this man was his.

Out of all the scenarios he'd pictured in his head and all the places he'd imagined meeting his mate, a bar at a boring charity event was the last one he'd expected. And yet he couldn't be mad. Not when he was finally standing in front of him. After all the years of waiting and picturing what it would be like, he was stealing his breath and looking him right in the eyes as he did it.

Rio glanced up and down, dragging his eyes deliberately over the strong figure. He was just slightly taller than him, but broader, sturdier. His messy honey-brown hair didn't look like it came in any other form than windswept, and warm hazel eyes held mischief and joy in them, accentuated even more by the boyish smile stretching his lips. But the most stunning detail on him, the most eye-catching, was his wings.

Fire.

Living, breathing, all-consuming fire.

They were the most vibrant shade of red he'd ever seen, gleaming and shimmering under the lights. They looked larger than most wings, stronger, more agile as they shifted restlessly behind the man.

No, not just any man.

"So..." He gathered his wits and tilted his head in a way he knew made him look attractive. "You're mine."

He had expected the man to swoon. To swoop in and declare his undying love for him. To hop on the bar top and proclaim his happiness at having such a perfect mate to the world.

He did not expect him to quirk an eyebrow at him, smirk, and lift his glass in salute.

"Apparently so," he said, taking a sip before lowering the glass and extending his hand. "Fire."

Miffed, Rio took his hand and gave it a dainty shake. "Your parents named you Fire?"

"My parents named me James," he said with a chuckle. "Yours left you nameless?"

"That would be absurd."

"So..." At Rio's arched brow, Fire seemed to bite down on a noticeable grin. "Are you gonna share?"

"Uxorious Archibald Charmichael III," he said, and the man stared at him for a long moment, eyes wide and jaw slackening before he seemed to shake it off.

"Absolutely figures I'd be mated to an Uxorious," he said. "Mind if I call you Rio?"

"Of course I mind," Rio said, refusing to admit it sounded nice. It sounded like something just between the two of them. Something nobody else could touch. "That's not my name."

"With all due respect, gorgeous, I don't have time to pronounce all of that," Fire said. "And Rio sounds nice, don't you think? It's cute."

"I am not cute," Rio said indignantly.

"Okay," Fire said, moving close enough that they were almost touching, eyes skirting every inch of exposed skin at his waist and chest. "Maybe not cute."

Rio felt an answering shiver rise up to meet that hot gaze.

"Did you come here with anyone?" Fire asked.

Rio turned his gaze to face front, feigning aloofness. "What if I did?"

"Well you'll be leaving with me, so it kinda sucks for them."

Rio swung his head around at the pure confidence in those words. Fire gave him a cocksure smile and picked his glass back up. He took a slow sip, eyes locked on Rio's.

Rio watched his throat work around the amber liquid and felt a spike of heat in his gut. Rio knew the steps to the dance they were engaged in, but it had never felt quite like this before. Never so electric, like the tiniest spark could light him up.

"So sure of yourself," Rio murmured, reaching for Fire's wrist.

He wrapped his long fingers around the thick width, making sure Fire felt every. Single. One. Fire paused, allowing the glass to be guided from his mouth to Rio's, who leaned in dangerously close.

Rio tipped his head back, knowing how he looked, and drained the glass. The burn of the alcohol seared the whole way down, still cooler than the heat of his blood. He let the rim of the glass pull at his lower lip, wetting it before cleaning it up with a quick swipe of his tongue.

Fire eyes were locked on to every movement, pupils blown and dark, and Rio fought off a victorious smile.

"Thanks for the drink," Rio quipped, releasing Fire's wrist and turning to leave.

A hot hand grasped his bare waist, large fingers snaking under the fabric, and a hard body followed, pressing up against his side. Rio's breath hitched.

"That's it?" Fire asked into his ear.

"Maybe that's all I wanted from you?" Rio challenged.

"You haven't even seen half of what I have to give to you, gorgeous."

"Soooo so sure of yourself," he repeated, turning his head to meet Fire's eyes, noses brushing. "But is it justified?"

"Why don't we find out?" Fire asked.

God, but his name suited him perfectly, Rio thought as Fire's lips consumed his. He was holding him up by the hips, Rio's long legs wrapped around him as they kissed.

He could barely believe what he was doing, in public, at a social event. But he couldn't stop. He didn't want to stop when it felt so good.

Fire's lips descended on his neck, and he felt teeth pull at the bow around it.

"Don't ruin it," he panted as his nails looked for purchase on Fire's back, finding fistfuls of feathers and pulling at them desperately.

Fire hissed and backed them both up until Rio was glued to the wall, his wings fluttering for a few moments before tucking back into his back. Rio wanted to protest, but Fire lifted his head up to look into his eyes and smirked.

"I'm clearly doing something wrong if you're still thinking about clothes," he said, and Rio huffed, pushing his fingers into Fire's hair and guiding him back to his neck.

"I'm always thinking about my clothes," he said. "Now shut up and do your job."

Fire chuckled, canting his hips forward and pressing Rio between the wall and his own hardness, making him gasp. It felt so good. Better than anything else ever had, and Rio struggled to keep his voice steady and his eyes steely when all he wanted was to close them and let Fire consume him.

"My job?" Fire asked, tongue sneaking out to lick the shell of Rio's ear. "And what is my job here, gorgeous?"

"Me," Rio said. "I am currently your job, and you're not doing it. At least not right."

"Now that's just mean," Fire said. "You're bruising my ego."

"And you're bruising my back and wrinkling my suit with zero payoff for me," Rio said, unwrapping his legs from Fire's hips and wiggling down until he was standing on his own again.

He stalked forward until he reached the coats hanging on golden hooks and sifted through them.

"Ew." He discarded a black knee-length man's coat and reached for the next one. "No...no...oh, absolutely not."

The pile next to him grew.

"What are you doing?" Fire asked, picking up the coats and hanging them back up, probably on the wrong hooks, but Rio didn't really care enough to correct it.

"Looking for something to put on the floor so we can lie on it," Rio said, throwing another coat on the pile in Fire's arms.

"And this is a procedure that lasts for how long?" Fire asked.

"Until I find something worthy."

"Worthy of what?" Fire asked, and Rio glared at him.

"Of me," he said, discarding the final coat he had to choose from and huffing. "None of these. Change of plans. I'll be on top."

"Oh, really?" Fire asked, voice gravelly as he threw the coats down and wrapped his arms around Rio from behind. "I didn't realize you were the one calling the shots here."

"Then you're incredibly slow," Rio said, reaching back to poke at one of Fire's buttons. "Off, please."

He watched in silent fascination as Fire obeyed him, discarding his blazer and shirt in smooth moves until he was standing in front of him, chest bare and ripped. Those shoulders were so broad.

He ran his fingers over the grooves, satisfied with the ripple in muscle and the goosebumps his touch left in its wake. His mate liked him. Desired him. He felt primal in the knowledge he could make him react that way.

"Like what you see?" Fire asked, and Rio looked up into his eyes, biting his lip for a split second before catching himself and giving him a shrug.

"It'll do," he said, and Fire threw his head back, laughing.

"Oh, you're gonna be a handful, aren't you?" he asked, and Rio tilted his head again.

"Probably," he said, wrapping his arms around Fire's neck and hopping up until Fire was holding him again. "But I'm worth it."

Fire lowered them to the spread coat on the floor, settling Rio on his lap. He rushed to get rid of Rio's clothes and complained minimally when Rio insisted on folding them neatly before going back to kissing.

Before he knew it, they were both naked, their panting loud in the empty coatroom, the music from the main event hopefully keeping them a secret from the rest of the world.

Fire's hands were everywhere. On his chest, his back, his hips, and his thighs. They were spreading his ass cheeks and letting the pearls from his wings fall in between.

He hissed at the cool sensation on overheated skin, nails digging into Fire's pecs as he tried to push himself onto his fingers.

"We don't have lube or condoms, gorgeous," Fire said as he used his thumb to press one of the pearls against Rio's entrance. "How do you want to do this?"

"My pocket," he panted, too far gone to give the thought of how he was going to clean his jewelry more than a split second of attention.

"Prepared for this?" Fire asked as his hands left Rio's body to look for the items.

"Galas like this are boring," Rio said, lowering his head to bite at Fire's nipple as he rocked their stiff cocks together. "And sometimes people are attractive enough to make them less boring."

He heard the crinkle of the lube packet being ripped open.

"Is that what I am?" Fire asked. "A distraction?"

Rio lifted his head up and attempted a glare, but Fire's slick fingers found his entrance, and all he could do was moan as they breached him.

"Mine," he gasped, and then no words were possible.

He was reduced to whimpers and moans as Fire fingered him open, the filth of the coatroom floor and the musky smell of the air around them making him feel like an animal.

He didn't recognize himself. He didn't know why he was able to let go of so many of his own barriers, but as Fire pulled the condom on and lifted him by the hips to lower him onto his cock, he realized he didn't care.

He couldn't care. There was no nerve ending that wasn't burning inside him as he braced himself on Fire's chest and met his hips with his own. He didn't want to be manhandled. He wanted to give as good as he was getting. He wanted to leave a mark on Fire the way he could feel Fire leaving marks on him.

He wanted to be remembered by him. Wanted to brand him so the world knew Fire was his now.

Helped by Fire's hands gripping his ass, he bounced faster, adding a tiny sway to his hips whenever he dropped, knowing it would drive Fire crazy.

He was close, so close, and he didn't want to burn alone.

"Gonna make me come, gorgeous," Fire said, fingers on Rio's flesh tightening, grabbing, and pulling forcefully until one sharp push inside tipped Rio over the edge.

He spilled on Fire's chest, his wings dropping for a split second in ecstasy as he felt Fire's cock pulse inside him.

Fire was lying beneath him, chest heaving, head tilted back, and eyes screwed shut as Rio milked the last drops out of him.

Rio felt pride swell in him at the sight of his mate so satisfied because of him. He felt accomplished and smug. His wings fluffed back up behind him, pearls dragging over his naked back and helping the sweat cool. He stretched his hands up and tilted his neck, rising up above Fire with his cock still inside him.

"You're something else," Fire panted as he slowly came back to his senses and Rio looked down. Fire's eyes were glowing even in the dim light, and Rio wasn't sure he was ever looked at the way Fire was looking at him just then. He lived to be the center of attention, but he was pretty sure this was the first time in his life he truly was. Everything around them had shrunk to just the two of them and how their breaths synchronized. Rio felt cut open. He felt exposed and vulnerable, and he wasn't sure he liked it.

He pursed his lips, standing and picking up Fire's discarded undershirt to clean himself off.

He tossed it onto his chest once he was done and pulled his clothes back on before heading for the door.

"Hold on a second," Fire called after him, hopping into his own pants. "Are you leaving?"

"Obviously," Rio threw over his shoulder.

"You're just gonna up and ditch me here, no phone number, no date arranged?" Fire asked, and Rio smiled.

"You know, I always thought I was worth a bit more effort than a quick romp in a dusty coatroom of a boring gala," Rio said. "And I always wanted to be swept off my feet. Worked for. You're my mate. All of that is now your job."

"You want me to..." Fire trailed off, and Rio nodded.

"Work for it, yes," he said. "Good luck."

He flounced out of the room, leaving a stunned Fire behind.

CHAPTER THREE

FIRE

Work for it.

Now, Fire wasn't a stranger to hard work. He loved hard. Hard was his favorite state of being. But there was a line between hard and impossible.

Fire had pulled his clothes back on after the tryst with his mate—because getting off in the coatroom of a charity gala could only be described in such words—and he'd exited stage right hoping to catch up to his wayward mate.

Rio had been long gone by then, which put Fire a little on edge, while at the same time it got his motor running from the audacity.

Next time he caught Rio, he was getting a spanking.

Fire had driven himself home buzzing and high on mating chemicals. He'd collapsed onto his bed in his temporary house of the month and pulled out his laptop.

What he had expected to be a quick search-and-acquire had him up until 3 a.m., when he promptly passed out in his fancy clothes and shoes, drooling onto his keyboard.

Turned out Uxorious wasn't that easy to track down, even though that fucking name appeared in every gossip column he clicked on. His Uxorious was partying, schmoozing, donating money left, right, and center. But that was where information about him stopped. No number, no address, no email.

He had even text some of his racing buddies, but while some had heard of his illustrious mate, nobody really knew him.

Which put him at square one with a big fat nothing.

Fire hated to lose.

But he didn't have the time to spend searching other avenues. Today, he had an appointment with Doc Nelson, and he couldn't miss it. Not even for his mate. He needed to get the all clear so he could race again. He hadn't been in the air for a month already, and he could feel himself atrophying.

He wasn't meant to be on the ground this long.

Anna let herself in while he was in the shower, not *not* thinking about Rio and how it had felt inside him.

She perched by the open bathroom door carelessly, dark hair scraped back into its customary severe bun and tailored suit pressed perfectly. "You left early last night."

"You're lucky I showed up at all," Fire said, the frosted glass sparing her an eyeful, not that she particularly cared.

"You got your picture taken, at least," Anna allowed, perusing them on her phone. "And you gave the check over?"

"That was the only reason I put up with the thing in the first place. You think I was going to forget?" Fire asked, leaning forward and rinsing out the conditioner from his hair, being careful not to get his wings wet.

"Doc will be here in fifteen minutes."

"You know what they say—a watched Fire never gets ready on time."

Anna scoffed, but her heels clicked away.

Fire smirked. Anna was the best in her business, and her no-nonsense attitude truly helped keep Fire on track, but man was it fun to rile her up.

He hurried through the rest of his washing and stepped out, drying himself off roughly and wrapping a towel around his waist. When he padded into the bedroom, he saw Anna had laid out a pair of sweats and a matching top in navy with his logo running up the arms. His sponsors wanted to create a Fire-inspired athletic-wear line, and their usual arrow logo was set against flames to represent the collab. He thought it looked sick.

He undid the snaps at the back and slipped the top on, closing them up before pulling the sweats on without underwear, because hey, who cared?

He grabbed his hairdryer and set to work drying his hair, feeling over his day-old stubble and deciding it could wait another day.

"Have you eaten this morning?" Anna asked over the noise as she stepped back into the bedroom.

Fire shook his head. "Order in?"

"Since there's nothing in the fridge, we'll have to."

"Well, it's kinda hard to stock all these places I keep moving to," Fire said dryly.

Anna sighed. "You can move back to your apartment soon. We just needed to throw people off the scent. Did you enjoy the fans camped outside on the street?"

"Better than having no place at all."

Anna didn't look unaffected, and Fire immediately felt bad. She was doing her best for him. And this was the price of his newfound fame. "I'm sorry."

She gave him a look. "It's my job, asshole. I don't need to be coddled."

Fire smirked at her bite and turned off the hairdryer. "I know that apartment isn't that fancy, but I paid for it with my first big win money. I don't wanna get rid of it."

"I know," she said, rolling her eyes. "I'll see if enough time has passed for you to go back."

Fire grinned, lunging in and giving her a kiss on the cheek that she retched at.

The doorbell rang before she could castrate him, and Fire skipped toward it.

"Oh no you don't," Anna said, bodychecking him out of the way, even though she was a hundred pounds soaking wet.

"Isn't this counterproductive?" Fire complained, rubbing his shoulder.

They jostled down the stairs.

"Stay up there, Fire. I mean it!"

"It's just the doc. It doesn't matter if I open the door," Fire said.

Their arguing got cut off by the sound of more arguing beyond the door.

Anna frowned and strode that way, unaware of Fire dogging her steps still.

The closer Fire got, the louder he could hear the heated words, only for them to abruptly stop when Anna threw the front door open.

To all of their surprise.

It was the doc, looking as charmingly bedraggled as usual in his white coat, his single white wing a little mussed. But he seemed to have acquired a limpet somewhere along the journey. A bronzed, hot limpet with legs for days and a hard-on for glaring straight at Fire, apparently.

"You're not a spurned lover looking for revenge, are you?" Fire asked, frowning bemusedly. "Because I gotta say, it's a shame I can't remember it."

The guy spluttered. "As if!"

At the same time, Anna snapped, "Fire, leave!"

"He's with me. He's my mate," Doc said, and there was a slight tinge of possessiveness there. Not overt. He wasn't that sort of guy. But it was a clear line drawn. One Fire had no intention of overstepping in any serious way. Especially now he had his own lines to handle.

"You're violating your NDA," Anna said coolly to the doctor.

"I'm aware. I apologize. Bailey was following me," Doc said, giving his mate a glare.

Fire raised his brows, thoroughly amused.

"I wasn't following you!" Bailey defended himself. "It was my day off, and I was just making sure you got to this sketchy-as-hell address safely in person instead of looking at the tracking app."

"So...tracking him isn't following him?" Fire said.

"No one asked you!" Bailey hissed. "You're the sketch in question."

"Everything was fine the last three times, Bailey," Doc said. "Why couldn't you trust me?"

"I do trust you," Bailey said. "I was just tailing your car, which sounds bad, I admit...but I was gonna drive off as soon as I saw everything was all good! I work in security, Heath. Paranoia is encouraged and required. I didn't want to interfere with your job. I just wanted to make sure you were safe and then I was gonna ghost... Hitting the speed sign with the car wasn't a part of the plan."

Doc sighed.

"It's kind of romantic in a messed-up way," Fire said. "I know this arrangement would raise red flags for me."

Anna cut him a scathing look. "Why are you still here where everyone and their mother can see you through the door?"

"You mean the graffitied wall, the stray cat licking its ass, and the broken sign?" Fire asked dryly. "I'm sure they won't tell."

Anna pinched the bridge of her nose, muttering some obscene things.

"I truly apologize," Doc said. "If you would like to take legal action, I totally understand."

"It's no biggie. Like I said, I get it," Fire said magnanimously.

"You have no say in what is a 'biggie' and what is not," Anna said. "Your identity has been compromised."

"I don't care who he is," Bailey said, meaning it. "He could have invented the wheel, and the amount of shits I'd give would still be less than zero. I just don't like when my mate leaves on business trips to weird locations with little to no info."

Fire laughed, wholly refreshed. "You guys are fun."

"Fire!" Anna snapped.

"Anna, it's fine. We can get Bailey to sign an NDA as well, and it's all gravy."

"Because I just have NDAs prepared in my asshole that I can whip out at a moment's notice," Anna said.

"Well…you have many talents," Fire said.

"Bailey will be waiting in the car and will sign whatever you need him to if you're still happy for me to continue your care," Doc said. "I can recommend someone else—"

"You're the best there is," Fire cut him off. "I don't want someone else."

"Hell yeah he is," Bailey said. "But watch your mouth."

"Bailey," Doc said sternly, pointing. "Car."

"I'll just take a tiny peeksee inside first…" Bailey said, inching forward.

"No you won't," Doc said.

"You definitely won't," Anna concurred.

"Just a quick sweep," Bailey said, holding his hands up. "It'll take two seconds, promise."

"Bailey—"

Bailey tripped over the worn welcome mat and landed straight on his face in between all of them.

"I gotta say, I wasn't quite imagining my day going like this," Fire said, watching Bailey get patched up by Doc in his temporary bedroom five minutes later.

The guy was sat on an ottoman and had his head tilted back while Doc inspected his nose. Dried blood was smeared around his face. Anna was in the corner of the room silently fuming, taking her rage out on her phone.

Doc went about cleaning Bailey up and then laid some strips down over the bridge of the swollen appendage. Fire noted with growing amusement that they had cute bears on. A punishment?

"How's it looking, Doc?" Bailey asked gravely. "Am I still pretty?"

Doc kissed the tip of his nose gently as an answer, and Bailey blossomed under the attention. Bailey pulled out his phone and turned the front camera on when Doc stepped back.

"Awwww. Bears!" Bailey grinned.

Not a punishment then.

"Sorry about that," Doc said, changing his gloves over. "I'll be with you in a moment, Fire."

"Take your time," Fire said, leaning back on his hands, wings sprawled behind him on the bed.

He wondered if he was looking at the future in a way. Would Rio kiss his injuries after he faceplanted in training? It was a little hard to imagine the uptight priss doing anything but telling him to stop rolling around in the dirt, and it made him smile so wide he probably looked insane.

The promise of excitement Rio held the potential for was like a drug to Fire. He lived for the challenge, the natural friction, and the rush of blood as the adrenaline pumped. Talking to Rio and taking him apart was like one big hit of that.

And like any good addict, he wanted more.

If he could just find the beautiful asshole.

"Okay," Doc said, approaching. "If you'd like to stand, we can run through our usual checks."

Fire blinked back into focus and shimmied off the bed. They ran through his range of movement, and other than the odd twinge, his wing moved smoothly.

"You've made good progress," Doc said, sounding pleased as he combed through his primaries.

"I may look like a bit of a flake, but I take this shit seriously, at least," Fire said. "I did everything to the letter. I need to get back into training as soon as possible. The next comp is around the corner, and I barely scraped in with that DNF on my record."

"Your usual training routine is off the table," Doc said frankly. "You'll have to ease into it. I've written a comprehensive guide for your coach and your sports therapist. You can start with that and build it up. As for any competitions... It's hard to say."

Fire pursed his mouth, sighing out through his nose. "If I can fly, I'm ready."

"You'll risk doing more long-term damage if you fly before it's fully healed."

Fire threw his head back and groaned. "I'm going stir-crazy here, Doc."

"I understand it's frustrating," Doc said. "If there's anything you want to talk about, I'm here to answer any questions you have."

"You found your mate recently, right?" Fire asked.

Doc's hands paused on his wings, eyes widening. "Not what I was expecting you to say."

"Hey! I'm still in the room, racing boy!" Bailey said, looking like he wanted to fight, only slightly offset by the happy bears stuck to his face.

"I'm not coming on to him. Chill, dude," Fire said, laughing. "It was a genuine question. The first time you came, we had a conversation about mates, and I'm pretty sure you didn't have one then."

"Well...in a sense, I suppose that's true," Doc said evasively, a slight flush traveling down his neck.

Fire's brows drew closer. "What does that mean?"

"Weeeeell..." Bailey started.

"Why do you ask?" Doc asked instead, talking over him, the redness growing deeper.

"I found mine the other night," Fire said.

"*What?!*" Anna screeched.

Oh yeah. He hadn't told her yet. Oops.

"Surprise!" he cheered.

"When? Where? How?" she spat out, almost too apoplectic to speak.

"That charity event you made me go to," Fire said. "Turns out it wasn't so bad after all."

"Who?" Anna demanded.

"Rio," he said, the name rolling off his tongue so pleasantly. He hadn't realized how much he'd wanted to say it to someone until now. And now he didn't want to stop.

Anna scrambled for her tablet, pulling up the guest list, no doubt.

"So you found your mate. Congratulations," Doc said, giving him a genuine smile.

"Found him. Fucked him. Now he wants me to find him, and I have no idea where to start," Fire said, crossing his arms over his chest. "So I'm feeling a little...pent up. Usually, I fly shit like this off."

"Patience is a virtue," Bailey sing-songed.

"Hush," Doc chided him, giving him a helplessly endeared smile.

It seemed like a private joke was passing between them.

"There are no Rios!" Anna burst out into the silence, hair becoming more frayed by the second.

"It's a nickname," Fire said. "That I gave him."

"What is his real name?" she said between gritted teeth.

"It's a mouthful."

Anna narrowed her eyes. "Try me."

"Uxorious Archibald Charmichael III...I think."

Bailey blinked. "That is a mouthful. Rio is cuter."

"Right?!" Fire said.

"Did you say he wants you to find him?" Doc asked, confused. "Even though he knows you're mated?"

"I think he might be a little high maintenance," Fire said with a grin before his annoyance took over at his lack of results. "But I looked him up, and all I got was a million gossip pages about his outfits and past conquests. There were some charity articles and a few spots he's been seen at, but nothing concrete."

"Tough deal, man," Bailey said, snagging Doc's coat so he could pull him closer and rest his head against his hip.

"Hey, you're in security you said, right? Could you get me his number?" Fire asked in a sudden bout of inspiration.

"Weeeeell..." Bailey started again.

"No," Doc interrupted once more, tugging gently at his hair in warning.

Fire huffed. So close.

"A Charmichael," Anna was murmuring while rubbing her temples. "You mated with the Charmichael heir."

"Wait, wait, wait. You know him?" Fire asked, perking up. He grabbed Anna's tablet. "Do you have his number on here?"

"Don't touch that," Anna snapped, taking her precious tablet back and cradling it like a baby.

"Anna, c'mon. Don't leave me hanging."

"I should have quit years ago, you know that? You don't pay me enough for the shit I have to deal with," Anna told him.

Fire pouted at her and blinked his puppy eyes. "Please. You love me really."

"Says who?"

"And listen, there's a bright side! Now I found my mate you don't have to deal with all the false mating claims! I can go back to my apartment and no more moving around!" She pursed her lips, looking slightly thawed. "I can settle down into that nice-boy image you want me to have. Picket fence, seriously mated, the whole nine yards. My unruly days are behind me!"

Anna gave him a shrewd look.

"Well...mostly."

Anna sighed, fingers moving around her tablet. Fire's phone pinged in the next second, and he looked down to see a string of beautiful numbers.

Rio.

CHAPTER FOUR

RIO

"rious!" Rio jumped up at his grandmother's loud voice and looked at her in wonder, heart jumping to his throat.

"Since when do you call me Rio?" he asked, the name sour sounding when it came from her. She shouldn't be calling him the same thing *he* did.

"I have never, and will never, call you Rio." She huffed in indignation, horrified at the idea. "What is the matter with you this morning?"

He mulled her words over in his head, certain he had heard her call him Rio, but, if he was being honest, he'd been pretty much disengaged for the past half an hour so it was anybody's guess. It could have also been his brain stuck on Fire since the moment he left the gala.

Finding his mate when he least expected him had shaken Rio enough to feel off kilter. Few things in his life managed that.

He was happy, of course he was. But the worry that had settled in the pit of his stomach as more time passed won. Who was Fire? Was he someone Rio's grandparents would approve of even if they didn't pick him themselves? Would they find him acceptable enough to drop the long list of potential mates they had been compiling since Rio hit puberty?

Fire had been at the charity gala. Which meant he was invited. Which meant the organizers thought he had enough money to be worth inviting. That had to count for something, right?

He sighed and picked up his tea, taking a small sip before looking at her apologetically.

"I'm sorry, Grandmother," he said. "I haven't really slept well these last few days, and I'm feeling a bit off."

"Yes, I can tell," she said dryly. "And apparently, I'm not the only one. Catherine had some choice words about your decorum at the charity gala."

Rio suppressed an eyeroll and forced a smile. "I was nothing but polite to Mrs. Avery. As I always am."

She narrowed her eyes at him. She looked so much like a bird of prey, with her large nose and narrow, long face. Her eyes were round and bug-like, and her entire body was made of sharp angles and harsh lines.

"Why am I not convinced?" she asked, and he felt the urge to shrug his shoulders in dismissal but knew it would make her even more annoyed. He chose his words instead.

"I'm afraid I don't know," he said. "I greeted her, complimented her jewelry, and then went to socialize like one is supposed to do at events like that. I can't remember a single wrong thing I said to her in those two minutes of conversation."

"And yet she left feeling insulted and dismissed," she insisted, and Rio crossed his fingers.

"I'm very sorry to hear that," he said.

"You don't sound sorry," she accused again, and this time he bristled.

"That might be due to the fact I have nothing to be sorry about," he said sharply.

"Uxorious!" she gasped, and he took a deep breath to get himself under control.

"Grandmother, I realize Mrs. Avery is your friend, but we both know she was never fond of me. Whatever she sensed from me that night was most likely just her looking for any excuse to further put me down," he said. "And her own issues are not mine to apologize for."

She stared at him for a long moment, desperately trying to find something to counter with, something to have the last word over him and win as she usually did. He felt his skin prickle with anticipation, knowing he had pushed enough in one conversation and she was a step away from snapping.

"No point in you dawdling around here if this is how you'll behave. You're excused."

She waved him off with her hand, and he swallowed a sigh of relief. He nodded his head and swished out of the room, saved from inane conversation and guilt trips.

Sure, he'd probably been a bitch to Catherine Avery, but she absolutely deserved it, and he'd done it in a way that granted him an out should he need one. He'd said all the right things. Not his fault she was good at reading body language and took his words the way he meant them—as insults.

He walked up to his room and locked the door behind him, reveling in the peace and quiet. He looked around what was supposed to be his sanctuary and, as usual, felt none of the comfort he should have felt. The room was beautiful—all soft pastels and rich wood—but it was devoid of anything Rio was attached to. Anything he felt was truly his. Except one thing.

He took off his shoes and padded over the soft carpet to his favorite armchair.

It stood out between all the fancy furniture and posh decoration. It was old. Worn in places and just a little bit too plain to belong in the otherwise grand-looking room.

But it was his late dad's favorite chair. And no matter how much his grandmother complained, Rio refused to get rid of it.

It smelled like his dad's favorite cologne. Both because Rio had memories of him sitting in it, and because he sprayed it on the ratty upholstery every once in a while to avoid losing it.

He sank down into it, curling his legs underneath himself and throwing a cashmere throw over his knees. He reached for his phone on the small coffee table next to it and checked his texts.

He saw a few from Kalie and some others, but his mood had turned a bit sour, and he didn't really feel like talking to them. So, he opened his favorite shopping app and scrolled through his wish list.

There was a pair of boots he had been eyeing for a while, and he figured what better occasion to get them than a gloomy Thursday afternoon? He clicked the little green button and smiled when the transaction went through.

New boots.

Exactly what he needed.

His phone pinged in his hand, and he looked at the unknown number when he had been expecting a confirmation email.

Unknown: *Found you.*

Rio frowned. It wasn't like he was a hard man to find. His face was in the tabloids every other day being accused of one inane thing or another. And it wasn't like he was hiding.

Rio: *Well done you. Whoever you are.*

Unknown: *Ah, so I'm guessing you fucked more than one mate in the coatroom of a fancy event, so you're having a hard time remembering who I could be.*

Rio's heart skipped at the words.

Fire.

He had found him. Sneaky. Exciting.

Rio: *Not mate...no.*

Fire: *You're evil.*

Rio: *Sometimes.*

Fire: *I like it.*

Rio: *You don't exactly have a choice, now do you?*
Fire: *If I did, I'd make the same one.*
Rio: *Smooth.*
Fire: *I thought so too. So, date this Saturday?*
Rio: *You think you've earned a date just because you sent me a text?*
Fire: *I also complimented you and threw a great line. You gotta give me some credit, at least.*
Rio: *I guess it earns you a few points.*
Fire: *There's points now?*
Rio: *There have always been points. Do try and keep up.*
Fire: *And how do I earn them?*
Rio: *I'll let you know once you do.*
Fire: *That doesn't seem like a good system.*
Rio: *Yes, well...you can always back out.*
Fire: *Oh, gorgeous, it's like you don't even know me.*
Rio: *I don't.*
Fire: *And that's what dates are for. Saturday?*
Rio: *Nice try.*
Fire: *Pretty please with a blowjob on top?*
Rio: *Places to be, people to see.*
Fire: *I'll wear you down.*
Rio: *Maybe...*

He put his phone down, trying hard to fight the smile that bloomed on his lips. It was exhilarating. Everything about Fire lit a flame in Rio.

He gave as good as he got. He wasn't awed or intimidated by Rio. He didn't simper in front of him. He sparred with him and made his mind work a mile a minute after just one meeting and one short conversation.

Rio was excited. He couldn't wait to see what came next.

And what came next was a delivery for him a couple of days later.

A tiny little package wrapped in brown paper. Nothing descriptive about it. No return address, no note to go with it.

Rio took it to his room, putting it next to his ear and rattling it a little bit to see if he could at least recognize the sound.

None of his favorite sounds came from it. Not pearls tinkling, not clothes rustling, nothing. The package was just quiet and light in his hands.

He frowned at it lightly and grabbed for a small letter opener from his desk to cut through the tape holding the package closed.

The paper fell open in front of him, revealing a light pink, shiny, toy-sized shovel similar to ones his grandmother used while pretending she was the one to uphold their gigantic, award-winning garden and not the army of gardeners they had on their payroll.

Rio stared at it, completely baffled. What in the world?

Why would he need a shovel?

Cute as it was with the bedazzled handle and the lovely color that reminded Rio of his wings, he had absolutely zero use for it.

His talents were not related to anything that required digging. Not even if he went digging for treasure. He'd probably just pay someone to do it faster and with a larger shovel than the one he had in his hand.

Confusion grew, and Rio hated not being in the loop. He didn't like not knowing what his response or reaction should be.

And there was only one person that could have sent something so bizarre to him and not explained it.

Fire.

He grabbed his phone, and instead of typing up a text, he hit dial.

Fire picked up after only two rings.

"*Rio! What a lovely surprise*," he said, and Rio bristled at the teasing tone. He felt shaken by the fact that he already knew what face Fire was making at that moment. He had only seen him once, and yet he remembered those mischievous eyes and crooked smile.

"Did you send me a shovel?" Rio asked, voice clipped and impatient.

"*You got my gift?*" Fire said, sounding delighted. "*Do you like it?*"

"I can think of one singular use for it," Rio said. "And that is to use it to bury your body."

"*Mean!*" Fire said. "*You're being mean to me again.*"

"Well deserved," Rio said.

"*But you don't even know the meaning of it!*" Fire said. "*It's so romantic I'm practically blushing just thinking about it.*"

"A shovel is your idea of romance?"

"*No, a shovel is a symbol,*" Fire said.

"Of your imminent demise at the hands of an annoyed mate?" Rio asked, and Fire had the audacity to laugh at him.

"*Of the work I'm going to put in to make sure you're getting what you dreamed of,*" Fire said, and Rio sputtered.

He had not been expecting that. After the verbal sparring and the jabs thrown both ways, sweetness from Fire that came out of nowhere rattled him.

"You're not all right in the head," Rio said finally, but it didn't come out as harsh as he wanted it. It sounded a bit breathy. A bit winded and uninspired.

"*Caught you off guard, gorgeous?*" Fire asked, and Rio coughed to hide the awkwardness and buy himself some time.

When he said he wanted to be worked for, he...well, he didn't know what he truly wanted. He'd never been in a situation like that before, and he just wanted to be difficult. He wanted to make sure his mate knew exactly what to expect with him. He was high maintenance on a good day. There was no denying that.

He didn't know Fire would take that and run with it.

Turn it into possibly the silliest, sweetest thing anyone had ever done.

"No," he said because nothing better came to mind at that moment.

"*If that's all you have to say, I have a question for you,*" Fire said, and Rio contemplated just hanging up the phone to get out of whatever ridiculous thing would come out of Fire's mouth next.

But...curiosity killed the cat, and Rio had been compared to a cat far too many times in his life to pass it up.

"What?" he asked.

Fire chuckled. "*What are you wearing?*"

Rio almost dropped his phone.

The audacity.

"Something is seriously wrong with you," Rio said, but he still looked down to double check his outfit. It looked as perfectly coordinated and fashionable as usual, thank you ever so much.

"*Relax, I'm not trying to have phone sex with you,*" Fire said. "*Although it could be fun.*"

"Get to the point, James," Rio said, and Fire groaned.

"*Oh, my name sounds so good coming from you,*" he said, and Rio suppressed a shiver that raked through him at the sound of that voice turning deep and shaky for him again.

"Today," Rio said, unable to form a longer sentence than that.

"*I just want to know if you're decent?*" Fire asked.

"I'm always decent," Rio replied. "You'll have to be more specific than that."

"*Decent to be seen in public?*"

Rio frowned. "My outfit is perfectly acceptable to be seen, but I wasn't planning on going out today."

Fire hummed. "*Plans change. Get your cute butt outside.*"

"What? Why?" Rio said, hating how squeaky his voice sounded.

"*Because I'm waiting for you in front of your gate. Dark blue car. You can't miss it.*"

Rio rushed to his window that looked toward the front gate. He pushed the curtain away and peeked through, hand going to his chest when he realized there was indeed a dark blue car just off the side of the main entrance to their estate.

"What are you doing?" Rio asked. "When have I agreed to this?"

"*You haven't,*" Fire said. "*And you wouldn't have for a while longer if left to your own devices. I just decided to speed things up a bit. Take you on a date. I promise I do a much better job wooing people in person.*"

"I don't need to be wooed," Rio said.

"*Not what you said the other night, gorgeous,*" Fire said. "*Now, I'm gonna hang up, and you'll be a good boy and come outside. See you in a bit.*"

The line cut off, and Rio was left glaring at the phone in his hand, heart pumping loudly and every nerve ending in his body screaming at him to just go and throw himself into Fire's arms.

His mate was waiting for him. His mate came for him.

But Rio wasn't ready to just give in like that. Fire was in for a hell of a first date.

CHAPTER FIVE

FIRE

Rio stepped out of the gates to his house—ahem, mansion, who the hell needed a house that big?—looking like another magazine cover, of course. Fire was less stunned but no less appreciative this time around. Dressed in tan trousers that were perfectly tailored to his legs, a white shirt, and a blue checked blazer that had more of the same tan accents, he managed to be both perfectly put together and indecent at the same time. Or maybe that was just Fire's brain on the second one.

He had to remind himself that it probably wasn't a good idea to tackle Rio to the floor and have him right there on the driveway, but it was a close thing.

Seeing him again even after only a few days was like taking a sip of water in the desert. He hadn't realized just how wilted he had been. He was instantly revitalized.

Man, this mate thing is a trip.

Rio stopped outside the passenger door and crossed his arms, waiting.

Fire rolled down the window and leaned over to see him better. "The door's open. Jump in quick."

Rio arched an entitled brow. "Do you not have *any* manners?"

"I know how to say please. So please get in the car," Fire said with a grin.

Rio refused to move, examining his nails now, and Fire racked his brain for what his fussy mate could possibly want before it occurred to him. "Oh, you have got to be kidding me."

"I most certainly am not," Rio said, still refusing to look his way.

Fire rolled his eyes so hard he feared they'd get lost inside his skull. But still he got out of the car and rounded it, taking the handle for the passenger side and swinging it open. He flourished an arm with a half bow.

"After you, princess."

Rio *humphed* but slid into the seat. Fire laughed to himself and slammed it behind him, running back around to the driver's side. He settled in and noticed Rio had pulled the visor down to look in the mirror, checking his hair was still styled away from his forehead to his satisfaction.

"You look hot," Fire said, pulling away and turning the car to face the direction of normalcy.

Rio shot him a side-eye. "I know."

Fire held his hands up in surrender, smirking. Rio's antics were unendingly funny to him.

"Both hands on the wheel please," Rio snapped.

"Yes, princess," Fire said, doing as he was told.

"And cease calling me that."

"Yes, princess."

Rio scowled, and Fire chuckled.

"What, no compliment for me?" Fire asked. "I'm crushed. After I dressed up all nice."

Which was true. Rio might have first seen him in a suit at the charity gala, but Fire lived in sportswear 90 percent of the time. Today was definitely a deviation from the norm for him. The jeans he had on now were one of two pairs he owned total, the top was a promo from an up-and-coming graphic designer, and the jean jacket he'd had since college. The rips and distressing were all signs of age and time, and he'd patched some up with a few pins he'd collected over the years from comps or fans.

Rio took all this in in one long, slow sweep of his eyes. "You look...adequate."

"Adequate?" Fire burst out, laughing. "I've never been adequate in my life. And I know you know that."

Rio's mouth dropped open. "Crude!"

Fire laughed again.

"Tell me where we're going," Rio said, sounding petulant now.

"It's a surprise."

"I hate surprises."

"No you don't. I'm one big surprise, and you're mated to me," Fire said.

"How does one negate the other?" Rio said casually, turning away from him.

"Ouch. Right in my feels."

Rio refused to talk to him the rest of the drive, pouting and protesting in equal measure. Fire let him sulk, so happy he could float.

They pulled up outside the botanical garden—a huge glass dome that was frosted on the outside—not long after, and Fire found a parking spot away from other cars. He reached over and popped the glove compartment as Rio peered around them, pulling out a plain black cap to tug on. While his wings were the most recognizable thing about him, he was notable enough now that his face got recognized in public pretty frequently.

Fire didn't want to be interrupted by fans on his first date with his mate.

"Is this...a *garden*?" Rio's horror was so dramatic it was bordering on silly.

"You have a problem with gardens?" Fire asked. "They're pretty."

"They're dirty," Rio corrected.

"They have curated paths. It's a *botanical* garden. It's not like I've taken you to a field," Fire said, rolling his eyes and getting out of the car.

Rio followed after him. "I was expecting dinner."

"I'll feed you," Fire promised, coming around to grab his hand.

"With tables."

Fire tugged him along easily. "I'll hand feed it to you. You won't know the difference."

"And ambient music."

"I can sing to you."

"Fire!"

"They have a butterfly exhibit here. You'll love it," Fire said merrily.

"*Bugs!*" Rio screeched.

He sounded like he was gonna pass out, but they were approaching the entrance, and Fire needed to show their tickets. He kept his head down as the lady scanned them in. She seemed more curious about Rio's gaping shock than him, and Fire smiled.

"First time here. He can't believe his luck. He loves gardens. And bugs. Can't get enough of them," Fire said.

Rio growled, and the woman raised a confused brow.

"Oh...well, we have plenty of both, so he'll have loads of fun. Make sure you close one set of doors before you open the other, so the butterflies don't escape. And just a reminder that no flying is prohibited if that applies to you."

"Got it." Fire grinned sunnily, tugging Rio along.

They entered as instructed and immediately felt a wave of heat that made the air sticky and heavy. Fire barely concentrated on that, however. He was too awed by the view. All around them in the glass dome was greenery and the vibrant colors of plants he'd never seen before, let alone knew the name of. And among them, as dancing pieces of living art, were the butterflies. They fluttered around in all directions above their heads.

Fire turned to see Rio had lost his dread and was instead looking around himself in surprised wonder, the unguarded expression clearly getting away from him. Fire's heart felt bright to see it. It had been a risk to come here, but instinct had told Fire to pick it.

Rio looked perfectly in place surrounded by beautiful scenery, and Fire found himself pulling out his phone and snapping a photo to remember this exact moment.

The sound drew Rio's attention, and he glanced around sharply. "What are you doing?"

"Taking a picture of you," Fire said.

"Without me readying myself?" Rio said, horrified. "Let me see it. Delete it if it's bad."

"No can do. This is the start of my private collection. I'm the curator, not you," Fire said with a smile, pocketing his phone.

"You think you can stop me? What's yours is mine, mate of mine," Rio said, dangerously low, leaning in.

The tone made Fire all hot and bothered, but he ignored it to be serious for a second. "If you really have a problem with the photo, I'll delete it. I'm sorry. But if the only issue is that you think you look bad, you don't have to worry. You're beautiful. Posing or not. I just wanted to try and capture it."

Rio seemed to simmer down at his words, softening visibly from his bristly exterior before he caught himself. He readjusted his shoulders to appear more poised. "Well, of course I am," he mumbled to himself.

Fire grinned at his self-confidence. "So I can keep it?"

Rio huffed. "Fine. But you need to take at least fifty photos of me over there to make it up to me."

Fire followed his pointing finger to a really beautiful backdrop of teardrop-shaped flowers covered in tiny butterflies. The flowers were the exact shade of Rio's wings. Fire smiled. "I'm at your command."

"Naturally," Rio drawled.

They did their impromptu photoshoot, Rio not moving for anyone until he was wholly satisfied with his picture. He was still examining it happily as they walked further in.

"Have you really never been here before?" Fire asked.

"It never occurred to me," Rio said distractedly.

"Well, I'll try and come up with more firsts for you," Fire said.

Rio shot him a look before turning back to his photo. "Don't trouble yourself. Truly. Don't."

Fire laughed delightedly at his dry tone, already planning in his mind for the next thing as he let Rio have a moment longer with himself on his phone.

Fire instead glanced around. He'd been here once before, a long time ago, but it had changed and expanded massively since then. The butterfly exhibit was new too, and he found himself chasing their fragile bodies with his eyes, admiring their grace.

Ahead of them there was a young father around his late twenties, and what Fire was guessing was his daughter, who couldn't be more than four. She had cotton-candy wings, one baby blue and one baby pink, that were still curly at the ends and downy all over, which told Fire more about her age than her height did. She was dressed in a blue smock dress with an adorable ruffled white bib that tied at her throat, and sparkly jelly sandals that seemed impractical and mismatched to the outfit. Fire wanted to pat her cute little blond head.

They continued to peruse the garden, Fire watching Rio contemplate each flower, tree, or butterfly studiously as if to judge it by his exacting standards. It made Fire laugh under his breath, happy, despite Rio's fervent protests, that he was unable to hide his enjoyment and interest.

Everything would have been perfect if not for the oppressive heat.

He was sweating under the brim of his cap, unable to risk removing any article of clothing in case he got recognized. It was like they'd stepped into the fires of hell.

Fire dabbed at his forehead with his cuff, knocking it high accidentally and scrambling to tug it back down. He took a furtive look around

Fire saw the little girl notice him, her eyes widening in recognition. She reached up and tugged on her father's jacket, but was waved off by her distracted parent, who was deep in an uncomfortable-looking discussion on his phone.

Fire quickly put his finger to his lips, and she stopped tugging, tilting her head at him like a puppy, pigtails bouncing.

Fire thought quickly, then took a bird pin from his jacket and placed it on a rock in one of the flowerbeds, near a monarch butterfly that was slowly beating its wings.

"What are you doing?" Rio asked.

"Bribing a four-year-old. C'mon."

He grabbed Rio's hand, then gave the girl an encouraging smile and waved before walking away. He hid them around the corner, behind some bushes, and watched as the girl disengaged from her dad and hurried over, picking up the pin in her tiny hands. She grinned with all her baby teeth, turning it over and over like a shiny treasure.

Her dad, noticing she was missing, frantically looked around before he spotted her and rocketed over. "Piper, what are you doing running off?!"

He grabbed her hand and she scowled at him mightily. "You were ignoring me."

"Good girl," Rio murmured approvingly, and Fire shoved at him.

"You would think that."

"She needs to make the rules early," Rio declared primly.

The dad looked suitably contrite, whiskey-colored eyes bracketed with stress.

"I'm sorry, baby. No more running off, okay? Your mom would kill me," he mumbled the last part.

"And then she won't let you see me?" Piper asked dully, her ponytails sagging along with her cotton-candy wings. It caught Fire in the heart and doubly so for her dad, it looked like.

"You don't have to worry about that, okay? I'll always find a way to see you," he promised. Piper sighed sadly as she was hauled up onto the guy's hip. She tucked herself under his chin, looking down at her hands and fiddling with her pin. "Oh... What have you got there, Pip?"

Piper held out the pin excitedly, her attention diverted from her sadness. "It's Fire's treasure! He gave it to me!"

"Fire?" the man asked, bemused.

"Yeah. He went that way!" she said, pointing at the corner, and Fire fell backward into Rio to avoid notice.

"My shoes!" Rio cried as Fire accidentally stepped all over them.

"Time to go!"

"You're not pulling me agai—*Fire!*"

Fire rushed them along the paths.

"This is the worst first date I've ever been on in my life!" Rio said loudly, drawing the attention of all the passersby as they exited the exhibit into the cooler gardens.

Fire kept his head low, both for privacy reasons and because he didn't need that declaration on his rep. He was great at first dates! He'd had nothing *but* first dates his whole life. He'd turned them into an art form!

He slowed them down when they reached a private spot with no people, and Rio snatched his hand away, fussing at his clothes and hair.

"You look great," Fire said, hoping to mollify him. Rio shot him an arch look, then turned back to his primping. "I think that went successfully, all things considered."

Rio got immediately red in the face and whirled on him, shoving a manicured nail into his solar plexus. "You take me to a garden, you have bugs crawl all over me, you ruin my shoes and my hair, you make me *run*, and you have the audacity to try and compli—"

Fire cut him off with a kiss.

Rio mumbled against his mouth before giving in, not without biting his lip in spite, however. Fire smiled briefly, the sting of pain only making his cock harder as he dove in further. The push and pull of their connection made Fire's heart hammer in a way not even racing could do.

They lost time kissing in their secluded part of the gardens, nothing but the gentle tinkle of running water and distant sounds of talking surrounding them. They couldn't go too far, though, despite his cock straining against his jeans. The answering press of Rio's a temptation to get on his knees for. Fire was up for a lot of stuff, including public sex, but there were children around, and he didn't want to risk scarring them for life.

He tapered the kisses off with regret, until they were just quietly breathing against one another.

"So, when do you wanna plan our next date?" Fire asked, thumbing at Rio's swollen bottom lip.

Rio slapped his hand away, though he didn't move. "You think I want to date you again?"

"Well, I guess if you refuse, I'll have to take drastic measures," Fire said, looking around and spotting a huge water feature.

"I do refuse!"

Fire shrugged. "You asked for it."

He walked over and hopped on top of the edge that was barely wide enough, teetering back and forth until he found his center of gravity.

"What are you doing?" Rio hissed. "Get down before someone comes!"

"Not until you agree to date me again."

Rio crossed his arms. "No."

"Then I guess I'll just stay here until I lose my balance and fall in," Fire said casually, waving his arms around.

"Fire," Rio said warningly.

"Yes, princess?"

"Get down."

Fire gave him a shit-eating grin. "Make me."

Rio growled at being defied, then strode over with purpose, grabbing for his hand to yank him. Fire moved it out of the way playfully, only for the move to make him actually lose his balance with no wings to help him. His eyes widened at the same time as Rio's, and remarkably, Rio reached out for his hand again to tug him back.

Only problem was, Rio was made up of sass and little else, and Fire was about double his weight.

They both went toppling in, Rio's horrified accusation of "*James!*" lost to the water that rushed up to meet them.

The pool itself was shallow, but it was enough to cover both their prone bodies until they could untangle themselves and push up on their knees.

Breaking the surface, Fire wiped the water out of his eyes briefly, only to find himself dunked again as Rio screamed bloody murder and tried to drown him.

"*I hate you!*"

Fire got a mouthful of stagnant water as well as water up his nose, but he was able to right himself even with Rio pounding at his chest with his fists. Rio's hair had been destroyed, falling over his forehead in straggles, and his clothes were soaked, losing all shape as they clung and hung in random spots.

"Stop laughing!" Rio screeched.

Fire couldn't stop, unsure whether what was running down his face was water or tears of mirth.

Rio growled furiously, redoubling his efforts to beat him to death.

Fire ignored the onslaught, snagging Rio around the waist and pressing a kiss to his flushed cheek. "You tried to save me."

"I wish I had left you!" Rio said, shoving against him still.

"No you don't," Fire said, smiling softly at him. Rio looked nothing like he had when he picked him up. Stripped of all adornments and armor, he sat miserably in a water feature.

Fire had never been so enamored by him, his heart beating loudly in his chest.

"Thank you for the rescue," Fire murmured.

Rio huffed but didn't snap back. In fact, he had stopped fighting altogether, and Fire leaned in to taste his lips again.

"Um...excuse me?" a young man's voice said. "You can't be in here."

Fire diverted course and ducked his head behind Rio, searching around for his lost hat. It slapped onto his head with a *squelch*. Fire grimaced.

"Would you get us some towels, if you please?" Rio asked in his poshest, snobbiest tone.

"I guess I can check in the staff room?" the man said, sounding completely confused but reacting to Rio's tone.

"That would be marvelous, thank you."

The guy's footsteps shuffled off, and Rio rose from the depths with as much dignity as he could muster. Fire smirked and followed him up, jumping out completely dripping and offering Rio a hand.

Rio looked like he was going to protest at first, but then acquiesced.

They stood there making puddles, Rio desperately trying to fix anything and failing completely.

"At least your last first date is one you'll never forget," Fire said proudly.

"This is going to be your last date. Period," Rio hissed.

"Do we need to go for another dip, princess?" Fire asked, chuckling at Rio's horrified reaction.

Rio began to shiver, and Fire tucked him in close as they waited for their towels.

"This doesn't mean I forgive you," Rio mumbled into his collarbone.

"Yeah, yeah, princess. I'll make it up to you next time."

Before he could fire back another protest, the guy was ambling back, a couple of small hand towels and blankets in tow.

They got dried off as best they could, Fire hiding away. Fire paid for matching t-shirts from the gift shop to change into that said, "Cact-I + Cact-YOU = Cact-US."

Fire loved them. Rio decidedly did not.

They walked out of the gardens soon after to the sun setting, a plastic bag full of sopping clothes in hand, bottom halves still wet. Rio was trying to hide inside his blanket to avoid anyone seeing him.

"You're being dramatic," Fire told him, opening his trunk and pulling out a spare pair of sweatpants for Rio and a pair of shorts he usually trained in for himself.

He got a glare as an answer.

They saw Piper again in the parking lot, tuckered out in her dad's arms as he carried her to their car.

Fire glanced back at the girl and found her looking straight at him. She waved lazily, her fist still closed around his pin.

"Daddy, look," she said. "It's Fire."

"Baby girl, I doubt a racing star is hanging around butterfly exhibits," her dad said as he put her in her car seat.

Next to him, Rio stiffened, a gasp leaving his lips. Fire turned to him, finding him pale and frozen in place, lips working around silent words.

"You're a racing star?" Rio asked suddenly, the words whip-sharp when they finally tumbled off his lips.

"I assumed you knew," Fire said. "How else would she know my name?"

Rio looked like he was internally going through it, maybe questioning any preconceived theory he'd had about him. Eventually, he said, "I don't follow that scene anymore."

"Okay?" Fire said like a question. When Rio didn't answer, he looked over again. "Is that a problem?"

He had a feeling it was even without a word from Rio. He just couldn't figure out why.

CHAPTER SIX

RIO

It should have come as absolutely no surprise at all to Rio that Fire would be a part of a world he truly didn't want to associate with. It made sense that his mate, the most important person in his life, would have ties to the world Rio had been forced to leave behind. Because that was just how his luck worked.

"So..." Fire said when Rio remained silent for a while.

"So..." Rio replied, not because he wanted to be a shit for a change, but because he truly didn't know how to talk about it, or explain to Fire why he'd reacted the way he had.

Rio tugged at the hideous t-shirt he was wearing, picking at the loose thread at the hem, racking his brain for an out he could use.

"I'm a racer," Fire said.

"I gathered that, yes," he mumbled, and Fire reached over to grip his chin gently and turn it until Rio was looking at him.

Hazel eyes searched his back and forth for a second. "That seems to be an issue for some reason."

"It's a really, really long story." Rio sighed, freeing his chin to look out the windscreen at the sign for the botanical garden, wondering how things had changed so fast. "One I'm not sure I'm ready to share until I've had some time to think everything over."

"Think what over, exactly?" Fire asked. "I'd like to at least know what's on the line?"

He sure did know how to ask a question, didn't he? Rio ran his hand through his messed-up hair, cringing at how rough it felt under his fingers without his usual hair wash and style routine.

"I need deep conditioning," he said.

"Nice try, princess," Fire said, snorting, "but we're not talking about your hair now."

"I am," Rio said.

"Rio," Fire said, tone clipped, and Rio let go of his hair to focus back on his mate through the dimming light.

"Look," Rio said. "I know this needs to be talked over, but I just found out something that might make my life a lot more complicated than it has to be. Can I just have a minute?"

"My job can make your life more complicated?" Fire asked, brows furrowed.

"Sadly, yes."

"How?"

"And that's where the thinking-things-over part comes in," Rio replied, knee bouncing with looming nerves. "I need to give this information time to settle and to think all of it over. I can't start a conversation I won't be able to finish properly."

"I'll repeat," Fire said, "I should at least know what's on the line. Am I losing you when I just found you? Am I changing my career? Am I slaying dragons to win your affection? What are we talking here, Rio?"

"Dragons won't be necessary," Rio said, but it sounded hollow to his own ears.

"I'm being serious," Fire said, no hint of any humor. "Am I losing you?"

And this time Rio could hear it in his voice. There was a hint of panic that hadn't been there before. It scratched at Rio's heart and made it bleed inside his chest. Instinct had him reaching out, cupping Fire's face in his hands.

He'd been holding him at arm's length the entire time since they met, and it had been fun. They both seemed to be enjoying it. The back-and-forth. But the curtain had come down, and it didn't feel like they were playing anymore. This was something that could make or break them. It was his mate, and in one split second, Fire had become one of the most important things in his life. For better or worse.

He leaned in and gave him a fleeting kiss. Gentle and short but it still left his lips tingling. He rested their foreheads together.

"No," Rio said. "You're not losing me. You won't lose anything. I just need to sit down and take everything into account before I can explain. Please give me that."

Fire held his gaze firmly, determination painted on his handsome face. He wanted to take it all away for Rio, he could tell. He was a problem-solver, and he wanted to fix the issues he didn't even know about just to make Rio's life easier.

Fire reached for what was in front of him instead and gripped Rio's waist, pulling him closer over the gearshift.

"I can give you anything you need," Fire promised, and Rio felt a shiver rush through him. "Just don't take too long. I won't be able to shut my brain up. It'll come up with the worst possible scenarios."

"I'll try and be quick, I promise."

"Will I be able to see you while you're thinking things over?" Fire asked.

"Yes, of course," Rio said. He looked down at his atrocious attire and cringed. "Just...no more spontaneous outdoorsy activities, okay? I'm a mess, and it's unbecoming."

Fire laughed at his words. "Only you, princess, would call chilling in a comfy pair of sweatpants unbecoming."

"Yes, well..." Rio huffed, scrunching up his nose. "Sweatpants are for people who sweat. I am usually not in the habit of sweating unless I'm in a sauna."

"Now that, gorgeous, is a blatant lie," Fire said, leaning in and brushing his nose against the skin of Rio's neck. Goosebumps followed the touch, erasing Rio's worries for a split second. "I remember distinctly licking your sweat from your neck in a coatroom just a few days ago."

Rio squeaked at the words, smacking his hands on Fire's chest.

"That is completely different," he said. "Sex is sweaty. There is no helping that."

"No, there really is no helping it," Fire said placing a kiss on Rio's neck, hands pulling the neck of the t-shirt aside to bite at his shoulder.

"Don't start anything. We're in a car in public," Rio said.

"That's the point," Fire said. "Never had sex in a car parked in a dark parking lot?"

"Of course not," Rio said. "It's..."

"Let me guess...unbecoming?" Fire said, and Rio grimaced at him mockingly.

"Uncomfortable is what I was going to say. Just legs and arms everywhere," Rio said with a small shudder, and Fire's arms around his waist slipped lower, hands going under his ass and lifting him up. Fire pulled him until he was sitting on his lap.

"Legs and arms everywhere is how sex should look," Fire said. "At least the fun kind of sex I like the most."

Rio felt fingers creeping up his thigh and smacked the top of his palm.

"Are you really trying to get me aroused right now?" Rio asked.

Fire nodded unrepentantly. "You don't get aroused in a car, princess. You get horny. Then it gets messy and sweaty, and everything starts smelling like sex."

"I don't like any of those things, to be honest," Rio said, and Fire chuckled, hand reaching between his legs and cupping his cock that stirred to life.

"That's not really true, is it?"

Fire gave his cock a soft squeeze, and Rio moaned, head falling onto Fire's shoulder.

"Fire..." he called out, and Fire hummed, fingers going for the waistband of Rio's borrowed sweatpants.

"Yeah?" he asked, and Rio rocked his hips up into his warm palm. He was desperate.

He could feel the beads of sweat forming at the back of his neck and any sense of decorum flying out the window. He didn't care they were out in public, his hair was a mess, or that he was wearing clothes that he usually wouldn't be caught dead in. He didn't even care about the fact Fire was a racer. He couldn't find it in him to worry or to stress about it when Fire was holding him so close.

All he cared about were Fire's hands on him, his lips on his neck, and the feeling of a hard cock underneath his ass.

"Hurry..." he moaned, tilting his head back to give Fire more access to his skin.

"But we're in a car, princess." Fire bit his earlobe, fingers finally making their way beneath the sweatpants and finding Rio's hard cock. "It's unbecoming."

He said it through his teeth, his fist circling Rio's cock and giving it a tug. Rio cried out, burying his head in Fire's neck and squirming on his lap.

He tried to spread his knees further, tried to make more room for Fire to go faster, but there was no space. He could just moan and take whatever Fire was able to give him.

"Want me to stop, gorgeous?" Fire asked teasingly, even though his hand picked up speed. "Want me to cover you up before someone sees you like this? Sees just how fucking hot you are? How desperate for me?"

"Don't you dare," Rio said, gripping Fire's wrist and holding his hand in place between his legs. "Don't stop."

"No?" Fire asked, adding a little twist to his upstrokes, using his thumb to spread precum over the head of Rio's cock.

Rio shook his head, turning it a little bit until he could get his lips on Fire's neck. He bit down, sucking at the skin until it was bruised for him. Bitten red and shiny with his spit. It made something primal in him preen at the sight of it. He'd left a mark on his mate. Everyone could see it and know Fire was taken.

He wrapped his arms around his shoulders, using the leverage to push himself down on Fire's cock to give him some friction. He wanted him to feel just as lost and out of control as Rio was feeling. He didn't want to be the only one losing his mind.

"Minx," Fire groaned, pushing his hips up, making Rio bounce on his lap. He pushed his other hand under the stupid t-shirt Rio was wearing and pinched his nipple, giving it a little twist, tugging it softly until Rio keened.

God, it felt so undignified, so filthy.

Why was every sexual encounter with Fire so wild? Why was he enjoying it so damn much?

The windows in the car fogged up from their harsh breaths, and Rio lifted his hand up to grip the handle above his head.

His knuckles turned white as he held on for dear life while Fire brought him closer and closer to the edge.

"Fire..." he moaned, wishing they were naked somewhere. Wishing he was lying down beneath his mate.

Wishing they could have their wings out and around each other. He wanted so many things from Fire.

"Call me James," Fire said through clenched teeth as his hips worked to rub his cock against Rio's ass.

"James," Rio cried out, tasting the name of his mate on his tongue. "Close."

"You can come anytime you want, gorgeous," Fire said, speeding up the movement of his hand, squeezing him just a little bit tighter.

"Not in these pants," Rio groaned, and Fire let out a desperate laugh at his words, using his other hand to tug the sweatpants down his hips until Rio was sitting naked in his lap. The humid air hit his overheated skin, and the steering wheel pressed against his hip, but Rio couldn't find it in himself to care at all.

He yelped when Fire pushed his hips up, lifting Rio in the air to tug his own sweatpants down.

He released his cock and lowered Rio on it, rubbing it in the crease of his butt cheeks. The precum made the slide smoother, made the feeling of it hotter.

Rio whined when Fire's cockhead tugged at the rim of his entrance, and that was all it took for him to spill over Fire's fingers.

He knew he was being louder than he should have been in public. He was crying out for Fire, shivering in his lap and grappling for purchase on his clothes and skin.

Fire released his spent cock and gripped Rio's hips with his come-stained fingers, pulling him down onto his own cock.

He made him rock back and forth, used his body to bring himself pleasure, and Rio wanted it just as much as Fire did.

He wanted Fire to come because of him. Wanted him to come all over him. God he wanted to be dirtied by Fire. Soiled by him.

"Come on," Rio said when Fire's breath sped up. When his fingers tightened on Rio's already-bruised hips and his cock slid further between his cheeks.

"Gonna come, gorgeous," Fire warned, and Rio nodded, gripping Fire's hair and pulling his head back to kiss him.

He thrust his tongue past his lips, sucking until Fire groaned, cock pulsing against Rio's entrance. Warm liquid spilled in Rio's crease, and it was the hottest thing Rio had ever felt.

The hottest thing he had ever done.

The entire car smelled of come and sweat. The fog on the windows beaded over and started sliding down in soft rivulets, mimicking the drops of sweat rushing from Rio's neck down his back.

Their harsh breaths echoed in the small space, and Rio's heartbeat was loud in his ears, giving rhythm to the world around them.

"Jesus, you're gonna ruin me," Fire said as his breathing evened out, and Rio nodded, hiding his face in Fire's neck again.

He didn't know why, but what they had just done made him feel bashful. Shy almost.

"Good," Rio said, fingers gripping Fire's shirt and holding on tight. "Because you're doing it to me too."

He didn't know what tomorrow would bring. He had no idea what would happen now that he knew Fire raced.

But he wanted them to find out together.

CHAPTER SEVEN

RIO

He rang the doorbell and waited for what felt like hours, the heavy gift in his arm making his shoulder ache. He wasn't cut out for physical labor, that was for sure.

Footsteps echoed from the other side of the door, and Rio straightened up, jutting his chin out and fixing his eyes to look straight ahead. Fire had made him wait, but Rio was determined to make him pay for it by looking as irresistible as he could.

He wore his best tan slacks that made his ass look amazing and a peach-colored shirt with a wide opening at the back to allow his wings to spread out behind him. He'd draped a set of golden chains with teardrop diamonds dangling from them on his wings, and a necklace with the same pendant perched in the hollow of his neck.

His hair was brushed to perfection, and Rio was confident he looked as perfect as he could get.

Confidence about the rest of his life, though, was a completely different thing. The aftermath of finding out about Fire's career loomed over his head like a cloud, making every moment of his every day feel heavy and exhausting. He still didn't know how to reconcile who Fire was with what Rio's life was supposed to look like.

The lock clicked and the door slid open, rendering Rio completely speechless and wiping all thought of anything else from his mind. The exact reaction he wanted to get from Fire, Fire pulled from him.

He'd turned the tables on Rio again.

His hair was wet from the shower, rivulets of water rushing down his neck and onto his chest. His ripped abs and pecs were firm and inviting Rio to touch, to bite, to lick the water off and taste his skin on his tongue.

He had a towel draped around his narrow hips, the slit in the side of it revealing thick thighs and sculpted calves. Rio wanted to touch.

"You're early, princess," Fire said with a smirk. "I assumed you were always fashionably late."

"There is a time and place to be fashionably late," Rio said, going for aloof but landing on shaky and dry-mouthed.

"I'm glad I'm important enough to make you on time."

Fire winked, and Rio huffed.

"Or are you not important enough to want to make an impact by being late?" Rio countered, happy to find his voice had firmed up, and he sounded more like himself and less like a blushing schoolboy with a secret crush.

He hoisted the gift higher and flounced past Fire and into the apartment he had only moved back into two days ago—a long story about rabid fans he'd explained to Rio over the phone while hauling his suitcases back.

The front entrance opened to a spacious living room, an arch at the far end of it leading into a decently sized kitchen. There was a staircase to the right of the entrance, and Rio guessed it led to a lofted bedroom. The apartment was relatively small but tastefully decorated.

Nothing over the top. Nothing like Rio would have picked given the choice. But the open concept, the dark wood of the floors and the furniture, and the light coming from floor-to-ceiling windows somehow screamed 'Fire.'

The furniture was massive, heavy, and utilitarian, the few art pieces on the walls simple and futuristic. It was tidy and organized. And best of all, it looked lived in. Loved.

Rio liked it. Despite the changes he felt would make it look even better. It had potential. It was a great canvas to create actual art with the place.

He walked farther inside, walking to a large wooden table and setting the gift he had brought with him down on it.

"I brought you a gift," he said, tearing the wrapping paper off the box and opening it in front of Fire.

"Was that for me?" Fire pointed at it, coming to stand way too close for it to be just interest in the gift. Rio looked at him.

"Obviously," he said, reaching into the box and pulling out a simple black bowl with a silver trim. It was asymmetrical, swooping to the right and large enough to fit on the shelf just above the TV.

Rio had seen the spot the moment he'd walked in. He took the bowl with him, placing it on the shelf and moving back a few steps, head tilted to examine whether it was as good of a fit as it was in his head.

"Perfect," he said happily, turning to look at Fire with a pleased hum. "Don't you think?"

"Sure," Fire said. "Looks kinda badass. And I needed a new bowl for snacks when I watch TV."

Rio recoiled as if slapped.

"Snacks?" he gasped, eyes wide and horrified.

Fire frowned.

"Yeah, snacks," Fire said. "You know, like chips and pretzels and stuff. Snacks."

"I know what a snack is, Fire," Rio snapped. "But this is a three thousand dollar Morray's bowl."

"I'm sure Morray won't mind," Fire said, coming closer and wrapping an arm around Rio's waist. He was entirely too naked and too wet for it to not drive Rio insane.

"He's dead, and if you put a single pretzel into that bowl, I'm sure he'll turn into a windmill from turning in his grave so much." There, that should put him back in control.

"But...it's a bowl."

"It's a decoration. A statement piece," Rio said. "It's a message."

"For whom?" Fire asked.

"Everyone who comes into your apartment," Rio said, spinning out of Fire's hold.

"And what is the bowl saying to them?" Fire asked, running his hand over his naked abs, nails scratching lightly.

"That you have style, that you know quality pieces, that you can afford them and know where and how to procure them," Rio said, trying not to stare. "These bowls are invitation-only items. Not everyone can just walk into a store and buy one. It's a privilege to own one."

Rio finished his speech triumphantly, expecting Fire to be happy and elated at the amazing gift he'd gotten for him.

Instead, he got a quirked eyebrow and a goofy smile as Fire walked to him, wrapped both his arms around his waist this time, and kissed the skin on the side of his neck.

"Having snacks is a privilege too, gorgeous," Fire said. "And while I'm super thankful you wrestled dragons and rich old ladies to get this bowl for me, I'd still rather send my guests home with full bellies than brains full of subliminal messages sent by a wonky dish."

"A wonky..." Rio jumped back out of Fire's arms, glaring at him as he picked the bowl up and took it back to put it safely in its box. "This is a piece of art! I will not have you defile it with...chips."

He spat the word out like Fire had said he'd offer dog poop on toast out of the bowl.

"Doesn't have to be chips. Nachos are also fine," Fire said, and Rio squeaked in offense, closing the box and cradling it to his chest.

"I'm taking this home with me," Rio said. "You don't deserve it at all."

Fire cackled as he walked to Rio again, fingers running over the top of the lid of the box.

"I'm kidding, princess," Fire said. "I love the gift, and I promise I won't be serving any chips out of it."

Rio looked up into his eyes, still tugging the box away from him. He narrowed his eyes and glared at Fire. "Promise?"

"Promise," Fire said, and Rio reluctantly released the box to him.

"It's staying here on a probation period. If a single chip touches it, I'm taking it back with me."

"Deal," Fire said. "Now put that down, unclench your butt cheeks, and come help me groom my wings."

"My butt cheeks are not clenched," Rio said, but he still put the box down and walked after Fire into the living room.

The short trip gave him a chance to watch the ripple of muscle beneath the skin on his back and the shift of his huge, sharp tattoos. They looked very representative of Fire's real wings. Outlined feathers pointed and cut across his back like arrows. They reached around his waist and disappeared down into the towel, making Rio wonder where the tips of them ended.

Before he could comment on them, Fire's shoulder blades rippled and his wings materialized around his body, fire-red and imposing.

Rio had noticed they looked powerful before, but now that he knew what Fire did for a living, the agility in the movement of them made so much more sense.

He frowned when he realized one of them was hanging a tiny bit lower than the other, the flutter of it jerky and staggered compared to the smooth shift of the other. The movement dislodged one of the feathers, which fluttered to the ground beneath Rio's feet. Molting wasn't unusual for racers, but combined with how weak Fire's wing looked, it worried Rio.

"Is your wing okay?" he asked, picking up the feather and setting it on the coffee table. Fire nodded as he sat down on a small stool in front of his couch.

"I landed on it roughly in my last race. It got injured, but it's getting better," Fire said, motioning for Rio to sit behind him on the couch and handing him a little basket with his grooming products inside. "I know I told you you'd help me groom, but you don't have to if you don't want to."

Rio snagged the basket from him and huffed.

"Please," he said. "As if I'd let you butcher the grooming of them on your own. Look at these."

He wiggled his own wings, catching the edges of them in the corner of his vision. They were beautifully groomed, shiny, and healthy-looking.

He turned to Fire proudly, breath catching in his throat when he noticed the expression on his face. Fire stared at his wings as if they were the most magical things he had ever seen. His eyes were slightly dazed, and he followed their soft movement as if he couldn't get enough.

"They're gorgeous," Fire said, and Rio resisted the urge to preen. He knew his wings were pretty, but having your mate compliment them was a completely different feeling.

"Yes, well..." Rio said, nose in the air, but he could feel his cheeks heating up.

"Aw, princess, are you blushing?" Fire asked, and Rio glared at him, gripping Fire's face and using it to twist his head away from him.

"Shut up. I'm not," he said. "Now do you want me to help you groom or not?"

He sifted through the products in the basket, noticing a lot of them were medicinal. There were also far fewer products than he usually used on his own wings, which didn't make a lot of sense. Wings the color of Fire's needed more than that to make the shine stay, to make them look their best.

"Is this all you use?" Rio asked, and Fire nodded.

"Yeah, it's the stuff Doc ordered for me. Most of it is to make sure my joints remain mobile while the injury heals. The rest is to help the feathers stay healthy and such," Fire said, and Rio frowned at how vague it all was.

"Are you telling me you don't actually know what the product you're using does?"

"I mean, I know they're helping," Fire said, shrugging. "I didn't really care to go into specifics."

Rio was going to get an ulcer. His own mate would give him an ulcer.

"I genuinely can't with you right now," Rio said, pinching the bridge of his nose with one hand and extending the other toward Fire. "Give me your phone."

"What? Why?" Fire asked. "I thought we were grooming."

"We will be grooming after I make a phone call."

"And you don't have your phone?" Fire asked.

Rio dropped his hand to glare.

"I do," he said. "But I don't have your doctor's number."

"You're calling Doc?" Fire asked.

"I am," he said, wiggling his fingers in Fire's direction again.

"Why?" Fire asked again, but still placed his phone in Rio's hand.

"Because one of us needs to be informed of what your product is supposed to be doing for you so we can track if it actually *is* doing it for you," Rio said. "Passcode?"

"Uxorious," Fire said. "I think Doc knows what he's doing."

"I didn't say he didn't," Rio said. "Just that I want to know as well. Passcode, please?"

"*Uxorious,*" Fire said. "Fine, do what you want."

"I would do what I want if you'd give me the passcode!" Rio said, at the end of his rope, and squeaked when Fire took the phone from him. He pulled up the keypad, turning it to face Rio, and very pointedly typed UXORIOUS to unlock it.

"My name is your passcode?" Rio asked, voice going breathy again when Fire nodded with a silly smile. How was this man making him feel so weak in the knees all the damn time?

"It is," Fire said. "Now make your call."

Rio pulled up Doc's contact info and hit dial, waiting for the doctor to pick up.

"*Hello?*" A soft, gentle voice came from the other end.

"This is Uxorious Archibald Charmichael III speaking," Rio said, ignoring Fire's eyeroll.

"Just call him Rio, Doc," Fire yelled to be heard. "He's my mate."

"*Oh my god, is he the dude you boned in a coatroom, who left you there with your dick out?*" came an unfamiliar voice that had Fire groaning and Rio recoiling from the phone before he put it back to his ear.

"I wouldn't put it so crudely, but I am Fire's mate, yes," Rio said, making Fire cackle.

"*Bailey!*" Doc admonished over the phone.

"*What? He did,*" the man said. "*Hi, man, I'm Bailey. I'm Doc's mate.*"

"Pleasure," Rio said, not meaning it in the slightest.

"*How can I help, Mr. Charmichael?*" Doc asked.

"*He legit told you to call him Rio,*" Bailey said.

"I did no such thing," Rio said, indignant.

"*Fire did,*" Bailey argued.

"Fire has no say in this," Rio replied. "Now, Doctor, I had a few questions about Fire's grooming products."

"*Is everything okay?*" Doc asked.

"*Are you questioning my mate's expertise?*" Bailey asked.

"Everything is in order," Rio replied to Doc, opting to ignore Bailey for the time being. "He is just completely unaware of what the products are supposed to be doing for him, and as such, it's making me wonder if he's using them correctly and what signs we're supposed to be watching for to make sure they're healing. Also, I'd like to add a few more products into his routine that are more for aesthetic purposes and was wondering if I could get your approval on them to make sure they're not interfering with the medicinal ones."

"*Has he not read the information package I sent over with the products?*" Doc asked, and Rio whipped his head to stare at Fire, who gave him a sheepish grin.

"Have you not read the information package Doc sent over with the products?" Rio said with a purposeful pause between each word, hissing through his teeth by the end of the sentence.

Ulcers!

"Nah," Fire said. "Just skipped to the routine steps and did that. I trust Doc."

"*As you should,*" Bailey chipped in again, and Rio closed his eyes to stave off the impending breakdown.

"So I'll read the information you sent over," Rio said to Doc.

"*That would be best, yes,*" Doc said. "*But I don't mind helping you figure it out should you need it.*"

"That won't be needed, thank you," Rio said. "Would you mind me sending over the names of some of the products I'd like to use for approval?"

"*Absolutely, send them over whenever. Usually, beauty products don't have ingredients that could interfere with the healing ones, but better safe than sorry.*"

"Precisely," Rio agreed, pleased to find at least one sane person in Fire's immediate vicinity besides himself.

"*If that's all...*" Doc trailed off, and Rio nodded.

"It is. Thank you so much for your time."

"*You're welcome*," Doc said.

"*BYE, RIO!*" Bailey screeched in the background.

Rio dropped the call and turned to Fire.

"Do you at the very least still have the information he sent over?" Rio asked, and Fire jumped to his feet.

"Sure do," he said, rushing upstairs and returning with a handful of crinkled papers, thrusting them at Rio. "Here."

Rio sifted through them for a moment, trying to make heads and tails of it, finally managing to find what looked to be the first page.

He read through it all carefully, matching the descriptions with the products in the basket. All of them seemed to be geared toward making sure the hairline fractures healed completely, the mobility of his joints stayed intact, and the strength he clearly had in his wings didn't diminish while he got back into his training routine. It all made perfect sense, and it settled Rio to know Fire's wings were being properly taken care of.

Fire flailed about next to him, clearly unable to sit still for longer than a few minutes.

"Okay," Rio said after reading the final page. "Turn around now."

"Finally!" Fire said, assuming position between Rio's knees, wings fluttering in his face.

"I can't believe you'd just slap things on your injured wings without even knowing what they do."

"A certified doctor told me to," Fire said, and Rio huffed.

"If he told you to jump off a bridge, would you do that too?" Dammit, he sounded so much like his grandmother, he cringed internally. "The spray you use on the roots on your feathers is to keep them nice, slick, and mobile while you're not actively training."

He took the bottle of spray and set off to move the feathers left and right, making sure to spray each and every spot on Fire's wings.

He put the bottle down and dug his fingers in like the instructions said, massaging the medicine in as gently as he could.

He noticed Fire flinch just a little when he touched certain spots, so he made sure to go over those spots more carefully while using the next product, which was an anti-inflammatory balm to make the aches in the wings lessen and allow Fire to move his wings about more.

Fire's wings felt strange and new under Rio's fingers, and as meticulous as he wanted to be with caring for them, he couldn't help but allow himself to enjoy the feeling of them. They were sharper than any other pair of wings he'd touched, the texture a mixture of coarse and soft—old feathers and newer ones that hadn't seen as much of the track yet. They were long, swooping from their roots in straight lines Rio knew made them more aerodynamic and helped in his racing.

"Your wings are one of a kind," Rio said while he smoothed down oils to the tips of the feathers, making them glisten under the lights.

"I'll take that as a compliment, gorgeous," Fire said, and Rio wanted to puff up in pride at how choked up Fire sounded.

"It was meant as one," Rio said. "I'm sorry you got hurt."

"I'm healing," Fire said. "Doc said I should make a full recovery and start competing again soon."

Rio felt worry settle low in his stomach, his heart picking up speed and pumping the anxiety through his bloodstream.

"Is that safe?" he asked. "Don't make it worse."

"Don't worry, gorgeous," Fire said. "I have a good team of people around me, making sure I'm safe."

Rio pushed his worries aside and buried his fingers in Fire's feathers again, trying to find calm. "As long as you're healed completely before racing again. I'll send Doc the list of products I want to get for you."

"Are they gonna be super bougie and made of unicorn tears and the blood of elves?" Fire teased, and Rio smacked the back of his head.

"They're going to be whatever I want them to be, and you'll love them."

"Didn't you kick up a fuss about me using products I didn't know what they did not five minutes ago?" Fire said.

"I do not kick fusses." Rio bristled. "I argue my points and make people realize they were in the wrong."

"Right," Fire said. "Well, I'm looking forward to smelling like unicorns."

"You're not going to be smelling like unicorns," Rio said, and Fire pouted, sprawling himself over Rio's knees and throwing a hand over his forehead.

"Disappointed!" he screeched, and Rio failed at hiding the smile that broke on his face.

God, his mate was ridiculous. He almost made the ulcers worth it.

CHAPTER EIGHT

FIRE

Fire was practically chipper on his way to training that morning.

Things with Rio were amazing. The sex was bomb, he was endlessly entertained, and they'd shared a few moments now that had brought them closer in a way Fire wasn't used to with relationships.

There was only one dark cloud looming in the sky that he was trying to avoid looking at. If he ignored it, then maybe it'd clear up on its own?

That's how that shit worked, right?

Whatever.

Rio had asked for time to explain his reaction to the racer thing, and while he'd given next to no details and that made Fire itchy as fuck, he didn't want to push him.

So he was getting back to what he knew, partly to take his mind off of it, but mostly because he fucking missed it.

Racing.

Maybe he was a couple days ahead of schedule, but his wing was practically good as new, Doc said. Noticeably weaker, but there was no real pain left and his X-rays were clear, and that's why he needed to get back into training.

He made it through the security gate easily, saying hello to Jim who was manning it and keeping the more fanatical fans at bay. He parked in his designated spot and grabbed his gear, barely remembering to lock up after himself.

The *beep* of the door scanner was like music to Fire's ears, and he rushed inside, greeting the receptionist as he beelined for the changing rooms.

The room was a huge rectangle, sterile and clean with the large Ace logo on the wall. Lockers were lined up and down, and half the back area was taken up by showers. Fire bypassed the first row and spotted a familiar face.

"Zero!"

The massive hulk of a Kriila was in the process of threading his equally huge raven's wings into his skintight black training top. He had more muscle groups than were possibly attainable and absolutely none of the typical alpha-male persona that went with it. Guy was the size of a house, with a mean mug and a shorn head, but was practically a ghost.

"How's it been going? I heard you won that race I crashed out of. Congrats. Better you than any of those other assholes. I bet Speed thought he had it all sewn up, that slimy little..." Fire lapsed into curses under his breath.

"Didn't you break your wing?" Zero said bluntly, voice pitched so low it could cause earthquakes.

"A little exaggerated." Zero grunted and turned away, done with the conversation. "But good news is I'm back to hand you all your asses again. You're welcome in advance."

Zaro closed his locker silently, not reacting to the overconfidence or shit talk. Fire could never figure out what the guy's malfunction was. He'd briefly considered whether Zero was an android for about three months after watching a chilling documentary on the advances in technology. It wasn't until drug test season came around and Fire saw them draw blood from him that he relented and decided that he probably wasn't.

"Nice talking to you," Fire called to Zero's back.

Zero let the closing door bookend his reply.

"Good to be back," Fire muttered to himself, shaking his head before heading to his own locker.

Their training gear was simple. Everything from tops to bottoms was skintight for aerodynamic purposes, and the gaps for their wings were tiny to make sure no airflow got into them.

He pulled it all on and let his wings loose, stretching them out before tucking them in and following the direction Zero took.

The Ace training facility was state of the art. With high-spec gyms and a huge racetrack inside the oval dome, it was one of the best in the world. Fire had only been allowed to train here after winning his first real comp. They didn't much like rookies hanging around. While the elitism grated, Fire needed access to the best of the best in order to be the best of the best.

And he got back at Ace in his own small ways.

Like hiring on his own team of staff instead of using the facility's. At first, the director of the place had flatly refused, but Fire had been able to leverage his newfound fame and prestige within the racing community to get his own way.

He didn't *have* to train at Ace. There were plenty of places that had offered him a spot that he could wear on his wings and promote.

Within a few days, that director had entered early retirement, and a new one had sat in his place. One that Fire thought was pretty chill in comparison and much more accepting. As long as he didn't make Ace look bad, he was free to train how he liked, with who he liked.

The heavy sounds of beating wings, shouted instructions, and the whir of gym equipment greeted Fire, and he breathed in the familiar smell of sweat and cleaners recycled by the air conditioning.

Fire said a few hellos to familiar faces as he walked toward the therapy and recovery rooms in the east of the building. He pushed inside and looked past the ice tubs, spotting who he wanted to see straight away. That bleached blond hair was impossible to miss, and even without that, the tattoos and piercings made enough of a statement.

"Vid!"

"Fire! What the hell are you doing here?" Vid said, brown eyes that were almost black widening. He dropped the mat he was holding to the floor and approached, pulling him in for a bro hug. "The email I got from your doctor said Monday."

"I'm good to go," Fire said confidently.

"Does Coach know? He's not here today."

Fire shifted. "Define 'know?'"

Vid's dark brows pulled together under his parted bangs. "Listen, I'm all for pushing the boundaries. I didn't get to this position without doing that. But you don't wanna risk everything over two days."

Fire smiled. Pushing the boundaries was right. Vid was the only human sports therapist Fire knew of within the circuit. Humans in general were rare within the sport for obvious reasons; wings were kinda a prerequisite.

"I know it looks like I'm too impatient to wait," Fire said, then tilted his head in acceptance. "And okay, waiting fucking blows and not in the way I like best. But I really feel ready."

Vid still looked skeptical.

"It's just easing in anyway. You've got my therapy plan, and if things start hurting even a little, I'll stop," Fire promised.

Vid sighed and shook his head, his chain helix piercing rocking with the force of it. "Let me print off your plan from Nelson. You're lucky I was even in today."

"You've had other clients booked in while I was out. Don't act like I left you without work," Fire said, following him to the office he shared with some of the other trainers.

"Of course you didn't. I'm not reliant on you. You're reliant on me," Vid said, bending over his laptop.

Fire couldn't argue. Honestly, having a good sports therapist was key in this game. They kept you in the air longer. Back in the day, the shelf life of a racer was brutally short. And even though Vid was human, he was one of the best.

"So what has you so busy then? Finally taking a holiday?" Fire asked, perching on a desk as he waited.

"I have a family commitment over the weekend. My nephew," Vid said.

"The cute little tyke on your lock screen, right?" Fire said.

Vid smiled. "Yup. It's his sixth birthday, and my sister is throwing a party."

"What kinda party is it? A racing one?"

"He has no interest in racing," Vid said, rolling his eyes.

"What kid doesn't like racing?" Fire said, offended.

"His reaction to me telling him I worked with you was a yawn and to ask for more snacks."

"Now that's just rude," Fire said. Bailey snubbing him was fine, but kids thought he was awesome. He had a reputation to uphold! "Are you sure you wanna turn up for his birthday?"

Vid laughed, walking over to the printer that was spitting out paper. "Not all humans revere Kriila just because you can fly."

"No, but all kids should revere me. I'm cool! I'm gonna be an action figure one day, just you wait."

"Well, Mr. Cool. Let's run you through this list," Vid said, smacking him on the back of the head with the papers that were still warm.

"Hell yeah," Fire said, eagerly following. "We've only got twelve weeks until AirCore X."

"AirCore is a circuit race, Fire," Vid said. "I doubt we'll get you in good enough shape to take turns and bends like that. If it was just a straight line sprint event I'd be more inclined to give you the green light to at least try."

"I believe in my team," Fire said. "Besides, look how reasonable I'm being. I'm not even suggesting we try getting me ready for an obstacle course."

"I wouldn't call that reasonable, man," Vid said. "That's like, just a step up from a full blown idiot."

"I can't not be ready for the final race of the season," Fire said after a moment of silence.

"You can always sit it out," Vid said, leading them to the gym. Fire gave him a look, and Vid shook his head in exasperation. "You'd rather come last instead of sit out a legit injury?"

"I won't come last. I've never come last... Well, not exactly accurate."

"I don't need to know about your sexual exploits, thank you very much. The Lazy Susan of fucks you choose from makes me dizzy."

Fire laughed, glancing around them covertly to make sure they were completely alone before leaning in. "Not so much choice anymore."

Vid's eyebrow lifted. "You got a boyfriend finally?"

Fire rolled his eyes. "So human. Don't you remember your Kriila lessons from school?"

"Honestly, I did my best to tune that shit out. No offense." Fire punched him, and Vid let up. "So you're trying to tell me you found your mate? Seriously?"

Fire nodded.

He whistled. "Damn, man. Congrats. Is that what people say?"

"They usually gift money."

"Nice try."

Fire grinned. "Worth a shot."

They walked into the gym. It was sparsely populated for right now, which was good. Fewer distractions and fewer prying eyes eating up the fact that he was out of the picture for now. Vid led him straight over to a wing trainer, and Fire grimaced at it.

"So you're still grounded for a couple days," Vid said.

"What?!"

"You'll be working on the machine to build up strength in increments until we get to a more even match with your other wing. Like this, you're liable not to even get off the ground, let alone control your angles in the air," Vid said.

Fire groaned. "You're just torturing me."

"Of course I am. Now get in position, and I'll hook you up and set your weight," Vid said cheerfully.

Fire sat on the bench, letting Vid help him thread his wing into the straps of the machine that were hanging down.

"Not too tight? Uncomfortable?"

Fire shook his head. "We're good."

"Okay, we'll start with no weight and just the straps and see how that feels. Then I'll start you on the lowest setting, and we'll do some sets," Vid said.

"This is so humiliating," Fire said, looking wistfully out the floor-to-ceiling glass panels on the right side of the gym that offered a view into the racetrack that ran around and made up the whole inside of the building. He could see the dark shadow that was Zero practicing maneuvers through suspended pylons.

"You'll get back up there," Vid promised. "But first you've got to put in the time here. Got it?"

"Yes, Mom."

Fire folded his wing forward in an imitation of how he would flap it for flying, and he felt the weakness immediately. Vid hadn't been kidding. He could feel sweat already beginning to bead on his forehead three reps in, but he gritted his teeth and pushed through it.

"Add some weight," Fire said.

Vid ignored him, eyes critically observing his wing as it struggled through the motions. "Three more and then you'll rest for a set, and then we'll go again with no weight."

"Vid—"

"Who has the degree here?"

Fire pouted. "You."

"There's nothing shameful about injuries, Fire. You've had them before."

"Not like this."

"We'll get you back in shape. Now, three more, let's go," Vid encouraged.

Fire pushed, wing shaking with the effort, and he was actually grateful to stop and rest. His wing was trembling like he'd just finished a full race, not a ten set with no weight.

"That you can even manage this is good, Fire," Vid said, making notes on the papers Doc sent over. "I'm pleased. We have a baseline to work up from."

"I suppose even this is better than sitting at home," Fire allowed, leaning his head back.

"We'll give it sixty and then go again," Vid said. "Then we'll move on to some light cardio. After that we'll heat, ice, and massage your wing so it doesn't seize. I'll book in some time with the infrared machine too."

Fire nodded. At least with cardio he could run some of his frustration out.

One hour later, Fire was dripping, a flush high on his cheeks and air burning in his lungs. It felt fucking fantastic.

"Definitely nothing wrong with your legs," Vid said, making some more notes.

"At least I have a little of my dignity left."

Vid shook his head with a half smile, putting the notes aside and reaching for his phone to check it. His brow furrowed at whatever he saw, and he began typing fast. Fire left him to it, walking over to the water dispenser on wobbly legs and grabbing a cup full of cool liquid. He downed it, refilling it one more time and grabbing a spare towel on his way back.

"So what does next week look like, training-wise?" Fire asked.

"I'll, uh, send you the schedule after I make it up," Vid replied, not looking up, thoroughly distracted.

"What's up?" Fire asked, toweling the sweat from his nape.

"The cover I arranged for fell through," Vid said, throwing his phone on top of a bench press in frustration.

"For Ace? I can speak to the staff," Fire said. "No worries, man. Go see your Fire-hating nephew."

Vid gave him another attempt at a smile that quickly fell again. "It's not for here. It's for the volunteer program I do a couple times a week when you aren't in pre-comp training."

Pre-comp was brutal and started two weeks before a big race. Coaches, trainers, and racers all slept, breathed, and ate nothing but racing as they prepared. It was a seven-day-a-week job in those periods.

"Well, what is it? Do you need credentials to volunteer?" Fire asked.

"It's a center for young kids. It offers a variety of classes, and one of them is flying. I know I'm no racer, but I've been around the circuit long enough, and I can help teach them proper safety and wing care."

"I'll do it."

Vid blinked twice. "Uh...what?"

"I'll cover you," Fire said simply.

"For real?"

Fire nodded. "Sure! Kids are great, and who better to teach them than the best racer in the Circles?"

Vid flicked him in the middle of the forehead. "Most humble too."

Fire grunted and swatted him away. "You want this favor or not?"

"Definitely want," Vid said quickly. "But don't you have better things to be doing?"

"Not with my wing all tied up. And besides, Anna will lap this shit up. Good for my image and all that," Fire said. "Wins all around!"

And he could bring Rio with him. Date round two was a go!

"Can I bring a friend?" Fire asked, just to make sure.

"As long as you both get background checked, then yeah, sure. Who are you going to—" Vid cut himself off. "The person who put an end to Lazy Susan?"

Fire burst out laughing. "If he heard you say that."

"Sensitive?"

"You have *no* idea."

"He must love you then," Vid said, snorting.

The words hit him in a way Fire was not expecting. Rio loving him? Finding your mate didn't immediately equal love, but god, did it sound good. Being loved by Rio. Being the one Rio turned to whenever he needed someone. Caring for him and Rio caring back. He was so impatient to get to that stage with him he was practically vibrating.

"Oh, you've got it bad," Vid said with a grin.

Fire shoved him.

Yeah, he did.

CHAPTER NINE

RIO

"Didn't you get my text last night?" Fire asked the moment Rio sat in his car. He didn't even get the chance to close the door or put his seatbelt on.

"I did," he replied with a quirk of his eyebrow, daring Fire to suddenly change their plans or add more to this 'surprise outing' he had sprung on Rio with zero regard to his personal preferences.

Rio hated surprises.

"Why are you dressed like that, then?" Fire asked, and Rio's jaw dropped as he looked down at the outfit he was wearing.

He'd put on his simple pale blue polo shirt and a sports blazer over it. He'd paired that with light cotton pants and comfy loafers he thought rounded the outfit out pretty well. His wings were tucked in, and his hair was just casually brushed over his forehead.

"You said to dress comfortably," Rio said, crossing his arms.

"And your idea of comfortable is a suit?" Fire asked.

"This isn't a suit!" he said, flapping his hands to encompass his outfit.

"You have on slacks and a blazer, gorgeous," Fire said. "That, in my world, is a suit."

"Well in the world of *adult* people, this is a casual blazer and cotton slacks that you wear for a casual day out. Which is what you said we were doing," Rio said and watched Fire pinch the bridge of his nose.

Fire himself was dressed in a navy sportswear set and a half-zip jacket with a high collar, all in familiar labels.

"Do you own jeans?" Fire asked.

Rio frowned, mentally flipping through his wardrobe. "I'm sure I have some, somewhere."

"What about a pair of sneakers?"

"I don't like sneakers," he said.

"You don't like..." Fire looked like he thought better of it and cut his sentence off as he started the car. "Okay. Well...I hope you don't mind getting your 'casual blazer' and 'cotton slacks' dirty."

"Dirty?" Rio exclaimed, turning in his seat to look at Fire. "Why would I get dirty? Where are you taking me? Am I being kidnapped right now?"

"Yes, Rio," Fire deadpanned. "You're getting kidnapped from in front of your house, in the middle of the day, by a public figure who can't walk three steps down the street without being photographed."

Well, when he said it like that.

"No need to be sarcastic," Rio huffed, turning to look out the window.

He decided he was annoyed now. He stuck his nose up into the air and let out angry little puffs of air through clenched teeth every few seconds to make sure Fire realized that fact. He was dead set on counting the trees passing by, contemplating ways to garner more attention, when he felt something warm wrap around his fingers.

He looked down and saw Fire's large hand gripping his gently, pulling it up and placing a kiss on top of his hand.

"You look gorgeous as always," Fire said, and Rio's heart skipped treacherously at the warmth in his voice. There was no teasing, no crooked smirks. Just tenderness and a hint of awe Rio was pretty sure Fire didn't show too often.

He wanted to snark back. He wanted to keep being annoyed, but something in his chest spilled over, like honey, making him feel soft and safe.

"Thank you," Rio said, looking down into his lap, unusually shy and floored by a compliment he had heard thrown his way a billion times.

But it had never sounded like that.

It had never been said by his mate.

"We'll be there in five minutes," Fire said, stopping at a red light and looking at Rio.

He leaned in and gripped Rio's chin between his thumb and forefinger, lifting his face up a little bit. He closed the distance between them and claimed his lips in a soft kiss. It lasted a mere second, and yet it left Rio feeling shaky all over again.

Fire smiled at him when he pulled away, those hazel eyes so pretty up close.

Rio was left thinking about them even as Fire released him and started driving again, and he lost time like that until Fire was telling him they'd arrived.

Rio glanced around, seeing no familiar waypoints in the Circle he knew so well. He frowned. Fire had parked in front of a small-ish building painted a pale green and surrounded by a neatly maintained garden.

"Where are we, exactly?" Rio asked as he stepped out of the car.

"This is the Children's Recreation Center," Fire said, locking up and rounding the car.

"And why are we here?" Rio asked. "Last I checked, neither of us were children, and my need for recreation stops at recreational gin and tonic consumption."

Fire laughed with a shake of his head, arm sneaking around Rio's waist as he pulled him toward the building.

"We're volunteering today," Fire said, and Rio dug his heels in, bringing them to a halt.

"Define volunteering," he said.

Fire beamed, his excitement obvious. "Vid, my sports therapist, volunteers here as a flying coach for the kiddos who are interested. He had other obligations today and didn't want to disappoint the kids, so I said I'd do it."

Alarm bells started to sound in Rio's head. Flying lessons were just a little too close to everything he'd been pointedly ignoring about his past, and he didn't want to risk the precarious balance of ignorance that they'd found.

"That is very sweet of you," Rio said, glancing at his surroundings. "I'll be in that little café over there. You can join me when you're finished."

He took a step in that direction, but Fire actually picked him up and turned him back around. Rio squeaked and hit him on the shoulder for the manhandling, refusing to acknowledge the answering swoop of heat.

"You're helping, princess," Fire said, unaware of his dilemma, marching him to the entrance. Rio kicked and whined the whole way there, rationalizing to himself that it wouldn't be so bad if he just observed. But then the second part of the problem reared its ugly head.

"I don't like children," Rio said under his breath when they were finally inside, a receptionist taking them to meet the kids.

"I'm sure you'll survive for a couple of hours," Fire said.

"And they don't like me either," Rio said.

"Oh please, everyone likes you," Fire said with too much faux sweetness to be real.

Rio glared. "You won't butter me up to be happy about this. It won't work."

Fire laughed, throwing a look that promised nothing good Rio's way.

"How about I handle most of the training? You just hang back and look pretty," Fire said, and Rio bristled at the words.

"I am not just a pretty face," he said. "I can handle a few children for an hour."

Fire raised his arms in surrender and nodded. "Never said you couldn't, princess. I just thought you 'didn't like children.'"

"I don't," Rio said, narrowing his eyes. "But I can keep them alive until their owners come and pick them up."

"Parents, gorgeous," Fire said. "The word is parents."

"Whatever," Rio said, charging past Fire and into a large room. He'd show him!

The room was equipped with different foam obstacles, including crash mats and a foam pit. The ceiling was high enough for small children to fly under, and there were a bunch of hand-painted birds on the walls in midflight.

There were about nine children milling about, their chatter high-pitched and their fluffy wings ruffled and colorful against the monochrome décor of the room.

"Children, gather around if you please," the receptionist called. "We have an exciting surprise for you."

All the kids came stampeding like she'd announced a 50 percent sale and Rio stepped back to avoid being caught up in it. Children were dirty and sticky and loud.

"Mr. Vid is away today, but he's arranged for someone very special to come and teach you," the receptionist said.

"Hey there," Fire said, stepping out and manifesting his wings.

A torrent of gasps and a flurry of shrieks rang out.

"Fire!" chorused around the room.

The receptionist stepped out, smiling, and Rio watched in disbelief as Fire put his hands on his hips, wings in some kind of pose that was supposed to impress. And it did. The kids all clamored to be noticed, firing questions over one another as they surrounded him—and Rio, incidentally.

Rio cringed, hands in the air to avoid being touched unduly.

"So who wants to learn to fly from the best, huh?" Fire said.

There was one dissenter in the ranks, a little boy with a buzzcut who was about seven. "Zero beat you last race! That means he's the best now."

There was a ripple of confusion as that logic sank in among the children.

Rio covered his laugh with his hand, and Fire gave him a narrow-eyed look. "Zero only won that one race. You have to win more than that to become champion."

"My grandpa sayed your wings got breaked, and you can never race again," one of the youngest of the bunch piped up.

"That means Zero will be the new champion," Buzzcut declared.

"Nuh-uh! Speed is cool!"

"Who said that?" Fire burst out. "Speed is not cool!"

"Is too!"

"Is not!"

Someone started to cry.

Rio leaned into his ear. "Are you losing your adoring crowd?"

"How can they think those guys are cooler than me?" Fire said, scandalized.

Rio rolled his eyes and stepped up forward. "Listen, kids. You wanna learn from a real racer?"

They all quieted down and nodded, wide-eyed at his authoritative tone.

Rio crossed his arms and raised his brows expectantly. "Then what do you say to Mr. Fire?"

"Sorry his wings are breaked?"

"Sorry he's not the champion?"

"My wings aren't broken, and I *am* the reigning champion until the season is over!" Fire said indignantly.

Rio smirked. There were a few more mumbles as the kids tried to work it out. A girl with braids raised her hand, and Rio pointed at her. "Yes?"

"Please?"

"Well done." The girl perked up at getting it right, looking smugly at the crowd. Rio approved. "Now, do as he says. Otherwise, you'll be average the rest of your lives."

Someone else lifted up their hand. He looked about four. "What's average?"

"It's completely mediocre in all aspects of your life, and you'll never amount to anything aspirationa—"

"Ah, ah, ah! Something to learn another day," Fire jumped in hastily, coughing. "Now, uh, thank Mr. Rio and how about we go search the supply closet and set up some activities?"

"Oh! I know where everything is!"

"I do too!"

"No, you don't!"

They all tore off toward the closet, pushing and shoving and shouting, and Rio examined his nails, feeling Fire's eyes on him.

"You could command the whole Circle, couldn't you?"

"You underestimate me thinking it would only be the one," Rio said.

Fire laughed, placing a kiss under his ear. "We'll revisit this scenario later, and you can tell *me* what to do. It's hot."

Rio shivered, watching Fire saunter off and leaving him to cool down on his own. Asshole.

He watched from a distance as Fire wrangled the kids. Despite their chatter, they followed the racer like little ducklings, eager for him to pay attention to them. Rio refused to admit it was cute.

The squeak of the door snapped him out of his staring, and he turned. He wasn't expecting two familiar faces to peek around the door before slipping in sheepishly, awkward to be late.

They were the father and daughter from the botanical garden.

The man was dressed down in some blue jeans and a green sweater. His chin-length hair was tucked messily behind his ears. He looked a few years older than Rio, maybe approaching thirty. Definitely too young to look that tired.

"Piper, don't chew your clothes," the dad said, looking down at her. "That jacket is brand new."

Piper popped the jean jacket out of her mouth and hid more behind her father's leg.

"You don't have to be nervous, Pip. I thought you wanted to learn?"

She mumbled something Rio couldn't make out.

The dad looked around the room and spotted Rio, walking them over.

"Sorry we're late," he said.

Rio wasn't exactly one to speak on tardiness. "It's fine. The class hasn't started yet. We're still setting up."

"Great. Uh, it's her first time," he said, cupping his daughter's head. "Are you the instructor?"

He looked a little confused as he asked, obviously looking at Rio's attire, but he seemed to roll with it. His lack of judgment soothed Rio's snappy retort, and he swallowed it back.

"Filling in for the week unexpectedly," Rio replied.

"I know a little something about that," he said. "I'm Mateo, by the way, and this is Piper. I didn't think she'd be this clingy. She's been talking about flying lessons for months. It was hell to get her mom to even agree to let me take her."

Rio hummed, looking down at Piper, who was looking at her feet, fiddling with the pin Fire had gifted her. "I think she just needs a little motivation."

"Do you mind if I sit in on her first class? Just in case there's a meltdown."

"You're more than welcome."

Rio did not want to clean up snot and tears. He had his own breakdowns to worry about. Piper did seem sweet, though. The jean jacket that she'd obviously gotten her dad to buy her to copy Fire's was impossible not to thaw even the coldest of hearts.

"That's a nice pin," Rio said to her.

She peeked up at him. "It's from Fire."

"Fire," Rio repeated, then leaned in and said teasingly, "That good-for-nothing racer? Are you sure?"

She scowled, little wings standing up straighter as she forgot her shyness. "Yes. Fire gave it to me. And he's not good-for-nothing! That's mean!"

"Listen," Mateo started, frowning too, chest beginning to inflate like he was going to defend his daughter's idol's honor.

"Well, let's just go ask him," Rio said casually.

Mateo and Piper wore identical looks of confusion as they deflated like balloons. They really were father and daughter.

"He's just over there," Rio said, flourishing a single finger behind him.

Piper's eyes widened and her little jaw dropped.

Rio smiled and turned his head. "Fire!"

Fire came bounding over, leaving the kids where they were. "What's up?"

"Another one," Rio said, indicating.

"Hey...I remember you!" Fire said happily. "Thanks for not ratting me out the other day."

Piper looked like Christmas and her birthday had come early, and Rio hid his smile.

"Cool jacket," Fire said approvingly. "Wanna put it to the side and join in?"

Piper nodded her head shyly.

"Let's rock," Fire said, offering his hand for her to take.

She rocketed to take it, abandoning her dad completely and forgetting her nerves.

"I don't think you need to worry anymore," Rio said.

Mateo blinked, looking a little stunned. "Don't I? A race star apparently knows my kid. I thought she was joking!"

Rio laughed. "She helped us out the other day. If she'd announced it to the whole garden, we would have been mobbed."

"She's a good kid. I don't much like the idea of strangers leaving her gifts, but...I suppose it was an extenuating circumstance." Rio nodded. "Well, I guess I'll go take a seat now. I'm not needed anymore."

"Feel free."

Mateo waved and headed for the corner to be out of the way, eyes attached to his little girl and smiling.

"Right! Who wants to show me their proper flight positions? Vid said you've been learning that with him, right?" Fire said loudly, drawing all the notice. They all dropped down to their tummies, and little wings of all shapes and sizes spread out in answer, bumping into one another's. Fire laughed. "Okay, okay, make some room. Good job."

He ran over their positions and corrected some here and there, showing Piper in particular what she needed to do. Once he was done, he grabbed the wooden boxes he'd taken from the supply closet and set them up in front of the pit.

"How about today we practice it in the air?" he asked them.

A chorus of "YES" echoed around the room.

"Skipping the theory?" Rio said as Fire passed him.

Fire grinned. "Sometimes you just gotta feel it out in the air."

Rio rolled his eyes.

Fire set them into two lines, the older kids on the taller boxes and the younger on the shorter. He had them take turns jumping from the box into the air, unfurling their wings to glide a little before they landed in the safety of the foam pit.

It was a standard flying technique for all ages and one kids usually enjoyed immensely. Rio found himself drifting over as he watched Fire coach them through it.

Fire was a good teacher. He was patient and kind, and his enthusiasm for the sport was palpable in every word and action. But there were things that he overlooked in the grander scheme of things, especially with this many kids. He skipped steps, ignored smaller details that were important. Things he must have learned growing up that were so ingrained he barely thought about them.

Rio saw them.

"Jump higher if you can," Rio found himself saying to a smaller boy who just couldn't untuck his wings on time when he jumped. The boy listened and managed the correct move on his next try. Rio felt something warm tuck behind his ribs at the beaming "Thank you" from the boy.

And from there he couldn't stop. The kids looked at him expectantly, eager to learn, and Rio found he had a lot to say. The words just poured out of his mouth like he'd broken a dam.

"You're tucking your wings. You need full extension to catch the updraft. Don't expect the air to just do the work for you."

"Yes, Mr. Rio."

"Straighten your legs. Don't leave them dangling like a weight."

"Yes, Mr. Rio."

"Your feathers are messy. You can't fly with your primaries all mixed up with your secondaries."

"But grooming is boring," the seven-year-old said, rolling his eyes.

Rio was unimpressed. "Is not being able to fly more boring?"

"Yeah," he mumbled.

"Then take care of your wings. I want to see them perfectly ordered next week."

"Yes, Mr. Rio."

Rio nodded and moved on, beckoning the next child.

"Remember your positioning. Angles are everything in flying," Rio said. "They mean the difference between who comes first and who comes second."

"First?" the girl with the braids asked as she fought her way out of the foam blocks. "Are we going to be racing?"

Rio felt himself freeze. He'd gotten completely carried away taking a simple flying lesson into a racing lesson. And to make matters worse, he hadn't noticed Fire watching him shrewdly from the other side of the foam pit the whole time.

Rio's stomach dropped and he flushed.

"Well...carry on," he said to them, stepping away and cursing himself for a fool.

What the hell was he doing?

The class ended soon after, and all the kids filed out of the room to be picked up by their parents, stopping by to make sure to say goodbye to Rio, which was unexpected.

All except Mateo and Piper.

She was flushed with happiness as she bounded over to her dad, cotton-candy wings droopy with exhaustion.

Mateo's smile was huge as he responded to her happiness, soaking it up secondhand. It made him look younger, more like his real age.

"Did you see me?" Piper asked excitedly.

"Sure did, baby. You did so good!" Mateo said, gathering her up.

"She's a natural," Fire said. "You've got a little firecracker on your hands."

Piper beamed at the praise, and Mateo laughed. "She is that."

"Will you be here next week?" Piper asked shyly.

"Oh...uh." Fire rubbed the back of his neck. "I think my friend Vid is going to be taking back over next week. It's his class usually. I was just filling in."

"Oh," Piper said.

"Vid works with me. He takes care of my wings. He's really nice," Fire promised her.

"Hear that, Pip?" Mateo said, bouncing her. "You'll have fun with Fire's friend."

It clearly wasn't what she wanted to hear. "Okay."

"If we have time, we'll stop by," Rio asserted.

Piper glanced hopefully at him. "Really?"

"I...guess so," Fire said, giving Rio a questioning look that he ignored.

They said their goodbyes, and Mateo took a chattering Piper out of the room, leaving the pair of them alone.

Rio refused to turn back and look at Fire even though he could feel eyes on the back of his head. Questions hovered in the air, unspoken, yet seeping out a tension that was suffocating.

Rio knew he was at a crossroads.

"You seem to know an awful lot about a sport you don't follow," Fire said quietly.

Rio hunched his shoulders as he turned around. "It's common sense. I have wings. I had flying lessons when I was younger like any other Kriila."

The words felt bitter on his tongue. Asking Fire for some time to get his thoughts in order was one thing. He was being honest and just asking for a chance. This...was lying. He hated it.

"I would agree, of course. But a lot of those tips you were handing out were a little strange for plain flying," Fire said, hazel eyes taking him to pieces as he walked closer. He tipped Rio's face up with a thumb on his chin. "Talk to me, Rio."

Rio stared at him, willing his heart to move from his throat so he could give an excuse, buy more time maybe...but there was no avoiding it anymore.

Even if he wasn't completely ready.

But then again, he wasn't sure he ever would be. Better to get it over and done with.

He pulled his chin out of Fire's grip and walked toward the door.

"Not here," he said, and Fire followed him in silence, thankfully giving him precious moments to get his brain to settle before he had to bare all.

CHAPTER TEN

FIRE

"So...terminology on point, if a tiny bit old-school, wing positioning you got down to a science, maneuvering advice in line with what my own coaches dished out in practice..." Fire counted on the fingers of his hand, watching Rio sink deeper and deeper into the cushions of his sofa next to him.

His lips were pressed tight together, and the tension was obvious in his body, despite Fire doing his best to keep his tone light and not accusing at all.

Rio had had a life before they met. He was well aware of that and not the least bit resentful of it. He also didn't think he had an inherent right to know all of Rio's secrets at once, mate or not. But to be put on proverbial ice because he was a racer, to spend days around him wondering what it was that made Rio reserved and if it would cost him his mate, and then discover that Rio had a very obvious past related to racing was confusing and a little hurtful to say the least.

He didn't need details, but he did need answers.

"Rio..." he prompted when the silence stretched too long.

Rio cringed visibly and drew his shoulders up, messing up his usually impeccable posture.

"I guess you did give me time I asked for," Rio said, biting his bottom lip for a moment before he met Fire's gaze. "And I do owe you an explanation."

"You don't owe it to me, or anyone else for that matter," Fire said. "If you don't want to share right now, I can wait until you're ready like I said I would...but I will say it's pretty obvious you have experience with racing. You know your shit. You can't blame me for being curious."

"I don't blame you," Rio said. "It's just very complicated and includes a lot of details about my family that might paint them, and in turn me, in a bad light."

Rio looked smaller than usual, like he wanted to take up less space, when usually he commanded every room he was in. Fire didn't think he liked that very much.

Rio was boisterous and melodramatic but in the most endearing sort of way. It suited him.

"I won't think any differently of you," Fire said. "I like you, Rio."

"I'm your mate," Rio said.

Fire rolled his eyes. "Yes, you are. But you're also incredibly gorgeous, so my eyes would have been drawn to you that night, mate or not."

"I do like a good entrance," Rio said, and Fire cracked a smile at the very weak attempt at a joke.

"And you deserve one every time you go somewhere," Fire said. "I might tease you about being a posh little princess—and don't get me wrong, you absolutely are one—but I like you like that. I wouldn't change it."

Rio returned his smile, and Fire reached out to grip his hand between his fingers. He wanted to offer him reassurance.

Rio squeezed back and took a deep breath before he spoke again. "My dad was a racer."

Fire widened his eyes. He had been a racing enthusiast his entire life, but he had never heard of a racer with Rio's last name. Plenty of his competition came from the extreme wealth that just came with being Kriila sometimes, but he didn't think Rio's family was involved.

"Your dad raced?" Fire asked after a moment of silence, surprise making his voice fast. "Is he retired? How have I never heard of him?"

"He passed away," Rio said, and Fire felt his stomach drop in sympathy. "I was about eleven."

"I'm so sorry," Fire said, and Rio shrugged his shoulders.

"It was a racing-related injury that cost him his life. He took a tumble during a race and hit his head on one of the obstacles," Rio said. "He never woke up."

Fire watched as Rio's throat worked, and his eyes glossed over. He ran his thumb over the top of Rio's hand and waited patiently.

"I have my mother's family name," Rio finally continued, voice thick and quiet. "The Charmichaels are really old and almost seen as royalty. My grandparents wanted my mom to marry someone close to their status, but my dad was her mate."

Fire smiled at that—he couldn't help it. It seemed Rio took after his mother. Or at least the universe wanted their stories to mirror each other when they gave them mates from similar backgrounds.

"Sounds romantic," Fire said, and Rio snorted.

"Not exactly. My mother wasn't the best person. Still isn't, I imagine. I haven't seen her in a while," Rio said. "She wanted the wealth and the status the arranged mating brought, but she also wanted the thrill of being with her real mate."

Fire's smile dropped.

"She pretended she was ready to leave everything behind for my dad," Rio said. "She told him she loved him and she was just figuring out how to tell her parents she didn't want to marry their choice. The wedding preparations were in full swing when she realized she was pregnant with me."

Fire saw how much of a struggle getting the story out was for Rio. He recognized the pain and the reluctance in his voice.

"You can take a break if you want to, gorgeous," Fire said once again, desperate to ease the tension and make Rio smile again.

"It's okay," Rio said. "It won't be any easier if I wait."

"I'm here," Fire said, and Rio nodded.

"Anyway, she told my dad she was pregnant, and he was over the moon," Rio said. "My grandparents, on the other hand, were appalled. They arranged for her to go on a 'vacation.'"

He put finger quotes around the word *vacation* and snorted an ugly laugh at it.

"She gave birth to me and then, with the blessing of my grandparents, deposited me on my father's doorstep," Rio said with a wry smile. "She never called or asked about me. She married the rich guy and started her socialite fairytale life in another Circle."

"Without you?" Fire asked, and Rio nodded.

"As far as Nadine Charmichael was concerned, I never existed. Apart from the name, she had never given me anything," he said. "I spent my childhood at the racing tracks with my dad. Learning from him, watching him do his thing. God, he was so good at it."

"Can I ask who he was?"

Rio smiled. "Theodore Perkins."

"Bullet?" Fire gasped. "The king of obstacle courses?"

Rio actually laughed at the nickname. "The one and only."

"Oh my god, I watched all the recordings of his races when I was a kid, trying to figure out how he passed the obstacles. He literally made it magic," Fire said, practically bouncing in his seat. "He was one of the best racers ever."

"Mhm," Rio said. "He truly was. Sucked at speed and circuits though."

"Everyone knows speed and circuits are just there for point accumulation for those who aren't good at obstacles. Your dad was an artist."

Fire noticed the tight smile and mentally slapped himself for letting his inner fanboy rear its head when his mate needed him.

"I'm sorry," Fire said. "I will table the fanboying for now. But we're circling back to it. Keep going."

Rio nodded and shuffled closer, leaning back against Fire's arm, head lolling onto his shoulder.

"My dad started coaching me when I was about six or so," he said.

"Wait, you raced?" Fire said, looking down at the top of his head.

"I attempted." Rio snorted. It was an undignified sound from his mate, but Fire liked how cute it sounded. "And I wasn't bad, I don't think, but...it never felt like my thing, you know? Like, I watched my dad do it, and he'd light up whenever he took off the ground. I always felt like it was a chore."

Fire hummed in understanding. He lived and breathed racing. But not everyone was like that. "I get it. If your heart isn't in it, talent means fuck all."

"Beautifully said," Rio said dryly, and Fire grinned into his hair. He adored riling him up.

"Thank you," Fire said. "So...no racing for Rio."

"Not competitively, no," he said. "I still practiced with my dad. Accompanied him to his races whenever I could, watched on TV when it fell on school days. I learned all of his strategies. I know all of his drills, all of his tips and tricks to fix the weak spots. Bullet had the best coaches money could buy."

"And you grew up with them," Fire said.

"And I grew up with them," Rio said, and Fire fell silent, understanding slowly settling in.

Everything Rio had shown the kids that day was well thought out, strategic. It came from someone who knew racing inside and out. Being the son of Theodore Perkins explained all of it. The man had been an icon while he raced. And he'd turned into a legend once he passed.

"So how did you end up with your maternal grandparents?" Fire asked, and Rio sighed.

"The pain of being rejected by his mate caught up to my dad," Rio said. "He tried to train and compete like he usually did. He showed up for all his races, but his performance started suffering. His coaches suggested taking the season off, letting the pain dull before coming back, but racing was his life. He miscalculated one of his moves, and it ended...how it ended."

Fire held him closer, aching for him and hating not knowing how to help him. He remembered Bullet's last race. Had seen videos of it countless times. Every racer had. He remembered not understanding how someone like Bullet could have made the mistake he made. It felt too stupid for someone of his calibre. When Fire had crashed out on his own obstacle race he'd thought he could understand a bit better. But he realized he had no actual idea until that moment.

The pain of losing a mate would have done it. Having his own mate in his arms made it perfectly clear to Fire.

"After Dad passed, I went into a group home for a bit," Rio continued. "They found my grandparents and informed them I was alone and needed guardians. They were hoping to get in touch with my mother through them. But she wanted nothing to do with me, still. And apparently, she never wanted anything to do with any child. Which would absolutely not work for my grandparents, as carrying the family name was of the utmost importance. So they took me in. Pulled strings to get my last name changed, erased my dad from my life in any way they could think of."

Fire bristled at that, his heart aching for his mate, who had no actual family to speak of.

"Did they give you a good life?" Fire asked, desperate for something to be good. Something to hang on to to make himself believe his mate was happy.

"I never lacked anything," Rio said. "Anything money could buy I had."

"Money can't buy everything," Fire said, and Rio shook his head.

"No, it can't," Rio said. "But it does teach you to think you get everything you set your mind to. Their mind is set on me. I am to take over their estate, company shares, and chairs on charity boards. I am to continue living the way they lived, carrying the Charmichael name to the next generation."

"Next generation?" Fire asked.

"Yup," Rio said, breathing out a laugh. "Oh, they had a meltdown when I came out, but calmed down fairly quickly when they realized it's not exactly a dead end when it comes to children. Like they tried to do with my mother, they have a list of eligible Kriila they'd be okay with me marrying."

Fire's throat closed, and his heart skipped a beat. Their story did mirror that of Rio's parents too closely for comfort. Rio had said he wouldn't lose him, but this didn't feel like it.

"Rio..." he started, but Rio lifted his head up off his shoulder to look into Fire's eyes.

"I'm not my mother," he said, voice shaking with the force he used.

"Why didn't you leave when you came of age?" Fire asked, and Rio lifted his shoulders to his chin.

"And go where?" he asked. "I know I seem near perfect, but I'm not very good at anything other than being a Charmichael heir. I can write checks, swipe credit cards, and preen at events. That's the extent of my talents, James."

"You're more than that, Rio," Fire said, pushing a stray lock of hair behind his ear.

"Maybe," he replied. "Maybe I am. Maybe there is more to me, but I never had the chance to find it. So when I asked for time, it wasn't to think about whether I wanted you or whoever my grandparents pick. There was never a choice there."

Fire's heart soared at the words. He cupped Rio's cheek and kissed him on the lips softly, resting their foreheads together after it.

"It's you," Rio said. "But that will mean my life as I know it now will come to an end. No money..."

"I don't exactly earn peanuts, gorgeous," Fire said, and Rio cracked a smile.

"You're very cute," Rio said. "I think my shoe collection costs more than what you earn in a decade."

Fire barked a laugh. "You'd get used to it."

"I'll be insufferable while I'm doing it, though," Rio replied.

"And if push comes to shove, we can always sell your shoes and turn a profit," Fire said, and Rio gasped, slapping him on the shoulder.

"You can pry my shoes from my cold, dead feet, you monster," he said, and Fire scooped him up around his waist, lifting him into his lap.

He nuzzled his nose into his neck and held him close.

"It's not just money," Rio said, leaning into the comfort. "Or the connections. I won't...I won't have a family anymore. They're the last family I have."

Fire caught the tremble in his voice. He caught the crack in his beautifully polished walls.

Uxorious Archibald Charmichael III was untouchable. He didn't need anyone because he could take care of himself. He had a sharp tongue and an even sharper glare that could bring people to their knees.

But underneath all that was Rio, his mate. And Rio was open and vulnerable. He was small and a little bit lost. A person who valued independence but craved belonging and family after having it ripped away from him so cruelly when he was young. And Fire wanted nothing more than to protect him. To care for him and keep him safe and offer him belonging.

There was only one place he knew where to do that, and he stood up, Rio still in his arms. Rio squeaked at being airborne suddenly and gripped Fire around the neck.

"What are you doing?" he asked as Fire walked them over to the staircase, climbing up and taking them into a large, lofted bedroom.

He bypassed it and walked farther in, coming to a closed door that he pushed open with his foot.

He entered, standing in the middle of the room, and then went down on one knee to place Rio gently on a large leather bean bag. He stepped away and watched as Rio took his surroundings in.

He looked, too, as if he had never seen the room before.

It had no windows, the only light coming from small lightbulbs fixed into the ceiling. The walls were decorated with signed racing uniforms from Fire's favorite racers. There was a glass display case filled with racing memorabilia he had collected over the years.

There were several beanbags strewn around the floor and a large flatscreen hooked to the wall.

Between it all, framed photos of Fire's family and friends filled in the gaps racing left with love and friendship.

It looked like the ultimate man cave, but it was so much more than that.

"This is your nest," Rio said, and Fire nodded.

"It is," Fire said, pulling a beanbag next to Rio's and sitting down next to him.

"Why are we here?" Rio asked.

"It's the safest place in the world for me," Fire said. "It's where I feel the most protected and calm. I wanted that for you."

Rio's cheeks pinked again and he looked around. Fire knew he was trying to hide the blush, and as much as he wanted to tease him about it, it wasn't the time. He'd let him get away with it this time.

"It's very you," Rio said after a while, and Fire smiled.

"Kind of the point of having a nest," Fire said. "I'm sure yours is very elegant and color coordinated."

Rio frowned, looking down.

"An interior designer decorated mine," he said. "I never had any input on how it looked. And I don't spend time in it because it doesn't feel mine."

Fire's heart nearly shattered at the words. He leaned forward and took Rio's hands.

"You're welcome into mine whenever you want," he said. "You'll always be safe here. And I want you here. But if you want it, I have a spare room that's sitting empty now. You can decorate it however you want and it can be just yours. I'll give you the key and stay out of it until you invite me in."

Rio stared at him, and for a moment, Fire was afraid he had said something wrong. Then he felt the softest squeeze of Rio's fingers on his hands.

"You'd do that for me?" he asked.

"I thought I made it pretty obvious I'd do anything for you, princess," Fire murmured, and Rio lurched forward to cuddle into his chest. His fingers gripped the collar of Fire's shirt and held tight.

"Even...even keeping us a secret until I'm ready to tell my grandparents?" he whispered, and Fire froze in place.

He didn't want to keep them a secret. He wanted everyone to know Rio belonged to him. He was proud to be with him, proud to be his. But underneath all the caveman desires to claim Rio in public, he knew his request made sense. He wasn't saying forever.

Rio was just asking for some time.

"Yeah," he said finally, words heavy on his tongue but true. "Even that."

Rio slumped against him, face buried in his neck.

"Thank you," he said, and Fire nodded.

"You're welcome," he said, hugging him as tight as he could. "We'll figure this out together. And I'll do everything I can to be the best family to you."

"You know," Rio said, "I always knew I was amazing, but I must have been better than even I knew to deserve a mate like you."

Fire pressed his lips together to keep himself from laughing, but there was no stopping it. It was such a Rio thing to say.

"What?" Rio asked as he kept laughing.

"I know you meant it as a compliment to me, gorgeous," Fire said. "I'm just impressed at how much praise you gave yourself while doing it."

"I'm telling it like it is," Rio said, and Fire nodded.

"Yes, you are," he said, letting a comfortable silence descend on them. He kissed Rio's hair and closed his eyes, inhaling the floral scent that lingered on his skin.

"Fire?" Rio asked after a few moments.

"Yeah?"

"Can my nest NOT have any beanbags?" he asked. "They're extremely uncomfortable, my pants will wrinkle, and there is no way to sit upright like a proper person in them."

Fire laughed again.

"Yes, princess," he said. "Your nest can have, or not have, whatever you want."

"Good," Rio said.

CHAPTER ELEVEN

FIRE

The rest of the weekend passed in a haze of happiness. Fire had refused to let Rio move further than the bed or his nest, a zero-clothes rule implemented. Though Rio pretended to hate it, he didn't protest nearly as much as he should.

He'd left early that morning, making sure to wake Fire to see him out the door as was his 'obligation.' Fire made sure to make it worth his own time and had taken half a dozen kisses and a grope of that fantastic ass as payment.

Once Fire was inside Ace, he changed quickly, not coming across anyone until he stepped into the gym. Vid was there already, leaning over a tablet with the salt-and-pepper head of Fire's coach, Rand, next to him. Not that anyone called him that.

Coach was a retired racer from Bullet's prime who had crashed out early due to injury. Back then, medical advancements weren't what they were now, and while he'd been able to fly still, he was never what he was. He'd turned to coaching as a lot of old racers did, and Fire was his protégé.

He'd scouted him young, when Fire was more interested in showing off and winning than technique. He'd quickly put him through his paces, however, and while Coach didn't completely knock the attitude from him, Fire gained a respect for racing he'd been missing as a kid.

Fire's parents loved him.

"Miss me?" Fire announced himself, throwing his arms wide.

Coach's blue eyes regarded him with little fanfare. "Sure, kid. Like a hole in the head."

Fire pouted. "So mean. You've had a vacation, and you're still so mean."

Coach looked heavenward, then came closer, patting him on the back. Fire grinned at him.

"Vid was just running me through your program...that you apparently started early," Coach said pointedly.

"You know me—an overachiever!"

Another eyeroll. "Let's get working."

He led the way, and Fire fell into step with Vid.

"How was the birthday?" Fire asked.

"Loud," Vid said, smirking. "I hear you were a hit at the community center. They've had parents calling up about you and a 'Mr. Rio.' They said you're supposed to be coming back next week."

Fire flushed, pleased more than he thought he would be. "It was fun. I may have to steal your class. Sorry not sorry, I'm cooler than you anyway."

Vid shoved him. "Not likely. But I suppose I'll let you take a class or two. And Mr. Rio is welcome to come too."

"Stop fishing," Fire warned him, remembering Rio's wish to keep quiet. "We're still on the DL."

Vid laughed. "Yeah, yeah. I'll stop. But I better not hear about this from the news."

"Not if I can help it. Anna would kill me."

"Too late," an arch voice drawled.

Fire's eyes widened, hearing the death knell of heels coming closer behind him.

"If I don't move, maybe she'll walk right by me," Fire whispered.

"You're on your own," Vid said, shuffling away to where Coach had disappeared to.

"Coward!"

Anna grasped his arm and twirled him around easily. She was dressed in all black like she was planning his funeral, hair slicked back like she didn't want it to get in the way of her murdering him so she could attend.

Fire pouted and rubbed his arm. "Why are you so freakishly strong?"

Anna leveled him with a flat stare. "I've been carrying around your bullshit for years."

"Touché."

She shoved newspapers under his nose. "You've been dodging all my calls, and then I see *this* in the papers."

"Pixels?"

"Explain," Anna demanded.

Fire moved her arm back and saw a faraway shot of Rio and him standing outside the community center, a few paces away from each other. It was grainy, but they were unmistakable. It was the last thing Rio needed at the moment, and Fire knew he'd freak out at seeing the photo.

"He's going to kill me," Fire said.

"He can get in line."

"Is this the only one?" Fire asked, grabbing the paper from her and crumpling it in his hand.

"Yes," Anna said testily, pulling her arm back. "You're lucky it was some passerby. They didn't stick around to see where you went. They just wanted the photo-op to put on their social media account. The paper bought it from them, as well as their 'eyewitness' account."

The photo itself wasn't incriminating. It had been one of the only times Fire had kept his hands to himself because he was still reeling from learning about the racing thing.

"It's hardly scandalous," Fire said, mostly to reassure himself.

"It's enough to start rumors, and rumors can be dangerous, Fire, you know this," Anna said. "And thanks for the heads up, by the way. Volunteering with kids and you don't let your manager and *publicist* know?"

"I didn't do it for that reason," Fire said, jaw set.

"Who said you did?" Anna asked, shoving a sharp finger in his chest. "But that doesn't mean you can't also publicize it. They write enough hit pieces about you in the tabloids. You're taking all the bullets out of my gun and giving them to someone else! I don't like playing defense, Fire!"

"Holy metaphor."

"Shut up!"

Fire held up his hands, palms out placatingly. "I'm sorry, okay? I didn't think about it. I was distracted."

"And we need to talk about that *distraction* too," Anna said, eyes narrowing. "Had many outings with your mate lately?"

"Well...I wouldn't say *many*—"

Anna cut him off. "We need to plan a statement."

Fire grimaced, scratching the back of his neck. "That's...gonna be a little complicated."

"How?" Anna growled.

"Rio doesn't want anyone to know yet. He has a complicated relationship at home."

Fire braced for the implosion.

Anna closed her eyes and took a few deep breaths. "Calm. Zen. Just breathe. Rainbows. Lakes. Rainfall... Stress. Anger. *Rage*."

"I don't think that's how that's supposed to end..." Fire ventured, stepping back a few paces.

"Can I have my racer back, Anna?" Coach said, interrupting. "I know he's a pain in the ass, but I'd like him to be in one piece as well, if you can manage."

Anna didn't open her eyes, but said between her teeth, "I'm sure you have some glue and a manual around here somewhere."

Coach grunted. "Fire, c'mon. You'll call Anna later."

"Gotta go."

He leaned forward and pressed a quick kiss to her cheek.

"*Fire!*" she exploded, but he was already out of range.

Fire made it through both Anna and training. Barely.

He was grateful to step outside again after three grueling hours. Not even Vid's sports massage could fully prevent the aches and pains he felt coursing through his body. He passed a silent Zero on his way out, his massive body barely fitting in the shower stall.

Zero didn't bid him farewell, just stared at him placidly through the spray of water.

"Like he's too good to talk to me. To me!" Fire muttered to himself as he pushed outside into the brisk afternoon air. "God, Rio is rubbing off on me."

He approached his car and unlocked it, throwing his shit into the backseat like usual. But thoughts of Rio eventually led to thoughts of the picture again, and he groaned. This coming on the back of their conversation and agreeing to keep them a secret just felt like a slap to the face. Rio wouldn't take kindly to it.

His phone rang, knocking him from his head. He fished it out of his duffle, insides turning as he saw Rio's name on the screen.

"Hello?" he answered, expecting things to blow up.

"*I'm guessing you saw the papers?*" Rio sounded strangely detached. Fire had braced for melodrama, not...whatever that was.

"I did," Fire said. "Are you okay?"

"*I am,*" Rio said. "*It's...well, it's not great that it came out, and my grandmother is in full 'give them something else to talk about' mode, but I told her we were accidentally at the same place at the same time and that we didn't know each other.*"

That stung.

Fire fell silent. He knew he'd given his word, but being denied like that hurt.

"Okay..." he said quietly, and Rio sighed.

"*You know I didn't mean it, James,*" Rio said, voice apologetic, and yes, Fire did know.

"I know," he said. "Just sucks to hear it."

"*I'm sorry,*" Rio said sadly, and Fire felt like an ass.

"No need to be sorry, princess," he said, doing his best to make his voice brighter. "We agreed to do this, and I know why we have to. Don't worry about me."

"*Sure?*" Rio asked.

"I'm sure. Go survive whatever your grandmother has planned."

"*Ugh... It's a party for all her friends so they have something to gossip about other than me,*" Rio said.

"Sounds like a nightmare," Fire said and could almost envision Rio nodding on the other side.

"*It will be,*" Rio said. "*Especially without you there.*"

His voice turned husky and raspy, and well...that did make Fire feel better.

But as they hung up, Fire couldn't help but still feel unsettled. He found his restless feet walking back into Ace, cornering Vid in his office.

The blond looked up at him in the doorway in confusion. "Something wrong?"

"Wanna hang out?"

Vid looked around. "In the middle of work?"

"Yup."

Vid looked back at his computer for a suspended second. "Yeah, okay."

Fire grinned, watching him pack up. It wasn't the first time he'd gotten Vid to bail out a little early, but he hadn't done it in a while.

Vid gave him a quelling glare. "Don't look so pleased with yourself. I don't have any clients scheduled, and I can do the paperwork at home."

"Sure," Fire chirped.

Vid grabbed his jacket and shoved him out of the doorway. "Dick."

Fire laughed. "It's not like I twisted your arm or anything."

"Because the puppy look on your face isn't the same thing," Vid said, rolling his eyes and threading his arms through the sleeves of the leather. "What's with the sudden invitation anyway? Ever since you and you-know-who started up, I've hardly seen you. I figured you'd be busy."

Fire made a face. "I didn't mean to go radio silent on you."

Vid shrugged and smiled. "It's okay. I can share you."

Fire smirked before it fell.

"Trouble in paradise?" Vid guessed.

"Yes? No? I don't know," Fire said with a sigh, opening the door to outside.

Vid hummed. "Well there's only one thing to do to achieve clarity."

Fire glanced over, eyebrows furrowing. "What's that?"

"Beer," Vid said decisively. "And burgers."

"Those are on the *consume and I'll shove my foot up your ass* list," Fire said.

"Since I made the list, I can make exceptions."

"This is sending mixed messages."

"Do you want it or not?" Vid asked, black brow raised.

"I bow to your wisdom as always."

CHAPTER TWELVE

RIO

"You could at least pretend you're pleased to greet our guests," Rio's grandmother told him through gritted teeth, lips stretched into an unnatural smile. She had been wearing that smile since the event at their house started. Rio's grandfather was standing just behind her, as usual, detached from the world and letting her dictate how they behaved. He looked dead inside.

It was as if someone was holding them both at gunpoint and forcing them to host these godawful gatherings. They were both snappy and irritable for days leading up to them, spending disgusting amounts of money on tasteless food and ordering drinks that would make the guests forget they hated each other.

"I am pleased to greet them," Rio said, smiling at one of his grandfather's business associates and his son Rio vaguely remembered from school. He hated the old man with a burning passion and wished one of the ornate chandeliers would fall on his head. "Good evening, Mr. Donnelley. Lovely to have you with us tonight."

He couldn't remember the son's name to save his life, so he just gave him a polite nod and what he hoped was a friendly smile. He got nothing but a blank stare in response.

"Yes, yes," the ornery little man scoffed, looking Rio up and down before he curled his upper lip in disgust. "Still playing dress-up, I see."

Rio was wearing one of his favorite cream-colored suits, the matching pants, waistcoat, and blazer offset by a floral-patterned shirt. The back of his suit was open to allow his wings to spread around as much as possible, golden chains draped over them. Rio had picked his most expensive set. Both because he knew it was what his grandparents would have wanted, and because he genuinely did like how they made him feel.

"Is it still playing if you're so good at it?" Rio asked with a smile, making several people around them chuckle and the old man bristle with rage as he pulled his son and stomped angrily away.

"You're funny," someone said as they entered the foyer, and Rio looked up to see another man his age accompanying an older woman Rio recognized from his grandmother's inner circle of harpies. She ignored him, already busy gossiping with his grandmother.

"I do try," Rio responded, extending his hand. "Uxorious."

"Bellamy," the man said, wincing. "Twenty-nine years with the name and it still sounds godawful to say it out loud."

Rio chuckled, thinking back on how Fire gave him his nickname and how much more like a Rio he felt these days than he did Uxorious.

"I hear having an easily pronounceable nickname helps deal with the trauma," Rio said, and Bellamy threw his head back in laughter.

"I'll try and come up with something," he said. "If you're not too busy tonight, find me and help me pick?"

It sounded better than half the activities he usually had to engage in at these parties, so he nodded.

"I'll bring a baby name book if you bring the alcohol?" Rio asked, and Bellamy gave him a thumbs up.

"You got yourself a deal, Uxorious," he said, pulling a face. "Although pronouncing yours makes Bellamy sound like a balm."

He scurried away before Rio could retaliate.

"Uxorious, focus," his grandmother hissed, and he straightened up like a scolded child.

"I am focused," he said. "I was literally talking to a guest."

"And missed several other guests who came through."

"Yes, well, I only have one head, Grandmother," he said as he fake-smiled and nodded at the next few people who walked in.

He noticed something of a pattern.

Grandmother's friends and Grandfather's associates. Accompanied by young men. He frowned.

"Why does it feel like I'm on a live rendition of *Clip Your Wings?*" he asked, referencing a godawful reality dating show that leaned heavily into every horrible stereotype of what a mated Kriila couple looked like. Hence the name.

"Don't be ridiculous," his grandmother said. "However, after those photos of you came out, we just felt it was high time for you to start thinking about your potential mate. After all, the Showing is coming up in a few months' time. You can use tonight to meet some potential mates and narrow down the list of who you might be claiming."

"Grandmother, for the millionth time"—Rio swallowed around a lump in his throat—"I was at the Children's Recreation Center to make a donation. The reason you sent me to that gala was to make a donation."

"And that young man was there because...?" she asked, and he played stupid perfectly.

"How would I know?" he said. "I don't know him. That was the first time I saw him, and I'm not in the habit of asking complete strangers about their day."

She side-eyed him and turned back to the door.

"Straighten your back," she scolded, changing the subject because she had no arguments to bring up. "Mr. Barrow, thank you so much for joining us tonight."

Rio suppressed an eye roll and shook the man's offered hand.

"Uxorious, my boy," Mr. Barrow said, smile not touching his eyes as he looked at Rio with barely hidden contempt. "Russel will be here a bit later. He told me to make sure you save him a dance. He's very excited to see you."

"I'm sure he is," Rio said, not sharing the sentiment in the slightest and cringing at the obvious struggle in the man's voice as he relayed his son's message.

"Mr. Charmichael," someone said from behind them, and Rio looked over Mr. Barrow's shoulder to see Kiran Castillo, their Council Leader, looking at him with a wide smile on his face. "Thank you so much for inviting me tonight. You remember my mate?"

"I do," Rio said, greeting them both, congratulating himself on hiding his shock at seeing them there. "Good evening, Council Leader, Mr. Hayes."

"Oh, please just call me Jude," Jude said with a smile. "I consider us friends already, so no need for formalities. Such a lovely evening, don't you think?"

He directed the question at Mr. Barrow, and Rio reveled in the awkward nod and the quick scurry away from the man. He was as prejudiced as they got, but he was also an opportunist.

He didn't approve of same-sex matings, but he'd sell his son to advance in life. Engaging with a human was beneath him, but antagonizing their Council Leader was inadvisable if he wanted his son to have the political career he had planned for him.

Profit came before ideals every time.

"Thank you for saving me from another boring exposé on the wonders of his son," Rio whispered to Jude, who winked cheekily at him.

"You looked like you needed saving," Jude said, before turning to Kiran and linking their arms. "Should we get something to drink?"

"Anything you want," Kiran said, smiling at Rio. "Find us once you've greeted everyone. I'd love to talk to you about some things."

Rio nodded, and Kiran ushered Jude further in, disappearing into the crowd.

"You invited the Council Leader to what is essentially a private Showing ceremony?" Rio asked, unable to hide the incredulity in his voice.

"I can't think of anyone more suitable or of a higher standing than him," his grandmother said, and Rio stared at her.

"He came with his mate," Rio said. "He has a mate."

"A human." She tsked. "The novelty of that will wear off, and he'll be on the lookout for someone more appropriate."

"But—"

"He told you to come find him," she said. "Go off."

"Grandmother..." he tried again, but she dismissed him with a wave of her hand in front of his face as she turned to the next person who walked in. Another family, with another bland-looking young man who wanted to be there just as much as Rio did.

Rio didn't even try to greet them as he walked away, picking up a gin and tonic from one of the trays being carried around and going to find a secluded little corner to drink it in peace. He'd mingle once he had some alcohol in him.

He watched the people milling around and, for the first time, saw them all through a different lens. Fire's lens, he supposed.

The superficiality, the shallowness. The fake smiles and the inane conversations that masked what everyone truly wanted.

To pad their bank accounts and show everyone else they were better than.

It was staggering how obvious it was when you paid attention to it, and how much of it Rio had managed to ignore over the years.

Fact was, he enjoyed being wealthy, he just didn't enjoy the way his grandparents went about becoming and staying wealthy.

"You look bored out of your mind, even with all these eligible mates turning up in droves just for you," a voice drawled from his left, and he turned to find a gorgeous girl standing next to him, smirking.

Kalie, one of the rare people Rio considered to be an actual friend, took his glass out of his hand and took a sip of his drink.

She was wearing a lavender-colored pantsuit, the blazer of it buttoned down over naked skin. Several necklaces decorated her cleavage, and her dark hair was pulled up into a slick ponytail. Her dark purple wings were slicked back with a glittery pomade, looking sharp and defined. She looked rebelliously put together. Walking that thin line of looking amazing while also being the talk of the older attendees at the party. She loved it. And Rio loved how she played their game almost as well as he did.

"Good, that means my face is doing exactly what I told it to," Rio said, snatching his glass back from her and taking a sip.

"You never did learn how to truly make the best of these shindigs." She shook her head, hand swiping out to grab a few cocktail sandwiches she stuffed into her mouth.

"Be a lady, Kalie," he said mockingly, and she opened her mouth to show him the chewed-up food inside.

"No, thanks," she said. "That's boring."

"Why am I friends with you again?" he asked, and she lifted one shoulder.

"Because every other person in our social circle is a condescending prick not worth either of our time, so we're stuck together?" she offered, and he guessed it was as good an explanation as any. "Also, I'm the shit."

She said that a little louder, earning herself a glare from two bedazzled old wenches that came to every party they heard of just to get the latest gossip and spread it around. They curled their lips at her and walked by, clutching their pearls and whispering among themselves. They didn't even have young family members to justify being there.

"And you're getting on a list for shits as well," he told her, and she fist-pumped the air.

"Mission accomplished," she said, waving a waiter over and grabbing two champagne flutes.

"I don't want champagne," Rio said.

"Who said it's for you?" Kalie asked, downing one flute and setting it down before cradling the second one gently in her hands. "The first one is an anesthetic. The second one for aesthetics."

She sipped from the second one daintily, pinky finger up in the air, making a subtle spectacle of it as she did with everything else. Surface level, she was perfectly poised. Underneath it, she was a menace, and she knew it.

"So, where have you been?" she asked. "I feel like I haven't seen you in ages."

"I've been busy."

"You...have been busy?" she said, tilting her head. "Doing what, exactly?"

"Things," he said vaguely.

"Things," she repeated, narrowing his eyes at him.

"Yes, I just had some things to do," he said again.

"Some things? Or some ones?" She grinned at him and he rolled his eyes, lifting his glass to his lips.

"I guess you haven't seen the tabloids then," he said against the rim of the glass, and she pointed a finger at him.

"I stopped looking at those ages ago. My own dating drama is exhausting to follow," she said. "So what did they say about you? Are you seeing someone? Are you going behind your grandvultures' backs and dating? How rebellious, Uxorious. I'm proud."

She wiped a fake tear off her cheek and sniffled.

"You're a cow," he informed her.

"Cows are adorable," she said. "Now spill. Who is he? Is he hot? Is he good in bed? OH! OH! I bet he's someone completely unsuitable for you, and that's why you're all hush about it when I know everything about every other dude you boned."

"He's not unsuitable, and we didn't bone," he said, and even to his own ears, it sounded too defensive. Too harsh of a reaction compared to how the two of them usually talked to each other.

She noticed too. Of course she did.

She narrowed her eyes again and leaned in until their noses were almost touching. She looked him over, scanning his entire body as if something on him would spell out exactly what she wanted to know.

He tried to lean back, but she was like a dog, almost sniffing him to see if he smelled of real information.

After several uncomfortable moments, she pulled back, a corner of her lip tilting up.

"Something is different about you," she said. "For all the glaring and the bitching at the party, you seem strangely relaxed and settled."

"I don't know what you're talking about," he told her, and she threw her head back in annoyance.

"Come ooooon," she whined like only a spoiled heiress to a multi-billion dollar company could. "Tell meeeeee. Tell me, tell me, tell me, tell me."

He grinned and let her whine and prod and poke for another few minutes, enjoying just being the focus of her attention and being the one with the juicy news.

"Fine," he said when he figured she had suffered enough. Kalie knew no larger torture than not being in on the gossip. "I'll tell you."

"Yes!" She bounced on her heels. "I knew I'd wear you down eventually. Spill!"

"I will, but if word of this gets to anyone," he said through clenched teeth, "and I mean this, Kalie. Anyone. Not your diary, not your reflection in the mirror, you are not even to dream about this and talk in your sleep about it. I will find a way to destroy every single pantsuit you own."

She glared at him but mimicked locking her lips and tucking the key into her cleavage.

"You're supposed to throw the key away," he said.

"There might come a time when you want me to spread the good word," she said. "I'm just keeping our options open. Now, enough stalling. What's up?"

Rio took a deep breath and looked around to make sure nobody could overhear. Several people were relatively close to them, but he doubted they could hear over the music playing and the guests chattering away. He leaned in closer just in case.

"I found my mate," he said, and she jumped back as if burned.

"WHAT?" she said way too loudly, drawing attention.

"Shhhh," he hissed, and she bit her lip.

"Sorry," she said, leaning back in. "You found him? When? Where? Who is he? Oh my god, your grandparents will lose it. Please let me be there when you tell them. I want to see the drama unfold."

He smiled despite his better judgment. Kalie hated his family almost as much as his family hated everyone on the planet.

"I'll see what I can do," he said.

"I'll accept a livestream as well," she said magnanimously. "Now tell me who it is. Where you met. Tell me all of it."

"We met at that charity gala you were supposed to come with me to," he said, giving her the side-eye.

"I got three pairs of bespoke boots on that shopping trip, and you got a mate. You will not make me feel guilty for ditching you to go on it," she said. "And you're not gonna change the subject. Who is he?"

"Okay, so...you might know his name," he said. "I didn't know, but apparently, he's a big deal and all that."

"You bagged a celebrity?" she said, eyebrows high. "That might make your family a bit mellower. Which is entirely disappointing."

"Not necessarily," Rio said. "He's a racer."

She dropped her jaw and widened her eyes at him, staccato breaths escaping as she tried and failed to form words. Rio was quite pleased with that reaction. He took a sip of his drink and watched her flail as she tried to regain composure.

"Well..." she said after a while. "You sure don't do things halfway, do you?"

"I'm not known for it, no."

"A racer," she said, shaking her head. "Your mate is the one thing in this world your grandparents hate the most."

"Yes," he confirmed, and she chuckled, sipping at her champagne.

"Wow," she said. "You said he's a big name? Who is it?"

"Fire," Rio said, and she had another moment of pure shock before a sharklike grin bloomed on her face.

"Of course you snagged the hottest one."

"Only the best for me," Rio said, and she cackled.

"Oh, this is the best news I've gotten in a while," she said, laughing for a few more moments before schooling her expression into a more neutral one and leveling him with a stare. "And you were in the tabloids? And the old ones are still alive and kicking?"

"We were photographed together, yeah, but far apart enough for me to excuse it as coincidence," he said, looking around the room. "I'm not sure it worked."

"Yeah, no, the mating ritual you have going on here means she did not buy it," Kalie said. "Cheap entertainment, though. They all look identical. It's perplexing."

He looked around once more and couldn't agree more. They were all variations on a theme of rich, posh, and boring.

"All joking aside, though." Kalie broke the silence again. "Your mate, he's good to you?"

And just like that, Rio was reminded of why she was a friend instead of someone he just tolerated. Kalie cared. In her own self-absorbed ways, she held her people close. Rio was one of her people.

"He is," he said with a soft smile on his face. "He's different from everyone we know, but he treats me well. He takes care of me. He wants me happy."

"Good," she said. "He should. You deserve the best."

"And the best he will get." A hand wrapped around his waist and pulled him close. "Uxorious, my darling, your grandmother told me you were hiding away so I came to find you."

Rio cringed at the sound of that voice, the visceral reaction enhanced by the fact he had just been thinking and talking about his mate. He turned to look at the intruder, finding himself face to face with a smarmy smile and beady eyes that leered at him. His father had announced his arrival earlier, and yet he caught Rio by surprise.

Russel Barrow.

His grandmother's first pick of Rio's potential spouses. His parents owned several lucrative hotel chains, had more money than they knew what to do with, and one sole heir to leave it all to. Rio's grandparents saw bling and prestige.

Rio saw an obnoxious little twatwaffle who had nothing else going for him but a slightly-above-average sized dick.

That he, according to word on the street, did not know how to use.

Rio tried to wiggle out of Russel's hold, placing his palm on his chest and giving it a push.

"Russel," Rio said. "No need to get physical."

"How can I resist when you look this delectable tonight?" Russel said, tugging Rio closer.

"You'll wrinkle my suit," Rio said, not wanting to cause drama, pushing him off again, and this time, Russel let go.

Smoothing his horrible suit down, he turned to look at Kalie, tilting his chin up to try and make up for the few inches she had on him. "Miss Marshall."

Kalie smirked at the insecurity, straightening up to her full height and staring at him down her perfectly contoured nose.

"Russel," she said. "What an absolute delight."

"Likewise," he said dismissively, turning back to Rio. "My father said he reserved a spot for me to dance with you. Would you care to join me, darling?"

"Not at the moment, no," Rio said. "Kalie and I were just in the middle of a conversation."

"I'm sure it was fascinating," Russel said condescendingly. "But it can wait. Just one tiny dance."

He took Rio's hand and tugged, stumbling when Rio refused to budge.

"I said not at the moment, Russel," Rio repeated, feeling eyes on him and turning to see his grandmother glaring from across the room. She whispered something to a woman standing next to her and zeroed in on Rio and Russel. She took a step toward him, and he plastered a fake smile on his face, returning her glare. He would not be forced into anything with Russel. She could stalk menacingly toward him all she wanted—he wasn't giving in.

"Don't be like that," Russel said, voice turning whiny. He sounded like a toddler gearing up for a tantrum. "We haven't seen each other in ages."

He tugged again, and Rio sneered at him, patience wearing thin, but self-preservation in the face of his grandmother's wrath won again. He could refuse to dance. But he wasn't allowed to make a scene. People would talk. And not in a way that benefited them. Rio had to keep the peace until he figured out how to detach himself from his family in a way that was sustainable for him. In a way that didn't ruin him.

"And while that's a shame, I haven't seen Kalie in a while either, and she found me first," Rio kept his tone neutral, wiggling his arm to try and wrestle it out of Russel's grip. The man wasn't letting go. "Let go of me, please."

"Just one dance. One tiny, itty-bitty dance," Russel pleaded, adding a little pout to his lip and a bounce to his knees. Rio knew he was going for annoyingly adorable, but he overcalculated and landed too far from the adorable to make up for the annoying.

Rio spent his life around spoiled, arrogant little pricks. Hell, he was one.

With a final eye roll, he jerked his hand back, Russel's fingers slipping off his elbow.

"Uxorious," he heard his grandmother admonish from behind Russel. She apparently materialized when he least needed her close.

"Yes, Grandmother?" he asked, plans to just grab Kalie and make a dash for it squashed with one raised eyebrow from her.

"Russel is a guest..."

"I just wanted one dance, Mrs. Charmichael." Russel said, that sweet mask still painted on his face. Rio wanted to end him. "Uxorious isn't in the best mood, it would seem."

"Uxorious would love to dance with you," his grandmother said, and Rio bristled.

"No, Uxorious would love to be allowed to make his own choices regarding people invading his personal space," Rio said.

He knew it was a mistake the moment the words left his mouth. His grandmother turned her smile into a tight line on her face, eyes going narrow and a small, barely visible clench to her jaw making her look ready to destroy any and all pushback from him.

"You will behave appropriately toward our guests," his grandmother said with that tone Rio knew she used when she wanted her word to be last. "Russel came straight from work to spend time with you, and you will grant him his wish."

"Thank you, Mrs. Charmichael," Russel said and tugged Rio's arm again.

Rio dug his heels in, holding his grandmother's look, refusing to blink, refusing to give in like that, but she was better. She had a lifetime of getting her way under her belt, and he was still weak when it came to opposing her fully. He still didn't know how.

His pupils widened the longer they stared, and Rio felt the resistance in him break.

He unclenched his body, and the next tug from Russel got him moving in the direction of the dance floor. Russel led him to the middle of it, as if he wanted everyone to see he got to be the one to take the man of the evening to dance.

"Smile, darling," Russel said as he wrapped a hand around Rio's back, fingers getting tangled in his gold chains and tugging at his feathers.

"Ow," Rio flinched when Russel pulled his hand free, and the man smiled in apology.

"I apologize," he said, hand finally finding Rio's waist and settling there awkwardly.

He spun them around with zero sense of rhythm or finesse, making other people move out of their way.

Rio tried to follow, but his brain was doing the best it could to just be somewhere else. With someone else.

He wanted his mate to hold him like that. He wanted Fire to sway him back and forth and show him off to the crowd. He wanted Fire to be there and to be the one to claim him with a hand on the bare skin beneath his wings.

Instead, he got a boring, spoiled man whose family saw Rio as a cash grab, not a person. He got someone who knew nothing about him, yet insisted on paying empty compliments that meant zero to Rio.

He got someone who wanted Uxorious, not Rio.

He wanted out.

"Uxorious?" He heard Russel call his name, and he came back to reality, looking at the man who was slowly spinning him around in a particular direction.

"Where...?" Rio tried to ask, but before he could finish the sentence, Russel stopped the spin and wrapped his arms around Rio from behind.

"Smile for the camera, darling," he said, and Rio froze, a flash of the camera blinding him for a second, leaving behind cold dread and regret.

That photo would be in the press by morning.

And just like that, Rio knew exactly what his grandmother's angle had been.

CHAPTER THIRTEEN

FIRE

Fire was leaning against the hood of his car, parked in front of the Children's Rec Center. He had his hands stuffed in his pockets, the right one clenched tightly around a crumpled piece of glossy paper.

He'd torn it out of a magazine that had been thrust in his face as he'd walked into a café close to his apartment to grab a coffee. He'd been standing in line, trying to be surreptitious while waiting for his order, and there it was. Stacked up on a little shelf. Fresh off the press that morning.

The lustrous cover reflected the early morning light, and the slick-looking man pictured had his arms wrapped around none other than Rio's waist too tightly, too intimately to be anything other than what it looked like.

Fire had felt disbelief, then liquid rage course through his veins the more he looked at it.

He'd grabbed it from the shelf and thrown the money for it onto the counter when he picked up his coffee. Locking himself in his car, he'd ripped the front page out, pulverizing it between his fingers and stuffing it into his pocket.

Rio's face said he didn't want to be in the man's arms. His entire posture was closed off and tense, his wings ramrod straight. Fire could see that. He could rationalize it to himself all he wanted.

But the beast that lived in his chest wouldn't let go.

Because he knew.

He knew how Rio smelled when he got all dressed up for an event. Fresh and clean and inviting. He knew that his suit would be open in the back to allow for his wings to stand out, and he knew that man's hand would be touching soft skin from the way it was positioned.

He knew how sinfully attractive Rio was and how his body arched when Fire touched his waist. He didn't want anyone else knowing that. He didn't want him touched by anyone else.

He told himself Rio wouldn't betray him because even after having known him for only a short amount of time, Fire knew he was a man of his word. He was loyal and seemed as invested in their relationship as Fire was.

And yet it didn't settle the rage in him.

He drove to the Rec Center on autopilot, clambering out of his car when the silence became too stifling to handle. Rio had called him mid-journey to his house and said he'd meet him there instead. A change of plans that spoke volumes, coupled with his tense voice. Fire knew he was aware of the photo being out, but Rio hadn't commented on it at all.

Fire didn't know if that was a good idea or a horrible one. He just knew he needed to find a way to get his emotions in check before Rio got there and they headed in to meet Vid and the kids.

"Hi." Rio's voice came from behind him and, well...emotions not in check at all.

"You made it," Fire said.

"I said I'd be here," Rio said with a quirk of his eyebrow.

"I figured your party wore you out." Fire shrugged, but his shoulders were too stiff for it to be anywhere close to casual. "Looked like you were having a lot of fun."

Rio sighed deeply and lowered his eyes to the floor.

"I take it you've seen the photo," he said, and Fire snorted.

"I had the pleasure, yes," he said, and knew the little stutter of Rio's breath was a reaction to his tone but couldn't stop. "I take it he's your grandparents' number one contender for your husband?"

God, but he sounded like a dick.

"I don't really care where he ranks on their scale," Rio said in a clipped tone.

"No, what matters is where he ranks on yours," Fire spat back, and Rio balked at the words.

He took a step back and stared at Fire for a long moment, those gorgeous brown eyes brimming with emotion. Fire knew he had hit a nerve. But he also knew Rio wouldn't back down. So he was prepared for the bristle and the bite in his words when it came.

"Keep it up and you won't rank much higher," Rio said through clenched teeth, glaring. "You think I'd go against what we are to each other and just cozy up to some random guy? That's who you take me for?"

Fire clenched his jaw, unable to speak.

"I'm flattered by your trust in me. Truly," Rio said flatly. "I'll be inside."

He turned on his heel and walked toward the entrance to the center, leaving Fire to look after him, shame and regret pooling low in his stomach, longing to touch, to pull him into his arms and not let go.

The contrasting emotions were difficult to keep up with. He felt completely off center, unable to recognize himself. He hated that his own instincts would make him snap so much at someone he cared about. He didn't like falling victim to the primitive parts of himself, and yet he couldn't help feeling the way he was, something driving him on and on, fueling the flames.

Fire took a deep breath and tried to think past the haze of jealousy and the need to break fingers. He willed himself to think rationally for a second, and he managed to see a glimpse of reason that told him Rio wouldn't lie to him. Rio was a lot of things, both good and bad, but he wasn't dishonest. And Fire had no reason to doubt him. He had no reason to be that bent out of shape because of a single photo, except his own lizard brain trying to make him think Rio was his property because he was his mate.

He felt a desperate need to hold on to Rio for reasons he couldn't explain. Like he would disappear if he didn't hold on tight enough. But Fire didn't want to be one of those people. He'd never thought he would be one of those people. He'd never had a mate before, though. He had no idea how intense it could feel. How all-consuming.

He ran a hand over his face and sighed, jogging after Rio into the center. He greeted the receptionist dully and made his way toward the training room, itching under his own skin.

He opened the door and stopped in his tracks, watching as Rio talked to Vid, who was already setting up an obstacle course for the kids.

Rio had his shoulders drawn up, his pink wings stiff and lips pressed tight, but he smiled at Vid as they spoke. Clearly trying to act like an adult about the situation.

Forcing himself to get out of his funk and do the same, Fire walked over to them.

"I see you two have met," he said, and Vid looked up.

"Hey, man!" he said. "And yes, I have met Uxorious."

"Just call him Rio," Fire said, throwing a look at Rio, hoping he'd realized that the standard joke about Rio's name was an olive branch. At least for the time being. Until he could properly apologize and explain.

The long pause after his words made him squirm under Rio's gaze.

"That's not my name," Rio said finally, and caught Fire's eyes. The corner of his lips turned up just a tick, and Fire wanted to bottle the feeling that small movement pulled from him so he could carry it around with him everywhere.

"Sure, sounds better than Uxorious," Vid said.

Rio snapped his head in his direction, giving him a glare fit to turn people to stone. "My name is unique."

"Sure, man," Vid said, nodding and wide-eyed, holding up a foam obstacle in front of him like a shield as he backed away. "Absolutely. Just gonna go set this down."

He rushed off, leaving them alone, and Fire shuffled over to stand next to Rio.

"I'm sorry," he said softly, looking down at his sneakers. "I didn't doubt you. I know you wouldn't do that."

"Well, you clearly did think it at least for a second," Rio said, crossing his arms over his chest.

"No, I don't think I did," Fire said, pinching the bridge of his nose as he tried to make sense of his own brain. Whatever had really been driving him wasn't *just* jealousy, but he didn't have any other answer to explain. "I just saw that photo this morning, and this blinding jealousy took over."

Rio looked at him. "Has it settled now?"

"Not really," Fire said, figuring honesty was his best way forward.

"So the truce was fake?"

"No, it wasn't fake," Fire said, reaching out to catch his sleeve between two fingers. "I just realized I can be jealous and not let it affect you and me. I can't help not wanting hands on you, Rio. I can't help wanting to lock you away from everyone and keep you just to myself. You're my mate."

"But..."

"But I can and should control myself," Fire said. "I can think past the jealousy and instinct and choose to believe you, remind myself that I trust you. And that you're mine. Are you?"

Rio looked at him, closing the remaining distance, and lifted his hand up to cup his cheek.

"I am my own person, James," he said. "But I am also your mate. I feel it. I accepted it. And I want it. I want you. But you already know it will take some maneuvering to get my life in order."

The words made him itchy again, but Fire was desperate for them to get back on an even footing. He didn't want to fight. "Can we compromise?"

Rio dropped his hand to Fire's neck, looking between his eyes. "How?"

"Can you wear closed-back suits in the future?" Fire asked. It wasn't even close to all he wanted to say. "I don't think I can handle hands on you like that all the time."

Rio actually giggled at that but shook his head.

"My wings are too pretty to put away," he said. "But I can wear waist corsets to cover up skin."

Fire's mind couldn't resist pulling up images of Rio's slender waist in those corsets, and he had to fight off the urge to whisk him away, to make him wear one just for Fire. Where nobody else could see.

"You're a damn tease, Uxorious," he said, and Rio lifted an eyebrow at him.

"Am I?" Rio asked, walking away just as the kids started pouring into the gym, leaving Fire to swallow everything down and just be grateful they'd reached some sort of an accord.

The kids flocked to Vid first, asking him how he was and telling him they'd missed him a lot. It seemed like they didn't really see anyone else but him for a moment.

But then their eyes found Rio, and Fire watched in amusement as they descended upon him, grubby hands wanting to high-five him and curious minds wanting to know if he'd train them all the time.

Rio tried to remain composed, replying to their questions seriously. He was tense and kept them at a distance, but he was also polite to them, treating them like adults with the way he explained how he might not be there every time, but he'd definitely make sure to keep track of how they progressed.

Rio took a few steps toward Vid, and the gaggle of children followed him like baby ducklings, tripping over one another to be the first one in line after him.

"Okay, kids," Vid called out, clapping his hands. "We have Mr. Rio and Mr. Fire here with us again, to help you learn to fly. Happy?"

The kids cheered happily, hopping from one foot to the other, and as much as he tried to keep his face neutral, Fire saw the little smile on Rio's face at the excitement.

One of the girls in the group—Fire thought her name was Maya—raised her hand.

"Yes, Maya?" Vid asked, and she looked around.

"Piper isn't here today," she said, and Vid frowned a bit.

"Piper?" he asked, looking at the kids first and then Rio and Fire.

"She joined the class last," Fire said. "Her dad brought her because she really likes flying and wanted to try."

"Oh, okay," Vid said, looking back to Maya. "Maybe she had something else to do today, and she'll join us next time, hm?"

"Okay," Maya said, clearly happy with the explanation, and Vid took over again.

"Right, attendance taken..." he joked. "I'll take you through your warm-up, and then today, we're working on our takeoff and soaring. Sound good?"

The kids cheered again, and Fire had a distinct feeling Vid would have gotten that reaction no matter what he suggested. They clearly worshipped the ground he walked on. They listened to him intently as he guided them to form a circle in the middle of the room, and then he led them through a thorough, total-body warm-up.

Now that he knew the truth about Rio's dad, Fire wasn't surprised that Rio had some really good suggestions of exercises once they came to the wings. He corrected the form for several kids and made sure they were stretching their wings to their full range before they finished with the routine.

Between Rio and Vid, Fire almost felt forgotten during warm-up. But then the flying part of the training kicked in, and between the three of them, Fire was the best flier, even recovering.

Vid set up wooden boxes for the kids again, teaching them how to lift and soar, explaining how to tuck their wings back in and gain momentum. Fire showed them by soaring from one of the higher boxes—nothing too strenuous, of course, with Vid in the room. But he was able to slow his motions deliberately so the kids could follow.

Several dared to try, and while they all kicked off the box neatly, there was no soaring to be found. They all landed softly, their wings stretched wide around their bodies. They didn't seem too bothered by it, clapping and cheering every time Fire landed on the ground after showing them how to do it.

Vid tried explaining too, but they were both falling a bit short on ideas as to how to make it click.

Fire turned to look at Rio, finding him flipping through a small notebook until he seemed to find what he was looking for. He read for a few seconds, then tucked the notebook into his back pocket and approached Vid.

"Mind if I try?" he asked.

"Go ahead," Vid said, flourishing a hand, and Rio stepped closer to the kids.

"Okay, how about we try something else?" Rio said, and they all turned to him, looking at him as if he'd hung the moon. Fire couldn't really understand what it was that they liked about him so much.

Rio treated the children like he treated everyone else in his life. Polite, aloof, detached, but there. Fire had no idea kids responded well to being treated like that. But they apparently did.

"I want you all to step on your boxes," Rio said, and they all scrambled to get up, curious little eyes staring back at him. "Okay, now, imagine your wings are like a little bowl. And you have to use the bowl to collect wind in it."

A little boy whose name Fire couldn't recall raised his hand.

"Yes?" Rio asked.

"Why are we collecting wind?" he asked.

Rio smiled. "Because the more wind you have in your bowl, the higher you can fly."

A chorus of "Ooooooooh" spread through the kids, and Fire chuckled to himself.

"So when you hop off your box, make your wings into bowls." Rio demonstrated how with his own wings. "And collect as much wind as you can. But, if a lot of wind helps you go up, how do we get down?"

They thought for a moment before another little girl named Ella beamed.

"We throw away the wind from our bowl?" she asked.

"Exactly," he said, nodding. "When you need to soar, first, you have to go very high, so collect a lot of wind."

He made his wings sit in the right position for takeoff.

"But when you need to go down fast, when you have to soar, you need to empty your bowl as fast as you can. Which means tucking your wings all the way back so no wind gets in."

He tucked his wings behind his back and turned them sharp and pointy at the ends, the perfect soaring position.

The kids all followed, their fluffy little wings pulling down and back as they worked on their positioning.

"Okay," Rio said once they seemed to all get how to make their wings positioned for takeoff and how to tuck them to soar. "Let's try the boxes again, hm?"

They all nodded, settling themselves on the boxes, toes hanging off the edge. Vid was supervising them, and several of them managed to perform something that vaguely looked like a soar after a few attempts.

Fire walked to Rio and nudged his shoulder.

"That was great advice," he said. "Is that from your notebook?"

Rio smiled, pulling the notebook from his back pocket. It was wrapped in brown covers and clearly well loved if the signs of wear and tear were anything to go by. Rio ran his thumb gently over it.

"My dad noted down every training program, both for him and me," he said. "He had countless notebooks with advice, best practice, regimes, and programs for every stage of learning to fly and competing. This is the first one he filled with things he taught me."

Fire smiled sadly at the longing in Rio's voice. "You really miss him."

"I do," Rio said quietly, clutching the book tighter. "But I know he'd be happy to know his materials are being used again."

"You said he had tons?" Fire asked.

Rio nodded. "He did. I have them all safely tucked away so nobody can get them."

He paused for a second before lifting his eyes to look at Fire.

"Would you like to see them?"

Fire almost flailed in excitement. "You'd let me see notebooks filled with Bullet's training regimes and advice?"

"Sure," he said casually, and Fire nearly vibrated out of his skin.

"But that would give me an unfair advantage," he said, and Rio quirked an eyebrow at him.

"And that presents an issue for you, oh moral high ground representative," Rio drawled, and Fire barked out a laugh.

It felt nice to be on the receiving end of his sass again. The air was still a bit cool around them, but Fire knew they'd be okay.

They wrapped up the practice feeling lighter, and Fire invited Rio back to his place for lunch. He wrapped an arm around his waist as they walked toward the door, refusing to admit he was reclaiming the spot from the smarmy guy in that photo. He just liked holding Rio's waist.

"Mr. Uxorious Charmichael." Fire heard Anna's voice coming from behind them, and he groaned. Just what he needed after the day he'd had.

"Walk fast. Don't look back," he hissed, but Rio was already in rotation, thrilled at being called by his first name.

"Hello," he said as Anna walked over to them, smile barely concealing the desire to end Fire in the most brutal way she could imagine. "I like her."

"Of course you do," Fire said. "She called you Uxorious unironically."

"I'm Anna, Fire's manager, personal assistant, babysitter, cleaner, and generally the voice of reason," Anna said, ignoring Fire and extending a hand to Rio. "You, I believe, are his mate."

Rio froze at the words, throwing a look at Fire.

"She's my manager and publicist. She has to know," Fire said, and Rio narrowed his eyes slightly before nodding.

"I am, yes," he said to Anna, shaking her hand. "It's a pleasure to meet you."

"I don't remember us having a meeting scheduled," Fire said, and she snapped her eyes to him.

"We didn't have one," she said. "I just did what literally every imbecile with a camera can do and followed you here to see you meeting the Charmichael heir in a dilapidated Rec Center for the second time. People talk, Fire."

"So let them talk," Fire said without thinking, feeling how tense Rio went next to him.

"You want me to let them talk?" she asked as if he told her to grow a third leg and teach only that leg to tap dance.

"No, he does not," Rio said. "We're keeping things under wraps for now, and I'd appreciate it if you could help us there."

"Not exactly what I had in mind," she said. "I was leaning more toward making a statement and coming out as a mated couple."

"Out of the question," Rio said, and that annoying, curling feeling settled in his gut again.

He watched Rio and Anna discuss their future, their voices sounding distant and muffled as the unfamiliar emotion raged inside his head. He wanted it to stop, but it felt like every time Rio pushed back on Anna's suggestions, it just ignited further.

As he listened to them bicker, he came to a realization that made his blood run cold. Rio didn't really have a plan at all. He had asked for time, but there was no deadline. No end to their secrecy in sight.

And however much Fire wanted to keep him safe and happy, he realized he didn't want to be a secret forever. He didn't want to hide behind walls and avoid touching him. He didn't want to pretend he didn't know Rio.

But it seemed that was the only option he had.

CHAPTER FOURTEEN

RIO

Rio didn't know what to do with himself in the weeks that followed.

Making it to practice at the Rec Center was a study in accomplishing the impossible each week he walked out the door. His grandmother had caught on to his scheduled departures and tried to stick her nose in countless times. When he refused to clue her in, she decided it must mean he was doing something he shouldn't be doing and went on the offensive.

She persisted in bringing up Russel or any number of other potential mate candidates, trying to hook him into dates or meetings, treating him to lengthy talks about how they would be good matches for the family. The upcoming Showing was a looming guillotine over his neck.

Rio became paranoid. Worried she knew something. Scared someone was watching or following him at every hour. Nervous about every text sent or received from Fire. Anxious about making any plans to meet. He found himself dodging calls, enough to make Fire notice and question if he was okay. Enough to make Fire clue in to his increased anxiety. Enough for him to respond to it.

And his response was to put up walls around himself when Rio was there. He still held him close and kissed him. He still fucked him until Rio couldn't breathe. But Rio felt him pulling away emotionally, and it hurt.

It was an unsustainable cycle.

Rio was already exhausted trying to balance these two lives he'd come to have. Rio and Uxorious. He was desperate to make them coexist, if only he could work out the formula. But inevitably, he always ended up in the same position.

Stuck.

But he didn't want to face the fallout. Surely, he could make it work. He just needed more time.

So he made his excuses. To Fire. To his grandmother. And holed up in his room trying to distract himself, finding himself drawn to his father's belongings for solace.

Once the box was open, Rio found he couldn't close it again.

He spent hours combing through old journals, refamiliarizing himself with every messy stroke of his father's handwriting and his own childish scrawl, reliving those memories he'd pushed down deep.

He lay on his bed and replayed old videos of private practices, watching his father try to perfect the same moves that would eventually make him famous over and over until he got them right. He got a new notebook and filled it with plans and ideas for the kids at the center. Moves he wanted to teach them, techniques he wanted to use.

He found inspiration in old videos of himself. Childish competitions with his dad behind the camera calling to him. He never used his name, not even a variation like Fire did. He always called him champ. An act of defiance to his family, no doubt. No one had called him that in so long and probably never would again.

Rio missed him. So much.

It was an ache that never went away—not really. He could only forget. Push it away like his grandparents wanted him to. Racing wasn't a part of his life anymore. His father was a footnote they wanted erased with the Charmichael name.

And yet here he found himself, staring at his father's smiling face, a trophy held high, confetti and champagne flying around him.

He swiped at the stray tear that escaped his control, slipping down his temple, and sat up. That life was gone. What was the use of being maudlin? He clenched his jaw and put the picture aside.

But his heart continued to throb, soft and wounded.

"What would you do?" Rio asked the picture out loud, then shook his head and smiled sadly. "Give 'em hell. That's what."

He stroked a finger down the side of the picture, whispering like a secret, eyes glistening, "But I was never as brave as you."

He looked around his gilded bedroom.

Would everything disappear?

His grandmother would never be called kind. His grandfather just blindly did what she asked. But they were the only family he had. Life with them was the only life he knew how to live.

Rio had nothing outside these four walls. Outside of the money he prized and the life that had been handed to him. He didn't know what he'd do. And he refused to let Fire just take over the role his grandparents held. His keeper. His provider.

He didn't want Fire to grow to resent him, and he was scared to see the person when everything he had was stripped away. Rio wasn't sure that person was as good as Fire believed him to be.

The sound of his ringtone made him jump, and he stretched to reach his phone on the bedside table. Fire's name lit up the screen, and Rio's throat grew tight.

"It's like you know," Rio said accusingly at the device, like Fire was actually inside there. He closed his eyes and took a deep breath before answering it.

"Hello?"

"*Princess.*" Rio half smiled, the endearment loosening some of the pressure on his chest, but the subdued tone of Fire's voice telling him things were going downhill. "*You busy?*"

Another excuse to join the three others this week was on the tip of Rio's tongue, but he bit it back. He didn't want to be in this house anymore. And he missed Fire. Every moment of every day he just wanted to be close to him. No matter how confusing it was. "Always, but I can move some things around, I suppose."

"*He finally deigns to see me!*" Fire said, and Rio knew there was some truth to the lighthearted joke.

"Or maybe something just came up." He donned his cape of snark and let it shield him from whatever came next.

"*Testy! I can swing by your place whenever you want,*" Fire said with a short laugh. "*I'm done with training for the day.*"

Rio jumped to his feet like Fire was right outside already. "No! No, it's fine. I'll drive to you."

"*You? Drive?*" Fire teased.

"I have my license!"

"*You have a chauffeur,*" Fire corrected.

"For convenience."

He could hear Fire rolling his eyes. "*I'll just come to you.*"

"I'll meet you at your place," Rio asserted. "You're probably tired."

"*I'm driving past your area anyway. It's not out of the way,*" Fire said, the sound of a car door closing in the background.

"Still..." Rio said, scrambling for an excuse. "It'll be more expedient to meet there."

"*Expedient?*" Fire repeated, bewildered, before falling silent for a split second. "*Okay. What the hell is going on, Rio? You've been acting strange all week.*"

"Nothing," he said hastily, sounding less than convincing even to his own ears.

"*Really? Because it sounds a whole lot like you don't want me within twenty feet of you,*" Fire said, and Rio clenched his eyes shut, hating hearing those words. He wanted Fire close more than anything.

"That's not true," he whispered.

"*Isn't it? You haven't accepted any of my invites to go out in a week. You refused to take any calls from Anna to talk about what we could possibly do to make this easier. And now, apparently, I can't even be seen in breathing distance of your house.*"

Each word made Rio's heart ache more and more.

"You've been to my house before," Rio said, deflecting. Hating himself for doing it.

"*So if I want to stop by and come in, I can?*" Fire asked. Rio was silent, heart hammering so loud he was sure Fire could hear it. Fire scoffed. "*Got it. Good to know you're apparently fucking ashamed of me on top of everything else.*"

"That is not what this is about," Rio said, not wanting Fire to think that for a second. "I promise I couldn't have asked for a better mate than you. You're the only thing that makes sense right now, James."

"*You have a very interesting way of showing that, gorgeous,*" Fire said quietly, ire diminishing and leaving just that tired, defeated note in his voice.

"Fire, please..." he whispered. "Things are difficult right now. I don't want to provoke my grandparents more than I have to before I'm ready for the fallout. I still want to see you. I need to see you."

"*But only in dark corners, right?*" Fire asked.

"That's not fair," Rio said, feeling his eyes water and looking up to stop the tears from falling.

Fire was silent. And the silence hurt even more than the biting words. They felt like Fire fighting for them. Silence meant giving up.

"I dug out the rest of my father's old books," Rio said quietly, taking a leaf from Fire's book and offering a truce. For the time being.

He heard Fire's sigh crackle down the line. "*Yeah?*"

"I can bring them and we can look at them together?" Rio suggested.

"*I'll see you at my place then, princess.*"

It was dispirited, but the nickname still gave Rio a little solace. They hung up, and Rio gathered his things and called his driver. He had the man drop him a block away for safety and kept his eyes peeled for anyone who could recognize him around the huge sunglasses and scarf he had on.

"You look ridiculous," Fire said when he opened the door to him. He had showered and dressed in sweats and a plain t-shirt that clung. His hair was drying over his forehead carelessly, and he looked effortlessly handsome.

"Impossible," Rio replied, removing his glasses daintily.

"You know people have seen you around my building already. Aren't you taking this a little too far?"

"For my vindictive grandmother? No."

Fire pulled a face like he had a mouthful to say but didn't comment, simply stepping aside to let him in. Rio felt tense in a way he never had before in Fire's apartment as he closed the door behind himself and set his bag down. The unresolved argument brewing between them made the atmosphere stormy.

Rio swallowed and walked up to Fire, grabbing his collar and bringing his lips to his. The tension immediately evaporated as Fire gave in to the natural rush between them, his frustrations showing in the harsh pull of his lips, the strength of his fingers on Rio's hips as he drew him closer.

Rio took all of it, keeping his own mouth pliant and soft, a silent apology until everything ebbed away, Fire settling into lingering kisses that stuck.

Fire sighed into his mouth when air became a problem, pressing his forehead to Rio's with his eyes still closed.

"I feel like if I don't hold you close, you'll fly away," Fire said suddenly.

Rio's heart thumped guiltily. "I'm right here."

It wasn't what Fire had meant, and Rio knew it.

"Have you eaten already?" Rio asked, changing the subject.

Fire was silent for a moment, and Rio wondered if he'd push it like he always did. Rio almost wanted him to. Eventually, Fire shook his head, pulling back but keeping his hands on Rio's waist. "I've gotta chug a protein shake in a bit."

Rio felt a mixture of disappointment and gratitude flow through him as Fire took the bait. "That's not food."

"It's not so bad. We can order in something else."

Rio nodded, extricating himself and grabbing his bag, settling on the sofa. He pulled the contents out and began stacking it on the coffee table. The sofa dipped as Fire sat next to him, eyes alight with interest despite everything.

"I still can't believe Bullet was your dad."

Rio smiled. "Of course he was. He was the best."

Fire snorted.

They settled in with shoulders and hands brushing, crossing arms as they each reached for the treasured pieces of history. Weirdly, both their childhoods were wrapped in these notes. Rio's firsthand and Fire's as a kid worshipping his idol and trying to copy his every move.

Fire devoured every page reverently, and Rio smiled, heart warmed to have *someone* to share this with finally. This missing piece of himself.

"Who's this?" Fire asked.

Rio glanced over and froze.

"My mother."

He'd seen pictures of her, of course. She was in some of the portraits within the house and some of the few photo frames his grandmother deemed acceptable to display. But Rio had never seen her like this.

Through the eyes of his father.

It was a candid shot of her laughing, and she looked beautiful. Happy.

But not happy enough not to leave him, mate or not.

Rio stared stonily at the picture, mind running a mile a minute.

"Rio?" Fire said softly. His palm folded around his inner thigh, squeezing to offer comfort.

Had Rio's father ever done the same thing for his mother? Had he realized that what she wanted was more than he could give? Accepted being pushed into the shadows, kept a secret pleasure so she could lead the life she wanted?

Rio had wanted nothing to do with that woman his whole life, but he was faced with the crippling realization that despite his vehement protests to the contrary...he might have been *exactly* like her.

It was suddenly hard to breathe.

"Princess?" Fire questioned, sounding concerned. "Talk to me."

Rio crawled into Fire's lap, taking his mouth in his own.

"Rio," Fire got out between presses. "Wait. Rio..."

Rio didn't want to talk. He didn't want to think.

Please.

Like Fire heard him, he finally leaned into the frantic kissing, picking Rio up around the thighs and walking him to the bed, where everything was said without words. Just for a little while.

Fire dropped Rio down onto soft blankets, covering him up with his body and smoothing his hair off his forehead.

"We can't keep escaping into sex," Fire said, and Rio closed his eyes tight, nodding in agreement.

"I know," he whispered. "But please, just this once..."

He canted his hips up, wrapping his arms around Fire's neck and pulling him closer.

It felt good having every inch of their bodies touching. Fire was strong and heavy on top of him, standing as a shield between Rio and the world he wasn't sure he was a part of anymore.

Rio wanted to melt into Fire. Wanted to become a part of him instead because he felt untethered and alone, and, for the first time in his life, he felt lonely.

"Please," he whispered again, and the little crack in his voice was what finally got through to Fire.

"Fuck, Rio," Fire said as he dove in to kiss him, lips bruising and branding Rio as his own.

Rio's lip caught on his teeth, the skin breaking a little and a drop of blood trickling down onto his tongue. It stung, but Rio wanted it. He wanted to run his tongue over the spot tomorrow and know Fire had been there, claiming him. Wanting him when he wasn't sure he wanted himself.

He returned the kiss wildly, biting at Fire's bottom lip, sucking on it, making Fire groan and push his hips down into Rio's.

Rio's hands ran down his back, sneaking to the bottom of Fire's shirt and pulling it up, nails digging into Fire's skin as they went.

Fire hissed and broke their kiss, resting their foreheads together.

"You'll kill me, Rio," he said, and Rio shook his head.

"Off," he demanded, pulling Fire's shirt up and out of the way until his mate was shirtless and beautiful on top of him.

Fire truly was a work of art. Rio would probably never sing anyone's praises out loud, but Fire took his breath away every time he saw him naked.

"All of it," he said, tugging at the waistband of Fire's sweatpants, pulling at it until he heard a few threads break.

Fire took his hands in his and pushed them up, wrapping his fingers around the headboard.

"Hold them there," he said, and Rio wanted to protest, wanted to bare his teeth and reassert his control, but...he just didn't have it in him.

He wanted Fire to take over. He wanted to close his eyes and lose himself in the pleasure Fire was so good at giving him.

Every single time with Fire was groundbreaking, and he needed that now. He needed the ground to break and swallow all of the things he didn't want to think about.

He just wanted to feel.

So he nodded at Fire and gripped the headboard as tight as he could, watching as Fire stood up and rid himself of the sweatpants.

He had no underwear on, and Rio licked his lips at the sight of him hard and leaking from the tip.

It was for him, he knew. All of that was for Rio.

"The way you look at me, gorgeous," Fire said as he approached the bed again, quick fingers attacking Rio's clothes until there was nothing left on him but a thin sheen of sweat.

Fire sprawled next to him, naked skin touching and sliding together as he kissed him again. He reached up and wrapped his fingers around Rio's wrist, then ran them down the exposed underarms, making Rio squirm.

He continued down Rio's neck and chest, thumbs catching his nipples, fingers squeezing and pulling at them until Rio whined.

When Rio's nipples were hard and red from Fire's fingers, he moved them farther down, wrapping them around Rio's aching cock and tugging, pulling slowly, so excruciatingly slowly Rio wanted to scream.

"Let me hear you, Rio," Fire said, speeding up the movement of his hand, giving it a little twist at the head of Rio's cock. "Let it all out."

He thumbed Rio's slit, and this time, Rio did scream. It was too much. All of it was too much, and he couldn't help himself.

He came all over Fire's hand, vision going fuzzy around the edges, the sounds rising in pitch until all he could hear was white noise, and he drowned in it.

He blanked out for a long moment, and when he came back, Fire was still by his side, his lips latched onto the side of his neck and his fingers playing with Rio's hole.

"Welcome back," Fire said, pushing a finger in. Rio was too sensitive, too spent, but it felt so good he didn't want it to stop.

"James..." he cried when Fire added a second finger, the muscles in his arms aching and screaming in protest, and he realized he was still gripping onto the headboard.

"Can I..." he started, but Fire already knew.

"You can," he said, three fingers working on stretching Rio as much as he could.

Rio let go of the headboard, arms going around Fire, cuddling up close, shivering from pleasure and oversensitivity.

"Ready... I'm ready," he moaned, pushing back onto Fire's fingers until he pulled them out.

He tugged Rio closer, turning him around until his back was pressed against Fire's chest. Rio felt Fire wrap him up in his arms, one under his head and across his chest, the other around his waist, hand lying between Rio's legs.

He cupped his spent cock in his warm palm as he entered him, the ache feeling like a blessing to Rio.

He closed his eyes and let himself be taken and pulled apart. He hoped Fire would put him back together. He hoped that whatever way Fire found to make his jagged pieces fit would be better than what Rio was at the moment.

Rio heard Fire's grunts in his ear, he felt his breath at the back of his neck and the thunder of his heartbeat against his back. He relished the strong hold around him and Fire's slide in and out of his body that gained speed.

The warm hand left Rio's cock and gripped his hip as Fire pushed inside faster, harder. He turned Rio onto his stomach, sprawling on top of him as he thrust, hips stuttering and breathing ragged. He was close. Rio could recognize it.

He pushed his ass up, desperate to feel Fire come, desperate to feel the warmth of him spilling inside of his body. He clenched around the hard cock, and it was that small movement that pushed Fire over the edge.

With an almost feral grunt, he spilled inside Rio, kissing him, tugging at him, holding him until Rio felt like they were one and nobody could untangle them.

It was what he wanted.

To be Fire's so completely the world slipped away.

To be his enough for him to know he belonged.

CHAPTER FIFTEEN

FIRE

They didn't talk.

When they did, it was about trivial things, nothing that could lead to the inevitable discussion that Rio wanted so desperately to put off. Fire was tired of silently fighting with him—a battle of wills he didn't want to win. He wanted Rio to want to lose.

The rest of their time was spent with bodies pressed together, the thing between them that had worked from the very start. A substitute for everything they didn't say. But like he'd told Rio, sex couldn't be the balm that fixed everything, and Fire found himself staring at the ceiling with their bodies cooling, wondering if this was sustainable in the long run.

When he wasn't with Rio—something that was becoming less frequent—he was thinking about him, but when that wasn't possible, he was at Ace, trying to take control of one aspect of his life.

Fire had managed to get into the air but could barely stay off the ground for more than a minute, immediately feeling the imbalance. Freefalling like he was showing the kids at the Rec Center was okay, but beating his wings and keeping level was still a nightmare despite the weeks of rehabilitation. Turning was off the table completely.

Fire could feel everything slipping away from him slowly, and there was nothing he could do about it.

"Okay, down," Vid said, grabbing his waist and helping him stabilize and lower.

"Let's go again," Fire said, desperate to fix it. To do something. "I can compensate."

"Not how it works," Vid said.

Fire growled, but it was ignored. Vid went back to making notes, and Fire stood there uselessly, wings trembling with exertion and spread over the floor behind him. Deadweight. Fire was beginning to hate looking at them, so he switched focus. He found Coach with his fingers on his beard, slowly stroking as he stared into space. It was a familiar visage, the one he had before all his big races, and Fire was apprehensive to know what he was thinking about.

"So what's our game plan, Coach? We're trailing a few points because of that DNF, but if I win with enough of a gap, I think we can clinch it at AirCore X," Fire said, all false bravado.

Coach's eyes refocused on his face, taking him in for a second, the whole miserable picture. His eyes settled on his wings before he shook his head. "We can talk about that another time."

Fire felt indignation rise, knowing others in the room were staring at him. "Why another time? It's not like I'm doing anything right now."

"Yes, you are. We have a massage scheduled," Vid said, smoothing over one wing arch.

Fire clenched his jaw. "Which doesn't affect my ability to speak and listen."

Coach sighed. "Look, we're not thinking that far ahead just yet."

"How can we not be?" Fire burst out. "It's right around the corner!"

"It's not worth your wings, kid. Trust me," Coach said, mouth settling into a wry line. "There's always next year."

Fire flinched, but his jaw was still set stubbornly. "I can race."

"We're concentrating on recovery right now. That's final, no matter how much attitude you give me," Coach said. "And if the press or the Racing Association asks me, that'll be my answer too."

Fire looked at Vid, but he just shook his head apologetically. "He's right, Fire. Look, you've been more stressed than usual lately. Maybe we should call it a day and start fresh tomorrow? And if you need to talk—"

Fire exhaled sharply through his nose to avoid saying anything he'd regret. Instead, he shrugged Vid off, gathered up his towel, and stormed away. He didn't bother showering or changing, he just dematerialized his wings with a wince, grabbed his shit, and left.

When he was in his car, he pressed his head back against the rest, slamming once, twice. He was so fucking frustrated. Didn't they believe in him? Did they not think he could do it? He knew everyone else in the circuit thought he couldn't, *hoped* he couldn't, but Vid and Coach giving up on him hurt like hell.

Racing was *the* thing he was good at. The only thing he could rely on. The thing he'd dedicated his life to, slowly slipping away.

"Fuck," he whispered, scrubbing his hands over his tired face.

Everything in his life was falling to pieces at once, and Fire felt helpless to stop it, trying to cup clumsy hands around the remnants of both his relationship and racing career.

His phone *pinged* with a new message, and he considered ignoring it, but he fished it out, feeling conflicted when he saw Rio's name flash across the screen.

Rio: *Come pick me up?*

He'd dropped his location, and Fire swallowed as he stared at it. It wasn't even a choice for him. Not really.

He tore out of the lot.

Rio

Rio was waiting with a pile of bags by his tapping foot, sunglasses covering most of his face. He wasn't trying to make it obvious he was hiding, but he couldn't help the paranoia that made him hide behind them.

Texting Fire to come pick him up had been an impulse decision. Stupidity, certainly. He was on a busy street; anyone could see him getting into Fire's car. But things were so dicey between him and Fire right now that Rio couldn't help but give in to the need to see him. To assure himself that he was still there even though *he* was the one holding them at a distance. It was beyond selfish, but Rio was feeling so lost—one step away from falling off the side of the planet.

Fire pulled up right alongside him ten minutes later, putting the hazard lights on before getting out. Rio settled to see him, heart reaching out for him even when he didn't dare.

"I've been waiting here forever," Rio complained instead.

Fire kissed his cheek, not commenting on the flinch and check Rio did instinctively. Rio felt horrible. He watched Fire grab his bags and put them into the back seat without a word.

"How are you?" Rio asked. "You had training today, didn't you?"

"It was fine," Fire said, clipped.

Rio frowned. "What happened?"

Fire smiled. It didn't reach his eyes. "Nothing. C'mon, before someone spots us."

Rio hustled into the car, hating that it had to be this way. Once he was in, he turned to Fire again.

"What happened?" he repeated.

"I'm starving, that's all. Didn't have time for breakfast," Fire said, pulling away.

Rio clamped his mouth shut, deciding not to press on his evasiveness. He didn't want to start their conversation with an argument. Instead, he looked out the window, lost in his thoughts until Fire stopped the car somewhere completely unfamiliar.

"Why did we stop?" he asked.

"I'm hungry," Fire repeated, reaching across to grab his cap from the glove box.

"Maybe I should wait in the car," Rio said, glancing around and gripping the seatbelt tighter. Rio had assumed they would be heading back to Fire's apartment to eat. He had no idea where they were, if they were in an area where someone could recognize either of them.

Fire rolled his eyes and pulled his cap on low, shielding his face. "Suit yourself."

Rio watched with a gaping mouth as Fire exited without another word, slamming the door behind him. Rio scrambled out after him, getting caught in the damn seatbelt he was just clinging to and nearly tripping onto his face.

"Slow down, princess. Where's the fire?"

He smirked at his own pun, and Rio's rage built tenfold. "You were just going to leave me!"

"You wanted to wait in the car, and I'm hungry. Do the math."

"You can't just leave me in an area like this to get—" He looked at the faded sign peeling at the edges, proclaiming Chick'N'Chill in black letters on a yellow background. "—chicken!"

"This is the best chicken in the Circle. And you're welcome to join me if you can stand to be in this *area*."

Rio flushed at being called out. He hadn't meant it that way, and he knew Fire knew that, but the jab still hit the mark, and his stubbornness rose up in answer, like always.

"Fine. I will."

He raised his nose in the air and pushed into the restaurant, hesitating once he passed the threshold. The smell of oil and grease and cooking meat filled his nose, and he refused to admit it smelled amazing.

The place was spotless. A little worn around the edges like the sign outside, but the gray tables and yellow booths were freshly scrubbed down, the scuffed, checked linoleum mopped to a shine in the less traveled places. The same logo of the red wing from outside was hung up in a huge neon sign over the counter that flickered a little on one corner.

Fire came around him as Rio swung his head left and right, raising a hand to the white-haired man behind the counter that Rio hadn't spotted. He was posted up against the wall dressed in a comfy black jumper, no uniform in sight, watching an old square TV in the corner that reflected off his glasses.

"If it isn't my favorite athlete," the man said, looking over the rims.

"Tobi. You know I couldn't stay away," Fire said with his first genuine smile of the day, which stung, clasping the hand that was offered and pulling in for a brief hug over the countertop. Fire already looked happier just to be in the building.

"And you brought company," Tobi said, sounding surprised as he eyed Rio, who was still standing at the entrance.

Rio flushed and walked forward. "I'm Uxorious Archibald Charmichael III."

Tobi blinked.

"Just...call him Rio," Fire said, leaning casually on the counter.

Rio scowled at him by rote. "My name's not—"

"He's never had fried chicken before," Fire cut off.

"I can tell," Tobi said.

Rio gaped, and Tobi and Fire shared a quick laugh.

"But don't you worry. We'll fix you up right," Tobi said with a sure nod. "I'll get you two orders of your usual."

"I don't want anything," Rio hissed under his breath as Tobi ambled away to the back.

"Yes, you do," Fire said.

"I think I would know if I was hungry," Rio said.

"You're hungry all the damn time."

Rio spluttered, and Fire ignored him, turning to find a seat. There wasn't anyone else in the restaurant, so he chose the booth in the corner by the window. He slid onto the peeling leather and relaxed, leaning his head back and rolling his shoulders out like they were hurting him. Rio frowned, walking over and sitting opposite him.

"You shouldn't push so hard after an injury."

Fire peeked an eye open. "Yeah?"

"It never did my father any good."

"Well, maybe this isn't race-related," Fire said, leaning forward. "Maybe it was left over from me holding you up to fuck you a couple days ago."

Rio's mouth dropped open, and his face flushed red. He looked around to see if Tobi had heard. "You uncouth, unsocialized... You can't just *say* that!"

Fire smirked, hazel eyes serious as they observed him over the table. "You're pretty when you're mad, you know."

"I'm pretty all the time!" Rio declared, even more offended than before.

Fire huffed. "Well, I won't argue with you there."

"You always argue with me."

It was all they seemed to do lately. Or pretend they weren't doing.

Fire tilted his head, leaning it on his fist as his eyes continued to take Rio apart. "Not about that."

Rio simmered down at the admission, allowing his feet to get hooked under the table and drawn closer to Fire, even though his sneakers were filthy and Rio's loafers were suede. It was another silent truce, not just to this, but everything between them.

Rio studied Fire across the table as they waited for their food.

He was relaxed in a way Rio only saw him at home. His body language was sprawled and lazy, and contentment radiated from him even alongside the fatigue. Rio began to realize that this place was more than just food to Fire.

"How long have you been coming here?" Rio asked.

Fire moved his gaze away from the window where he was people-watching to meet his eye. "Since I was about seventeen, early into my racing career. I stumbled across the place one day when I took a wrong turn headed for a training session. Safe to say I didn't make it that day. A quick bite turned into turning out my pockets to buy anything I could."

Rio found himself smiling at the visual. "I'm sure your trainers were impressed."

"They never found out. Only a very few trusted people in my life know about this place."

And now Rio was one of them.

His heart swelled, and he did his best to breathe past it.

"Surely people have seen you in here?"

"Don't worry. No one will take our picture," Fire said sarcastically.

Rio flinched back, unprepared for the sudden attack, drawing his feet away. "That's not what I meant."

Fire reached for him again, an apology in his eyes as he grabbed for his hands. "I know. I'm sorry. It's...been a long day."

Rio allowed himself to be coaxed. "You can talk to me about it."

"I'd rather finish talking to you about this place without being an asshole," Fire said.

Rio nodded. "I'm listening."

Fire stroked his fingers over Rio's knuckles. "The regulars have been seeing me in here since I was that bratty teen, so most of them don't see me as anything else. They all call me son and pat me on the head even though I'm taller than them. And anyone else—well, Tobi keeps them all in line, I think. I've never once come here and been mobbed or bothered. It's never been leaked to the press or on the internet."

"They're good people," Rio murmured.

Fire nodded. "The best. I keep trying to get Tobi to let me put their business as one of my sponsors, free of charge, but he won't have it. Says when he has enough, then he'll pay for it like anyone else."

"That's admirable," Rio murmured, more than a little humbled.

"I guess the only upside is that I get to come in here and escape for a little while longer. If everyone knew this was my favorite restaurant, I'd never get to eat here."

Rio looked around, seeing the place in a completely new light. Through Fire's eyes. Aside from his nest, this was his safe space, and he'd brought Rio right into the heart of it when he was feeling low.

"It's nice," Rio murmured. "Very you."

Fire smirked. "A little rough around the edges but bomb as fuck?"

Rio rolled his eyes, refusing to let his smile emerge. "I wouldn't go that far..."

Fire snorted, joining their feet again, tighter, focused on their hands.

"I didn't mean it..." Rio said suddenly.

Fire looked up from under his cap, questioning.

"What I said in the car...about the area..." Rio said, feeling heat prickle his cheeks.

"You're the most posh, pedantic, prissy person I know," Fire said. "But I know you're not like that. You give to charities and volunteer at rec centers."

Rio nodded, flushing, looking outside at the faded mural of flowers spray-painted on the wall. In the cramped balconies of the houses down the street, there were children's bikes and laundry hanging out and flower beds overflowing. Bright pops of color and life. "It's actually quite charming."

Fire smiled, pleased by his appreciation. Like he wanted Rio to like it. "There are definitely some rough spots around this Circle. There really is no avoiding that. It's like that in every Circle. But this isn't one of them. The community here pulls together so much—doesn't matter if you're human or Kriila, a race star or a nine-to-fiver."

Tobi arrived then with baskets of steaming chicken that was golden brown and coated in beautifully sticky sauces. Rio's mouth began to water from the smell.

"It's nice to see Fire bring a *friend* along," Tobi said offhandedly as he began unloading the tray.

"Friend." Fire laughed, eyes losing a little of their previous sparkle. "The best of friends, really."

Rio swallowed, bracing himself. "We're not exactly advertising anything."

Tobi nodded along amiably. "Nothing to advertise. Good friends are hard to come by."

"Yeah," Fire murmured.

"I expect to see you around more," Tobi said. "The annual family barbeque is coming up, and you're both expected to be there. You know Shay will beat your ass, son, if you make her wait to hear about the important *friendships* in your life."

"A party?" Rio perked up.

Fire huffed out a tired laugh. "Yeah, yeah. I got it. Let me get back to you on it, Tobi."

Tobi nodded and smacked a slab of napkins down as the final piece of the puzzle. He smiled at Rio. "Holler if you need any more."

Rio lifted a brow. "I can manage the trajectory of cutlery from the plate to my mouth just fine."

Tobi laughed. "Ain't no forks or knives here."

He ambled off, still chuckling, and Rio turned wide eyes on Fire.

"I'm supposed to eat with my *hands*?"

Fire snatched a chicken wing out of the basket, sauce dripping down his fingers that he licked off without a care. He split it apart and devoured the thing whole, clean bones the only thing left afterward.

Fire groaned in ecstasy. "Soooo good! Fuck yeah, I've missed you."

Rio was beginning to feel slighted. Had he ever elicited such a sound from Fire before? "It can't be that good," he grumbled.

Fire grabbed a drumstick and shoved it under his nose. "Never know until you try."

Rio frowned down at the offering, contemplating turning his nose up at it completely, but the quietly hopeful look in Fire's eyes kept him stationary.

With a dramatic groan, Rio leaned forward and took a tiny, polite bite out of the drumstick. Golden loveliness crunched between his teeth, and sticky flavor exploded across his tongue. His eyes widened, and he stared down at the drumstick in horror.

Oh no.

Oh no, oh no.

This was going to be a problem.

He snatched the drumstick out of Fire's grip and stared down at the mystical creation.

"Like it?" Fire asked innocently.

"Shut your face. And don't touch my food," Rio told him, cradling his basket closer to him protectively.

He dug in with gusto, ignoring everything else. It was the most undignified display he'd ever put on in his adult life, and he loved every second of it, licking his fingers and gnawing on the bones.

"Try this," Fire said, pushing a milkshake over and the fries that had largely gone unnoticed.

He watched as Fire dunked a fry straight in the mixture and popped it in his mouth with a little noise of happiness. One of the ones that he usually saved for the bedroom.

Rio wanted to be disgusted by the idea. Wanted to draw the line somewhere.

But.

He was grabbing a fry before he knew it and dipping it into the milkshake first and then his mouth. The salty and sweet flavor was heavenly.

Oh dear, oh dear, oh dear.

"You're so bad for me," Rio accused, grabbing a handful of fries.

Fire gave him a playful smirk, but it was tinged with something a little melancholy. "But I'm so good to you."

Rio did his best to ignore the tightening of his stomach, turning back to his chicken. The pile was getting smaller, and it was making him sadder. He tried to savor every bite before it was gone.

What had he come to that a plate of chicken was now a metaphor for his life?

"Coach doesn't think I'll be ready to compete," Fire said suddenly.

Rio glanced up sharply, seeing Fire's grimace under his cap. Fire's mood suddenly made so much more sense. On top of the stress Rio was putting him under, it must have been crushing to hear that when he'd been working so hard.

"And what do you think?" Rio asked. "Honestly."

"I can make it. Enough to race. It may not be in winning condition, but I can do it," Fire said.

"I believe you," Rio said.

Fire visibly swallowed, surprise lingering in his hazel eyes as they latched onto his. "You do?"

"You need it."

Fire looked so vulnerable as he nodded. Split open with every part of him on display for Rio to see.

"Not to make a point to anyone else, but to yourself. It isn't about retaining the title, or winning. It's about racing. It always has been, hasn't it?" Rio asked softly, speaking the realization out loud.

"Yes," Fire whispered.

"You can do it," Rio said. "Screw what your coach tells you."

Fire smiled, more himself. "You sound like my mom. It's what she'd say."

"She must be incredibly intelligent then."

Fire snorted. "Nice self-compliment."

"You hadn't done it in a while. I had to take matters into my own hands."

Fire smirked, playing with his fingers some more, despite their stickiness. "I want you to meet her. All of them."

Rio's heart began to beat double time. "Your family?"

Fire nodded, eyes downcast. "I know you want to scale things back..."

He trailed off, clearly giving Rio an out despite the excitement lighting his face. It was a look Rio hadn't seen in days. Open, joyful, hopeful. He wanted to give him that. No...he needed to give him that.

"When do we leave?" he asked finally.

Fire snapped his head up, his expression so hopeful Rio knew he'd done the right thing.

He could work this out. He could. He didn't want to lose Fire, and he could feel them reaching the edge of breaking something he was frightened could never be repaired.

"I'll set it up and let you know?" Fire said, breathless, like he still couldn't believe it.

Rio nodded, pretending that it wasn't a monumental moment that was scaring him shitless. It was worth it for that expression on Fire's face. He decided to stuff his face full of chicken and deal with it all later. Stress-eating wasn't a great habit, but it was what he had right now.

"Does this place deliver, by any chance?" Rio asked with full cheeks a few minutes later—completely offhand, of course.

Fire began to laugh, full-bodied and brighter than it had been since they first met. Rio was mesmerized. Fire leaned over, wiped a dollop of sauce from Rio's chin with his thumb, and popped it in his own mouth. He threw him a wink from under his cap.

"I'll give you the number."

CHAPTER SIXTEEN

FIRE

Rio's agreement to meet his family was a balm to Fire's festering agitation. Someone looking for an out didn't do the meet-the-parents thing, surely?

It finally felt like a step forward.

Fire was buzzing with barely repressed energy in the wake of it, something that was mirrored by his family. They'd been bugging him to meet Rio ever since he'd told them about his mating, but he'd always had to find an excuse. With Rio now locked in, all systems were go.

They settled on the weekend for a visit to avoid as many conflicting schedules as they could, and Fire didn't want to risk waiting longer in case Rio got cold feet. Not that it seemed likely. Rio seemed determined to do it, like he was challenging himself. Fire didn't know what had inspired the abrupt turnaround in his stance, but he wasn't one to turn down a good thing.

Rio slept over the night before, bringing far too big of a suitcase for one night at Fire's and one day at his parents. They weren't even staying there. Rio had given him a withering look that would have made a more insecure person cry, Fire was sure.

They left in the early hours of the following morning, the sun barely a purple-and-orange blur on the horizon.

The journey to his home Circle was about three hours by car, so they'd settled in for the long haul. Rio had been fussing with his appearance before Fire had even deigned to roll out of bed. He was currently on a rant about how his pants were bound to be wrinkled "beyond a state that was fit to be seen."

Fire simply hummed his agreement, secretly laughing to himself and loving every second.

This was what he wanted. Always.

Not the fraught tension. The uneasiness. The sex that buried feeling.

"Are you even listening to me?" Rio snapped.

Fire blinked and glanced away from the road. "Wrinkles?"

Rio glared. "That was three topics ago!"

"It's been like a minute."

"I can't help that you can't keep up with me," Rio said, sniffing.

"We can pull over and put it to the test," Fire said with a lascivious grin, slipping a hand onto his thigh.

Rio shoved him off. "We are *not* going to be late."

"No one would care," Fire said, signaling and switching lanes.

"I would!" Rio said indignantly. Fire swallowed a laugh as Rio shifted in his seat to face him. "Now quiz me on names."

"We did that, like, five times yesterday," Fire complained. "There's not that many of them, and none of them got a name change in the last twenty-four hours."

Rio glared. "You want me to fail."

"What?" Fire asked, looking over and laughing at his serious face.

"You want me to make a fool of myself. Well, I won't. Your parents will love me."

"They love you already. You don't need to do anything, princess. Trust me. You're my mate. You make me happy. That's all they need." Rio frowned, like he didn't understand, and Fire furrowed his brow back, trying to understand where Rio's head was at.

"Honestly, Rio. It's all going to be fine. You don't have to be anything but yourself. They just want to meet you. That's it."

Rio hummed distractedly, glancing off out of the window as he mulled over whatever thoughts he had. Fire left him to his privacy, sensing that he shouldn't press the issue. Instead, he clicked on the radio, and they drove in contemplative silence.

Rio was chatting again as they passed into Fire's Circle an hour later, spine getting straighter the closer they drew to home. He was practically a statue by the time Fire pulled up outside his childhood home.

"Too late to turn back," Fire said.

Rio huffed at him and got out of the car. Fire grinned and followed him out, taking a few moments to stare at his childhood home.

He tried to see it through Rio's eyes. The one-story beige house with a messy garden filled with kids' toys and gardening tools. It looked well loved. Lived in. Worn down over the years but kept in good shape by the people living there.

He knew it looked nothing like Rio's mansion, but Fire felt warm just standing in front of it.

Rio grabbed the gift he had painstakingly chosen from the backseat. He was straightening the gold gift bag meticulously when he caught sight of himself in the reflection of the window.

"I knew it! I should have brought my steamer," Rio cried out, staring at his pants in dismay.

Fire rolled his eyes and grabbed him around the waist, planting a kiss on his lips and letting it linger for a few seconds until he felt Rio slump into him.

"You look gorgeous," he murmured against his mouth, then slapped him on the ass. "Now let's go. My mom will let you borrow her iron if you really need it."

Rio made a token protest but allowed himself to be pulled along like always. Fire fished his keys out and opened the door with his spare hand.

"You're not knocking?" Rio asked, aghast.

"It's my house," Fire said.

"You moved out!"

"So?"

"Fire, no. This is so rude," Rio protested as the door swung inward.

Fire rolled his eyes. "I've done this a million times, princess. Get your cute ass in here."

He slammed the door behind them loudly, and a bobbed head peeked around the corner in answer. Then a hurricane was blasting through the house toward them.

"*My baby!*"

"Mom," Fire complained, feeling Rio tense at his back.

She was average height and build, but my god was she a bulldozer. He didn't blame Rio.

"Come here, let me see you," she demanded.

Fire avoided her grabby hands. "You can see me just fine from... Look, grab Rio instead!"

"*What?!*" Rio almost shrieked as Fire tried to use him as a shield.

It was all in vain. His mom got her hands on Fire's cheeks just like she wanted, and she smushed them painfully together, tilting him this way and that, not to be denied her fussing.

"You've lost weight," she scolded him.

"I'wve been twaining," he mumbled through duck lips.

"I'll have to call Rand and give him a piece of my mind," she said, nodding to herself before narrowing her eyes. "But you! You give me a heart attack watching you fall on national television, and then you don't text, you don't call, you don't visit! Do you want to send me and your father to an early grave, hm? Hm?"

Fire rescued his face, massaging his bruised cheeks and rolling his eyes at his mom's hyperbole. "We literally talk every day, Mom. You also talked to Rand, Vid, and Anna multiple times since I got hurt. No drama needed. C'mon."

Harriet clicked her tongue at him, then hip-checked him out of the way. He clattered into the coatrack.

"I'm sorry, dear. You must have your hands full with my son," she said to Rio.

Rio straightened his back, and Fire could feel his anxiety get replaced by smugness. He attempted to look sad as he replied, "It's a daily struggle."

"You poor thing. I'm Harriet. It's so nice to finally meet you, Rio. Come in, come in. Honestly, James. Leaving him standing in the hall! Where are the manners I raised you with?"

"You wouldn't let me move!" Fire yelled at her back, but she ignored him, pulling a surprised Rio by the hand and tugging him after her, all motherly hustle and bustle.

Fire shook his head, smiling.

"That was tame for her. She's mellowed in her old age," his older brother Eric said from the top of the stairs. He was rocking Fire's nephew, David, back and forth, obviously trying to get him to sleep. Fire looked a lot like Eric, only without a stupid beard and about five times as awesome, of course.

"Thanks for the save, big bro," Fire said dryly.

Eric shrugged, not the least bit remorseful. "You moved to a different Circle at sixteen. Take your lumps like the rest of us."

Fire rolled his eyes. "Mary around?"

"She gets off work at dinner. She's excited to meet your mate," Eric said. "You're lucky the day you decided to come home Lils was working a double she couldn't change."

Fire groaned at the mention of their little sister. She lived like the only purpose she'd been put on this plane of existence for was to annoy them. And their mother let her get away with everything. Not even her early mating and child had curbed her antics.

"Small mercies."

"You sure punched up with your mate, didn't you?" Eric said.

"Must be a family trait. Mary is an angel, and she should leave your ass in the dust," Fire said.

Eric snorted. "I'll make sure to give Rio the same advice."

Fire twitched, unable to formulate a response, and Eric raised a brow. "There's a story there."

"Maybe not," Fire mumbled, trying to push the pessimism of the last few weeks aside. Rio was literally in his family home right now. "I'm gonna go find them."

Fire walked in to Rio presenting his mother with her gift at the same kitchen island Fire remembered smashing his head on as a child. The chip was still there.

"Oh, you didn't need to, dearest," his mom cooed, pulling out the wine from the bag. "My, how fancy looking."

"It's a fantastic vintage," Rio said.

"Well, who am I to say no?" his mom said. "Let's try."

She bustled over to the cupboard and searched around for a moment before calling out, "Giles! Where's my good glasses?"

"Have you checked the cupboard?" his dad's deep, distracted voice called back.

"Of course I checked! Why do you think I'm calling you? For my health?" his mom said, exasperated.

"They must be there, love."

"Can't tear himself away from the television," his mom muttered.

"The game on?" Fire asked, announcing himself, and Rio spun to face him. He made a jerking motion to get Fire to come stand next to him, and Fire held in his laugh as he did what he was told. Rio latched onto his arm to make sure he couldn't escape anytime soon.

"Not even," his mom said, unaware of the pantomime going on behind her, still searching her cupboards. "Julie is into this new cartoon about talking cats or some such. Your father gets annoyed with her when she watches it without him."

Fire cracked up.

"How old is Julie?" Rio asked curiously.

"Five. Which is pretty much in line with Giles's very refined tastes in television, I'd say."

Rio seemed amused, pointing at the wine. "Maybe I should have revised my gift."

His mom giggled. "His birthday is in a month. Save it for then. I'm sure the whole party will be themed."

Rio laughed back. "I'm excellent at throwing parties."

"I'll definitely be giving you a call, then," his mom said with a cheeky smile, then threw her hands up. "Those darn glasses. Well, we'll have to make do. As long as it holds liquid."

She grabbed the nearest two cups and brought them back to the island. Fire hid his smile at Rio's horrified look as his mother poured that fancy wine into two plastic cups with ducks on them.

"Here you go, dear. Cheers!"

She clunked her glass against his and took an elegant sip. Rio gazed concernedly down into the cup before doing the same.

"What? No lecture for my mom on the history and etiquette of wine and how it shouldn't be defiled by plastic duckies?" Fire whispered into Rio's ear.

Rio elbowed him in the ribs, and Fire laughed, but curbed the teasing. It was adorable how worried and determined Rio was about winning his parents over, and Fire's heart was full of hope listening to them make future plans. Like Rio was sticking around for the long term. Like he was part of the family already, another thread weaving in seamlessly.

"So tell me everything!" his mom said, setting her cup down. "James is always so blasé about everything."

"About?" Rio ventured.

"Your mating, of course!"

Rio flushed a little pink across the bridge of his nose. "Well...it was all very romantic and proper, naturally."

"Naturally," Fire repeated and got another elbow.

His mom stared between them, amused. "Don't be shy now, dear. My youngest, Lilliana, mated at eighteen and popped out Julie nine months later. Eric crashed Mary's wedding! We've heard it all in this house."

"Her wedding?" Rio gasped, turning to Fire. "You never told me that!"

"Mary likes to tell it. She'd kill me if I stole her thunder," Fire said.

"Where is Mary? I need details!" Rio said, looking around.

His mom laughed. "She'll be here for dinner."

"Grandma, Grandma!" Julie's voice called, interrupting, and the little speed demon rounded the corner dressed in about fifteen layers of bright pink tulle and furry winter boots. "Grandpa is ruining it again! He keeps rewinding and rewinding and talking and talking."

His niece beelined for his mom's legs, pouting up at her. His mom patted her head, hiding a smirk. "Okay, darling. I'll go sort Grandpa out. Why don't you stay here and say hello to Uncle James and his new mate, Rio?"

Julie nodded, climbing up on a stool and then onto the island itself. She plonked herself down like an overdecorated confection, tapping her boots together. His mom walked out and Fire took the end of one of Julie's boots, shaking it playfully. She giggled, trying to kick him off.

"Dress yourself today?" he asked.

Julie primped her ruffles and nodded. "Mommy let me. She said it was a special day."

"Oh, it's very special," Fire agreed and tugged Rio closer. "Meet Rio. Mr. Special."

"Uxorious," Rio corrected.

Julie tilted her head like a puppy at the mouthful, and Fire laughed.

"You don't correct my mom, but you tell a five-year-old."

Rio shoved him, then turned back to Julie. "Rio is fine, I suppose. It's a pleasure to meet you."

He extended his hand for her to shake, and Julie lit up and took it, shaking it vigorously. It was ridiculous, but so *Rio* that Fire was in danger of keeling over as he watched them talk.

Fire hadn't realized how much he missed the familial chaos of home. He couldn't get back as often as he wanted, and having Rio there with him was like the piece he hadn't known was missing in the puzzle.

Everyone seemed to love him, but the most important thing was that he was a permanent fixture at Fire's side, making it obvious they were *together*.

A pair.

It worked Fire up so much that he had to drag Rio upstairs for a few minutes under the guise of showing him his childhood room. He reached for Rio as soon as the door was closed, grasping his hips and kissing his neck.

"Is that a poster of my dad?"

Fire froze with his mouth wrapped around Rio's earlobe. Talk about a boner killer. He pulled back with a grimace.

"We need to work on your dirty talk, princess."

Rio wasn't paying attention, though. Instead, he was devouring Fire's old room with his eyes. Everything about the room screamed one thing: racing. There were posters on his walls, trophies and medals on every available surface, pictures of him at competitions at all ages. His mother had never redecorated, and Fire had never bothered to update it when he visited.

"I keep telling you he was a hero of mine," Fire said. "But I kind of wish he wasn't now. Didn't know he'd be such a cockblock."

Rio slapped his arm. "That's my father."

"And I'm trying to defile his son in my childhood bed."

"I'm not having sex with your family downstairs, including your five-year-old-niece and infant nephew," Rio said, extricating himself from Fire's grabby hands and walking toward the shelves. He picked up a trophy and examined it. "Did your feet ever stay on the floor when you were young?"

Fire gave up on getting some anytime soon and hummed at the question, flopping down onto his single bed in the center of the room. "Not really. Honestly, this is the longest it's ever been because of the injury. I've never driven so much in my life."

Rio put the trophy down and approached him, climbing up and sitting astride his hips. It wasn't sexual—Fire could tell by the quietly contemplative look in his brown eyes—and so he simply took Rio's weight and rested his hands on his thighs.

"Doing okay?" Fire asked when Rio didn't speak.

Rio nodded, thumbing absently at Fire's shirt. "It's different."

"My room?"

"Everything."

Fire looked around, trying to see what Rio did. He wondered if he'd feel the same sense of dissonance if he ever entered Rio's home.

"Okay different?" Fire asked hesitantly.

Rio gazed down at him through his lashes and dipped, pressing a soft kiss to his mouth in lieu of an answer.

"Boys! Mary's here," his mom called up the stairs. "Dinnertime."

Rio broke them apart and rolled off of Fire to his feet. Fire followed him up and led him down the stairs to the cramped dining room. Garden chairs had been pulled in from outside to make up the seats, and a highchair had been squeezed in on the corner. Mary was there now sitting an excited David inside, still dressed in her nurses' scrubs, hair scraped back to collect low at her nape.

She spotted them as she finished strapping David in and threw them a megawatt smile that lit up her pretty face. Honestly, his brother had won the mate lottery with her.

"There you are! I'm Mary," she introduced herself, skirting around all the bodies and furniture. "It's so nice to meet the person who finally tamed Fire."

"One of my many talents," Rio said.

Mary grinned, and Fire rolled his eyes.

"How's the wing?" she asked him.

"Getting there."

"Are you going to be good to race?" Eric asked through a mouthful of pilfered bread roll.

Fire jutted his chin out. "I'll make it."

"So stubborn," his mom chided him, snapping a dishtowel his way, then turning to Rio. "Ever since he was little, he never missed a race. Didn't matter if he was sick or had to ditch his classes."

"Which we did not approve of, no matter how many trophies you won," Giles told him, taking his seat.

Fire grinned unrepentantly at his old man. Giles liked to pretend his hair loss was entirely Fire's fault.

"But no one could stop him," his mom said, her fondness creeping through despite her scolding.

"Does anyone else race in the family?" Rio asked.

"God, no," Eric said, scooping up some food to put in David's bowl. "No one knows where he got it from."

"Everyone always used to tell me he'd be a racer as a baby. He had wings twice as long as everyone else," his mom said. "I didn't actually believe them until he started trying to jump off the furniture to fly before he was even old enough for flying classes."

Rio laughed. "Sounds like him."

"Rio and I taught a couple pre-flight classes at a community center, Rio's really good at it," Fire said.

His mom raised her brows. "You're interested in racing, dear?"

"Oh no," Rio said, squirming in a way Fire had never seen him. "My dad used to race, that's all, so I know a couple things."

"A couple things," Fire said, teasing. "Suddenly so humble."

Rio glared at him. "Okay. I'm better at it than you."

The room burst out laughing and Fire clutched his chest. "Don't sugarcoat it for my feelings' sake, princess."

Rio sniffed.

"Who's your dad?" Mary asked curiously. "We've all been indoctrinated into the racing world one way or another. Is it anyone we would know?"

"Bullet," Rio said with a tinge of pride on his face, and Fire smiled at the sight of it.

The room exploded into chaos with questions flying left and right.

"Oh, so you are better at it than he is," Eric said, making Fire throw his napkin at him.

"Shut up, Eric," Fire said, but he still nudged Rio's shoulder with his own. "He's using his knowledge for good at the Rec Center, though."

"The kids must love you," his mom said, looking at Julie, who was practically glued to Rio's side.

"They're learning really quick," Rio said as they finally settled around the table, Rio between Fire and Julie, who insisted on sitting next to him.

She had decided she loved Rio. She asked him a multitude of questions ranging from his favorite cartoon characters to his opinions on hair bows and whether he thought a boy in her group might like her based on the fact that he'd spilled juice on her drawing. On purpose.

Rio regarded her like everyone else, answering her in serious tones, neither babying nor placating her in any respect. Exactly how he was at the Rec Center. And like those children, Julie responded to being treated like a grownup instead of a kid.

Fire could see how unused to family dynamics like his Rio was. But he took to it as he did everything else. With grace and confidence, inserting himself into a group of people and making a spot for himself there.

Fire had noticed him relaxing as the day went by. He'd stopped watching every step and every move, careful of his posture and everything that he said like there was going to be some kind of judgment passed upon him at the end. As they sat at the table, Rio fit into his family as if he had always been there.

The conversation lulled the more they ate, good food making them all heavy and slow. Fire glanced at Rio and found him looking around, wide eyes taking in his family and an expression on his face Fire had never seen before.

Like longing.

Fire took his hand on top of the table and squeezed, wanting to let him know he was there for him.

Rio didn't answer him, but Fire hoped he got the message anyway.

CHAPTER SEVENTEEN

RIO

He didn't think he had ever been in as much of a daze as he was in the days after meeting Fire's family.

He had come back home tired, full of good food and with his jaw hurting from laughter. Entering his own home was like getting slapped in the face by a block of ice. The perfectly polished marble floors, the carefully curated art pieces on the walls, the family portraits where all three of them just looked dead behind the eyes.

Fire's family home was an explosion of life. A celebration of it. It was small and humble and lived in.

Loved.

Despite Fire explaining how he wanted to move his parents into a better place once he had more money, his parents wouldn't hear about it. They'd made memories inside those walls. They'd created life and nurtured it until it grew into amazing people who went on to start their own, equally loving families.

Rio knew of supportive parents. He'd had one, however briefly. The memories were hazy with time now, but he knew what it was like to be loved without strings attached, without expectations or conditions. He knew what it was like to be supported and uplifted and praised by a parent.

But his dad wasn't there anymore. And Rio had grown up in a cold, detached, public image-oriented farce of a family and gotten lost in there.

He'd been raised to look perfect, sound perfect, and be perfect at all times. He'd been coached to say the right things and to make the right moves whenever he could. Everything was carefully calculated and done at precise times to be the most impactful it could be.

After years of the same, Rio was used to his life, even liked parts of it, but he now realized how stifled he was. How chained and restrained. How little of himself he got to keep.

He dove deep down into his own heart and found that little boy his dad had taught to be kind, and brave, and creative sitting hunched in a corner, forgotten. Exchanged for an adult version of himself he clearly didn't recognize anymore.

Rio wondered if his dad could see him. He wondered if he was still proud of him. If he could talk to him, he'd ask if he had disappointed him.

Was he truly a Charmichael more than he wanted to admit? Was he truly a carbon copy of the woman who had given birth to him and never cared for him?

No.

Rio refused to believe that.

He sprang out of his father's armchair and grabbed for his phone, typing up a short message.

Rio: *Meet me at Miroirs at seven.*

It was a suspended, heart-stopping minute before he got a reply.

Fire: *I had to research what that is.*

Before Rio could reply, another text came in.

Fire: *It's fancy, and it's very public.*

Exactly.

Rio: *Seven. Don't be late.*

He threw the phone down, walking to his bathroom, shedding clothes as he went. He stepped into the shower and ran the water as hot as it would go, hoping it would wash away the layers of everything he hated that had stuck to his skin over the years.

He splayed his palms on the tiled wall and let the water beat down on him until it ran lukewarm and raised goosebumps on his flesh. He shampooed and rinsed as fast as he could and walked out, wrapping himself in a fluffy bathrobe hanging by the door.

At his open wardrobe, rows upon rows of perfectly tailored suits stared at him. He ran his hands over them all. Each one had been custom made for him and he loved how he looked in all of them, but they were ghosts of memories laid out one by one. Parties, events, even Showings.

There was one specific one, though. One that he'd bought ages ago and just never found the time or place to wear it.

It was a three-piece suit with black pants, a black vest, and a black-and-white wool blazer. Rio's designer had paired it with a black shirt, a wide black-and-white tie, and a gorgeous silver brooch in place of a pocket square.

Rio knew he looked amazing in it. And while it stood out from any other suit, it was still monochromatic enough to allow his wings to shine.

He put the suit on, smoothing the fabric down over his skin, fixing it until every last fold was perfectly placed. It wasn't a suit tonight. It was armor. It was the hope of a new memory. A better one.

His wings stretched out behind him, and he walked to his jewelry cabinet to grab the perfect set of wing chains to go with the outfit.

The box was a rich purple velvet, and he pulled it out, opening the lid to find a set of thick chains, twisting in the middle and connecting with a large white pearl surrounded by smaller black ones—the only detail on the plainest set of chains Rio owned.

He draped them over his wings, fixing them in place with a small buckle. He fluttered his wings to test them out and found the chains sitting comfortably where they were supposed to.

Rio stood in front of his mirror and looked at himself, narrowing his eyes to try and find a single flaw in his look. He raised his head and tugged the bottom of his blazer down once again, the perfection he was seeing in the mirror failing to provide him the courage it usually did.

Dressed in his finest, Rio felt terrified.

But he walked out of his room and out of his house anyway. He had a point to prove. To himself, to Fire, to his family, to the world.

After all, courage didn't mean the absence of fear...or however that saying went.

Rio's driver left him on the street directly in front of Miroirs. He stepped outside, the heels of his shoes clinking on the pavement as he walked the few steps to the front entrance.

Fire was already waiting.

And he stole Rio's breath away. His hair was styled casually and pushed back from his forehead, displaying the handsome angles of his face and his hazel eyes to devastating effect. He was in a completely black outfit, from his shoes to his tie, his huge flame-red wings flared around him. He didn't wear jewelry on them. Rio knew he never would. But he didn't need it. Everything about him was eye-catching, and Rio forgot for a second they were in a public place.

His feet took him closer without his control.

He wanted Fire close. He wanted to breathe him in. He wanted his hands around him and his wings to shelter him from the rest of the world. For the first time in as long as Rio could remember, he truly didn't want to be seen. Not when his heart was on his sleeve the way it was. Not when he felt raw and exposed and vulnerable the way he did.

He came to a stop when he was so close a deeper breath from either of them would make their chests touch. He looked up into Fire's eyes, searching for reassurance. Understanding. Patience.

He knew he'd driven Fire up the wall with some of the choices he had made recently. He knew Fire's reactions, though hurtful, were just a response to what Rio was doing. And while he was doing his best to give Fire what he needed, he didn't think he could take Fire's biting resentment just then. They seemed to be in a better place since their trip, but he felt like he needed his mate more than ever.

"Rio," Fire greeted quietly, but the surprisingly empty street reverberated with it anyway.

Rio nodded, unable to form words. Too much inside him wanted to pour out all over the ground.

"You look gorgeous," Fire said, eyes running over him almost reverently. "But you always do, and you know that."

Rio did know. But he still needed to hear it.

"Thank you," he said, reaching his hand out and brushing Fire's fingers with his own. He was warm against Rio's skin. Comforting.

Fire returned the gentle caress for a split second, then pulled his hand back.

"We don't have to do this," Fire said, shocking Rio all over again. "Not like this, anyway."

"What?" Rio asked, and Fire grabbed his forearm, pulling him into a small back alley between Miroirs and the swanky new bar right next to it.

The alley was dark and smelled awful despite being situated right next to the best-rated restaurant in their Circle.

Rio scrunched up his nose and huffed. "I refuse to be here in this suit."

Fire let out a chuckle that sounded just a little bit too...unhinged to be amused. He exhaled and then took Rio's elbows in his arms, steadying him as he looked at him. "Tell me what's going on?"

Rio stared at him for a moment, knowing full well what Fire was asking but falling short on words to explain.

"We're having dinner," Rio said. "You took me to Chick'N'Chill and paid for my food and all that. Like a date."

"It wasn't like a date, princess. It was a date."

"Yes, fine," he said, hoping his heart wasn't beating loud enough to hear as he uttered the next words. "This is also a date. That I'm taking you to."

Fire was silent.

He was staring at Rio, making him squirm in place under the scrutiny. He didn't want to be scratched at the surface. He wanted to keep the layer of confidence he had put on with his suit.

Fire didn't even have to scratch. He could figure it all out just by looking into his eyes.

"Please?" Rio said before Fire could shatter the illusion. He was rapidly losing his nerve the longer they stood there.

Fire seemed like he had so much to say, face tightening from holding it all in. But it remained locked behind his lips, and Rio exhaled in shaky relief.

"Okay, princess. Take me on a date."

"I can't...I... No kissing or romance," Rio managed to stutter out, hoping Fire wouldn't hate him for the compromise. "But we are going in there to eat. Together."

Fire nodded. "Together is all I need. We can work on the rest."

Rio swallowed and nodded back. "Now let's go. I'm not wasting this suit on a dank alley and a depressing conversation."

He took Fire's hand and pulled him out of the dark and into the main street again, letting go as soon as they were lit up by the streetlights.

"You sure about this, gorgeous?" Fire asked.

"I am, yes," Rio said, straightening his wings. "Plus, I've been craving their escargot for quite some time now."

"You'd been craving snails?" Fire asked as they approached the door, and Rio lifted his nose up again.

"They're not snails, James," he huffed.

"Well, they're not burgers either," Fire said, settling into their usual banter as easily as breathing.

"Do you plan on complaining the entire night?" Rio asked.

God, I hope so. It made things seem normal again.

"No, I figured I'd get it all out in one go," Fire said with his trademark cocky smile. "Payback for Chick'N'Chill."

Rio rolled his eyes, opening the door. The sound of soft-stringed violins filled the air. "I tried the chicken and I liked it, so I assume you'll be trying the escargot then?" Fire grimaced, and it was Rio's turn to grin. "Fair is fair, after all."

"It's not remotely the same thing," Fire protested.

"You'll like escargot."

"I sincerely doubt that," Fire said, but followed dutifully as Rio gave the hostess his name and followed her to their table.

They were seated in a spot secluded enough to not be ogled all the time, but not so much as to make Fire think Rio was trying to hide.

He smiled when Fire went to pull his chair out but gave him a slight shake of the head to stop him. He had said no romance, but it warmed his heart to see Fire doing things he knew Rio liked.

They settled down at the table, the pristine white tablecloths long enough to obscure the view of their feet, so Rio allowed himself to stretch and push his foot between Fire's.

Fire gathered his feet closer together, trapping Rio's, and gave him a smile that made all the anxiety and worry about the night feel worth it. Like he was happy. Like he understood the effort, baby steps as they were.

They placed their orders, Rio getting his escargot and Fire absolutely refusing to get the same. He did promise he'd try it from Rio's plate after he ordered the first thing made of red meat he found on the menu. Rio got them both some good wine and settled in to wait for their food.

"This place is really fancy," Fire said, scouting around with his head.

"It is," he said. "But it's not as stuffy as some of the other fancy places around, I don't think. The food is good too."

Fire eyed some of the other guests, then looked down at his clothes.

"Am I underdressed?" he asked.

Rio shook his head, allowing himself to appreciate again the figure Fire cut with his massive red wings curled over the back of the chair. "Not at all. You look really good."

"High praise, princess," Fire teased, and Rio rolled his eyes, the corners of his lips ticking up.

"Yes, well..." he said. "Don't get used to it."

"Wouldn't dream of it," Fire said, then shifted in his seat, meeting his eyes sincerely across the candlelit table. "I know you don't want to talk about it, but I just want to say...I appreciate this. I know it's hard for you. And what you did for me, visiting my parents, it meant a lot to me."

Rio bit his lip, picking at his napkin.

Fire continued. "I want to be seen in public with you, and I want the world to know you're my mate...but I've been a dick to you, a little bit."

"A little..." Rio squawked indignantly, but Fire cut him off with nudge to his feet.

"A lot..." Fire corrected himself. "We were both dicks to each other."

"I was not a dick to you..." Rio justified himself, and Fire quirked an eyebrow at him. "I was...unpleasant."

"You were a dick," Fire said, reaching a hand across the table but not touching him. "But that's okay. I forgive you if you forgive me?"

"I do," Rio said.

"Good," Fire said. "Then if we both promise to each other we'll go home and talk things through like adults, and figure out together what we want to do, would you be okay with that?"

Rio thought it through for a second.

Was he okay with that?

It sounded like a solution to his problems. Fire was willing to see things from his perspective. He was willing to talk and come up with a solution together. Wasn't that what he had wanted from the start? What he'd been hoping to get when he'd asked Fire for some time?

He wasn't sure.

All he knew was that he had spent the day psyching himself up for what he wanted to do, and he didn't want all that hard work to go to waste.

Fire had come halfway toward him.

Rio had to start walking too.

"We can share a dessert," he said.

An intimate offering that Fire slowly smiled at, looking down at the table to try and hide some of his obvious delight. Rio's heart swelled to see it. It floored him every time how little it took to make Fire happy. How little he had to give to make his mate feel secure and treasured the way he made Rio feel every day. These tiny little things that cost Rio nothing, and yet made him feel like he could be the best mate for Fire. The mate he deserved.

Their food arrived a moment later. Fire received his medium-rare steak and the side salad he had ordered first. "This looks good," he said appreciatively.

Rio glanced down at his own meal; the round shells arranged artfully on a bed of mixed greens.

"That doesn't, though," Fire said, nose scrunched at the plate in front of Rio.

"They're really good," Rio said, taking the tongs and the fork in his hands, ready to dig in.

"It's also a hassle to eat," Fire said. "You got enough tools there to build a bridge."

"And I'm the melodramatic one." Rio snorted, pulling the first bite out and popping it into his mouth, moaning at the taste. "So good."

"I'll take your word for it," Fire said, taking a bite of his own meal.

"No, you won't," Rio said, pulling out another snail and extending the fork toward Fire. "You promised you'd try it, and now you have to try it."

"But..." Fire said, shaking his head, searching for an excuse. "I don't want to eat too much and ruin my own dinner."

"One bite won't ruin anything," Rio said flatly. "And if you hate it, you can chase it down with your steak."

Fire squinted at him for a second before sighing.

"Fine, put it in," he said, leaning forward.

Rio chuckled at the terrible innuendo, putting his fork against Fire's bottom lip, letting him wrap it around the bite and pull it into his mouth. Should it have been as erotic as it was? Probably not. But after days of not seeing his mate, the sight of those lips wrapped around something just did things to Rio.

He suppressed a moan when Fire licked his lips and was about to run his foot over Fire's calf to get back at him when a shadow fell over his plate.

"Uxorious!"
It couldn't be...

He turned his head up to find his grandmother standing next to him. All the warmth and tension Fire created evaporated from his body, leaving him feeling like someone had thrown a bucket of ice-cold water over his head.

His worlds had just collided.

She was standing too close. Too close for Rio to think she was there for any other reason other than to ruin everything. His grandfather, as usual, had her back, greeting Rio with a nod of his head and not a single word spoken.

"Grandmother," he said breathlessly, rising up from his chair to show respect the way he had been raised to do. "What a lovely surprise."

It wasn't. And he knew she knew it too.

"What is the meaning of this?" she bit through her teeth, voice coming out in a sharp hiss.

Rio knew there was nothing wrong with him having dinner with someone. Deep down, he knew nothing about him and Fire screamed "mated couple" to a casual observer. But the way she had asked him had too much knowing, and his knees began to shake against his will, a pit forming in his stomach.

"I'm having dinner with James," he said, trying to keep his voice steady. "James, these are my grandparents."

"Lovely to meet you," Fire said, standing up and extending his hand to his grandfather first, as he was standing closer.

His grandfather, meek as he was, opted to not rock the boat too much and shook Fire's hand, grip slack and disinterest written all over his face.

"Ma'am." Fire turned to his grandmother, who stared at the offered hand like it would burn her to touch it, sneering at him as she turned back to Rio.

"I know exactly who he is. If the photograph wasn't enough, the whispers following me as soon as I walked in here would be," his grandmother spat.

The people around them were blatantly staring. A few had their phones out and were pointing them in their direction. It made Rio want to run and hide under the nearest rock, but his feet were glued into place, and all he could hear was his heart drumming in his ears.

Fire stepped around the table, trying to get between them. "Maybe we should take this somewhere else?"

"This is between me and my grandson. I'll go nowhere with you," she said, staring him down even though she was half his height.

Her posture was threatening in a way only she could manage, and Rio saw Fire's hackles rising. It was instinct. A mate's need to protect. Fire's lips tightened, his wings sharpened behind his back, fists clenched at his sides.

Rio saw it. A second before it was spoken, he saw what would happen, and he was powerless to stop it.

"I think it has a little to do with me," Fire said, giving her a tightlipped smile. "He's my mate."

Rio closed his eyes as the bomb was dropped, getting a brief glimpse as his grandmother turned puce, beyond horrified. He had imagined the moment she found out a million times. Somewhere, in the tiny bit of naivety he had left, he had hoped she'd take it better. Hoped she'd find a way to accept it and let him have everything he wanted.

How could Rio have ever thought that he could join his worlds together?

"Uxorious," his grandmother gritted. "Follow me."

Her demand made him break out in a sweat, terrified. He opened his eyes when Fire touched his hand.

"He's going nowhere without me," Fire said, making Rio feel like he was being split down the middle.

"Uxorious!"

The tone made him stand at attention, too ingrained. He had listened to it directing his life since he was young. He was used to following it. Used to abiding by it. He didn't think he knew how to stop. He swallowed and detached his fingers from Fire's, meeting his confused gaze.

"It's fine." *It isn't.* "I'll talk to her privately." *I want to disappear from here any way I can.* "Maybe you should go home?" *Don't leave.*

"Rio..." Fire said, voice a little uncertain, gaze searching, tearing into Rio's skin and making him ache.

"I'll call you later, okay?" Rio averted his eyes and stepped toward his grandmother, who put her nose in the air, turning to find a server and demand a back room.

"We still have things to talk about, princess," Fire called to his back, and Rio closed his eyes, feeling his heart squeeze like a vise was around it.

They were quickly accommodated, a private function room with dishes still to be cleared being made available to them at the back of the restaurant. They didn't sit, simply stood facing each other in the room until the door was closed after them.

The muted sound of talking could be heard through the walls, glasses and kitchenware clinking. It all frayed Rio's nerves. He was about one thread away from snapping completely.

"I suspected something was going on with you. Maybe even a fling with that racer. God knows you've had enough of those. But this?" his grandmother said.

Rio clenched his jaw. "I've lived a lifetime of disappointing you. I don't know why the surprise is so great."

"This is not a game!"

"Who said I was playing at one?" Rio snapped. "Fire isn't a game to me. What we have is real. If you would just let go of your prejudice and get to know him, you'd see that."

"Do you really want to risk everything for him?" his grandmother asked in disbelief. "A racer with a short future?"

"You don't know it'll be short," Rio defended him instinctively.

"He's not your family, Uxorious. We are."

"He's my mate."

That word now made his grandmother roll her eyes. "Matings happen all the time. We both know they don't have to mean anything under the right motivations. Don't be naïve, Uxorious. He could up and leave you tomorrow if it suited him. Just like your mother did to your father."

"You didn't want them to be together," Rio said.

"Of course I didn't," his grandmother said frankly. "He was below us in every respect. Family, money, connections. But that had no bearing on what your mother chose to do. She didn't just leave him or you behind when she married again. She turned her back on us too. Just like you're doing now."

"No...I'm not..." Rio denied, shaking his head. "I just... I'm just trying—"

"We took you in," his grandmother continued. "Gave you everything. We raised you to be a part of this family. Not to leave it like she did."

The blow wasn't the glancing ones from before. It hit dead center, and Rio was stunned by it. His biggest fear was being like his mother. "I'm not her," he said out loud, to reassure himself.

"Then prove it. Come home."

Home. What even was home anymore? Was it four cavernous walls surrounding the only security he knew? Was it an old chair from the past that held ghosts of memories? Was it fiery wings that could both cause hurt and comfort?

Rio didn't know.

His heart felt like it was being torn down the center slowly, and he wanted to tape it back up. He didn't want the two halves to diverge; he didn't know where that would leave him.

"This is your life, Uxorious. Are you really going to throw it away so carelessly? Throw us away? We're the only ones that have stuck by you."

Rio couldn't think. Every thought conflicted with another, the swirling chaos impossible to make out. And then there was his grandmother standing there. Not always nice. Or nurturing. But a solid, steady presence that could be relied on. The foundation for his life had been made by her, and he was now trying to dodge the cracks and not trip.

"You can't choose both," his grandmother said. "Come home with us. With your family. We'll always be there for you. That's the only thing you can count on in this life."

Rio was so scared to be alone again.

He'd always thought he just needed some time. With time, he could figure this out. With time, it would fall into place. With time, he could avoid the destruction.

Running, running, running. Always running. Trying to outrun the clock.

But it had finally ticked down on him.

He had a choice to make.

And he wasn't sure he knew how to make the right one.

CHAPTER EIGHTEEN

FIRE

Should he have seen it coming? Should he have anticipated Rio just disappearing from his life as unexpectedly as he'd waltzed into it?

Maybe.

There had been signs pointing to it.

But the visit to his parents had allowed Fire to let his guard down. The dinner invitation had made him hope. As a result, the landmine he and Rio had been avoiding stepping on had gone off directly in his chest cavity, and Fire had been caught completely unaware.

He didn't know where to begin picking up the bloodied pieces when Rio sent him away, told him to wait yet again.

Despite that, he naively expected it to take a couple days before they were back together trying to work out what to do now. He found himself numbly watching the door or his phone for any sign of Rio.

They were mates. He had to call.

And yet it turned out that as much as Rio loved a grand entrance, he preferred a quiet exit.

The utter radio silence in the days after dinner was sobering. Rio was gone. Calls from Fire went unanswered, texts were read but never replied to, and Rio never showed up on his doorstep.

A headache started as a small annoyance that grew into blinding pain. His joints felt stiff and achy, and getting out of bed became the biggest chore.

Mate rejection, even without outright being rejected with words, felt like a fucking bitch. It had him woozy and off center, making him have to sit down multiple times a day just to fucking *breathe*. He hated it. He hated their situation. He hated Rio's elitist family. He wanted to hate Rio too.

But he couldn't.

Unable to properly process the hurt and loss he felt, Fire threw himself into the only thing he had left.

He spent every waking moment at the gym, going over Vid's and Coach's drills until he felt like he'd keel over.

His wings had never felt less like a part of him than they did at the moment. Shaky, weak, off-balance, and with no endurance. And yet he tried.

He lifted weights, and he threw himself in the air and landed like a beginner, growing more and more frustrated with each moment.

It took one week for Vid to say something.

At least he got a grace period.

"What the hell is going on?" Vid demanded, grabbing the strap of the weight machine he was using for his wing to halt the movement. "You're not scheduled to be in here until two o'clock, and I just checked the logs, and it seems you've been here out of your regular hours for the past week!"

"What does it look like?" Fire grunted, blinking the sweat from his eyes. The release of pressure made Fire tremble, a tingling sensation of static under his skin as his blood circulation finally caught up with the rest of him.

"Like you're training for a competition you shouldn't be training for."

"Gold star for you," Fire said, unhooking his wings swiftly and walking away.

"Fire!"

Several other athletes looked their way, Zero sparing only a single impassive glance before turning back to the treadmill that was straining under his bulk. The sight made Fire grit his teeth in anger, his own ineptitude a glaring spot in the room that everyone knew about.

No one expected him to be able to race.

Vid rounded him, grabbing his arm and saying in a lower tone, "We talked about this already and agreed—"

"You mean *you* agreed," Fire cut off, jerking his arm away. "And I'm not letting you guys take this from me."

"Take it?" Vid asked, eyes confused. "We're not trying to take anything."

"You and Coach don't want the stain on your records. Whatever. I get it. I'm not such a commodity after I took a nosedive, am I?"

"What the hell are you accusing me of here?" Vid growled, darkness settling over his usually bright features.

"You don't think I can do it, fine. Don't help me. But stay the hell out of my way," Fire said, clipping Vid's shoulder as he walked out of the gym.

He felt guilt surface, but it was soon swallowed up by the throbbing mire of feelings that made it hard to process anything else.

He barely remembered getting home, going straight for the liquor cabinet.

Numbness. All he wanted was some blessed numbness to take away the pain in his chest and blanket his raging thoughts.

He took a drink straight from the bottle, going to his windows to stare pensively out at the rest of the Circle. He watched people walk along in couples and families down below, cars driving past, probably taking their owners home to their loved ones.

He swallowed the envy down with another gulp and turned away, finding a seat at his table.

He set the bottle down and dug out his phone, letting the screen light up to the only picture he had of Rio. From the botanical garden. He stared at it for a long time, even though it hurt, even though a part of him wanted to delete it forever.

He couldn't, though. A part of him couldn't let it go. Couldn't accept that this was all he had left of him.

He put the phone on the table next to the bottle, staring at both of them blankly.

"You could call him again," Fire said to himself. "Or knock on his door."

And then what? Beg him to give them another chance? So they could end up back here again when someone else inevitably found out and told Rio's family?

But not trying felt like quitting.

Fire reached out and grabbed the bottle instead.

He woke the next morning, head on the table, empty bottle overturned, and a killer hangover making a home inside his stiff body.

He groaned, blinking himself back into some form of coherency and caught sight of his phone under his slack hand. He swallowed before tapping it.

No messages.

Cursing himself for a fool, Fire pushed it away from him and staggered for the shower, setting it to freezing. He braced his hands on the wall, inhaling shakily as the deluge of ice cascaded over him. It didn't help. He couldn't wash away what he was feeling. Couldn't trick his body into concentrating on anything else. Couldn't shock life back into something that seemed dead already. It didn't even dull the pain he was feeling. Just made it sharper. More prominent. Layered instead of one-dimensional.

He cursed loudly, slapping the tile.

He was crawling inside his own skin, scrambling at the edges of his mind to try and escape, and he needed to do something else that wasn't climbing inside another bottle. Something to release the pressure.

He stumbled out of the shower and threw on some sweats, body and wings still dripping wet. He walked to the living room, shivering and contemplating it. Everything reminded him of Rio now. The memories woven into the fabric of the couch, the small items Rio had left here and there, that stupid bowl on his shelf.

Feeling a wave of vindictiveness wash over him, he stalked over and grabbed the bowl, picturing throwing it before he paused. He ferried it over to his kitchen instead and reached inside his cabinet.

A party-sized bag of chips crinkled under his hand, and he upended the entire thing into that pristine lie. Not even halfway done, he opened his fridge and grabbed a variety of dips, opening them all and taking everything into his nest.

He sprawled into one of the beanbags Rio hated so much, kicking his feet up and turning on the TV. He settled back with the bowl in his lap, digging his hand in and crunching down spitefully, imagining Rio's face if he saw chips in his precious bowl.

"What message is it sending now, Uxorious?" he asked, but the silence was all that responded.

He looked down at the bowl, expecting to feel a sick sense of satisfaction to see it filled with crumbs. Instead, all he felt was sick.

He pushed the thing to the floor, where it dinged and spilled its remaining contents. Uncaring, he curled up into himself, wet wings cradling his chilled body and doing their best to comfort him.

He didn't move from that spot that day.

And he did something he had never done before the next couple of days.

He skipped practice.

Day four of his moping found Fire practically running for the door at the sound of a knock, yanking it open and visibly deflating when he saw Coach standing there.

"Don't look so disappointed, hotshot."

Fire schooled his face and stepped aside, not wanting to give himself away. "Here to ream me out personally?"

Coach raised an eyebrow at him as he passed, making himself at home by throwing his windbreaker on the back of the sofa. "Got a drink in this place?"

"No."

Coach gave him a flat look, eyeing the empty bottle still on his table.

"Can't blame me for wanting to cover my ass," Fire muttered, walking to his liquor cabinet that he definitely wasn't supposed to have.

"You drinking during the season is the least of my concerns," Coach said. "Now pour me a couple fingers with ice."

Fire did as he was told, making one for himself because why the fuck not. "I didn't think you considered me to still be part of the season. I should be able to do whatever the hell I want, right?"

"Don't get smart," Coach said, ignoring his petulance and taking his glass.

Fire settled on the nearby armchair and took a large swallow of his own drink, contemplating the amber liquid through the crystal.

"You know I understand your position, right?"

Fire set his jaw, but it was hard to find the necessary ire from before, the vitriol he'd flung in Vid's face. He was too exhausted. He let his head fall back against the cushions and contemplated the ceiling instead. "I know you got injured and couldn't come back. I know. But I can."

"I know you can."

Fire snapped his gaze to Coach's. "Then why...?"

Coach swallowed his drink and set it on the floor, leaning forward with his elbows on his knees. "I don't want you to end up like me."

"I'm not back to where I was, but I can race, Coach. I just want to finish the season out. That's it. It's not some ego boost where I need to retain the title or prove everyone wrong. I just want the chance to race. That's it," Fire said.

Coach hung his head and laughed. "You remind me so much of him sometimes."

"Who? Your younger self?"

"Bullet."

Fire swallowed hard, trying to figure out if that was a compliment or not.

"So he annoyed you too?" He tried for a joke, but his throat was constricted because thinking of Bullet meant thinking of Rio too.

"As much as Zero annoys you," Coach said. "He was competition. He was a drive to be better. He was relentless when he wanted something. And he wanted to race when he wasn't fit to do it. Not just race... He wanted to win."

"I don't..." Fire started, but Coach lifted his hand up to stop him.

"When I said I didn't want you to end up like me, I just meant not being able to race again. But I don't want you to be like Bullet either. He put racing before everything, and it cost him everything. You're like nobody I've ever coached, Fire. And I saw that the same day I picked you out at that competition as a kid and offered you a spot."

Fire looked away, unused to that amount of emotion from his usually gruff coach.

"I signed you up for the race," Coach continued.

"But..."

"I'm going to trust you with your own health. You're gonna race, and you're gonna end up in whatever place you end up," Coach said. "If I see for one second that you're pushing to win, I'll lasso your ass right out of the sky, are we clear?"

"Yes," Fire rushed out, an ember of excitement settling in his stomach.

"I'm not joking, kid." Coach pointed a finger at him. "One wrong move...I'll stuff my pillow with your feathers."

"Be a kickass pillow..." Fire said under his breath like the brat that he was, and Coach glared at him before shaking his head.

"One more thing. You need to apologize to Vid if you want a chance of keeping him on your team. I know it's a little harder for him to find work, but your name on his résumé would get him a new spot on a team pretty damn quick."

Fire grimaced. "I was an asshole. Been one a lot lately. I'm sorry."

"At least you have some self-awareness."

"Been going through a rough time."

"No shit," Coach said seriously. "Doesn't excuse the behavior."

Fire looked away, not really keen to talk about Rio. "How did you know?"

"The abrupt mood shift from ecstatically happy to angry and depressed may have clued me in," Coach said dryly. "The flinching in pain and flying like shit solidified it. But also, you've been dodging your mother's calls."

"She called you?" Fire groaned.

"Demanded to know what was wrong and why I hadn't fixed it yet, actually. She also had some choice words about your race and what I was and wasn't doing right."

Fire smiled. Trust his mom to yell at a seasoned racer and coach about what he should and shouldn't do.

"Sorry?" he said as a question.

"It isn't a new occurrence," Coach said. "I'm used to it."

"Yeah, I guess you are," Fire said with a dry chuckle.

"Just don't give her even more reason to worry, kid."

"I'll try not to," Fire said, and he meant it.

He would take back control of at least one thing in his life.

"Vid!"

The bleached blond looked over his shoulder, and his smile melted away, traded for a cool mask of indifference. He turned back around and carried on walking through the halls of Ace.

Fire cursed under his breath and jogged to catch up.

"C'mon, Vid, hear me out," he called.

"I'm busy. If it's important, email me."

"Email! You want me to fucking email you?" Fire said incredulously.

"Yes, email. We're in a professional environment. All my other clients email me with work-related queries," Vid stopped to say, and the line could never have been drawn clearer.

Client. Not friend.

"Now if you'll excuse me," Vid said, turning to leave, and Fire couldn't handle seeing another back turned.

"Listen, I'm trying to apologize here!" he shouted, drawing the attention of a few passersby.

Vid stopped, and Fire cleared his throat. They both waited for the eavesdroppers to leave, or at least hide better.

"Funny. I didn't hear the sound of apologizing," Vid said at length.

"You can be a real bitch, you know that?"

"And still blows through the sound of no apologies," Vid said, cupping his ear to the imaginary wind.

Fire grasped his bicep and spun him around to finally meet his eye. "I'm sorry, okay! I was in a bad spot, and I was taking it out on you, and I shouldn't have. Especially not after everything you've done for me. I was a huge dick."

"Don't self-compliment in the middle of your apology," Vid said, but the corner of his lips lifted.

Fire breathed a relieved laugh. "Does that mean I'm forgiven?"

Vid scrunched his mouth up and crossed his arms. "You questioned my integrity."

"I know." Fire grimaced. "I knew it was where it would hurt the most, so I aimed and fired. I told you, I was being a royal shitstick, and I'm really sorry. I understand if you want to transfer. I know Zero was shopping around for a new sports therapist..."

Vid hummed like he was considering it, and Fire braced himself for the hurt. What was one more blow at this point?

"I guess I don't want the hassle of breaking in another idiot racer."

Relief—brilliant, shining relief—blinded him, and Fire tackled Vid in a headlock that Vid struggled to wrestle himself free of. They both ended up crashing to the floor, a happier pile of limbs than before.

Vid punched him in the side before he sat up to glare down at him. "Worst apology ever."

Fire sighed out, exhaustion creeping in. He rubbed at the ever-present headache. "Yeah, well, that's all I got at the moment."

Vid frowned, turning to him and crisscrossing his legs like they weren't in the middle of a hallway. "You look like shit."

Fire smiled wryly. "At least the outside matches the inside."

"Look...I don't know what happened, but I can guess it has less to do with racing and more to do with a certain Lazy Susan who shall not be named?" Vid said, trying to broach it delicately.

Fire was infinitely grateful he didn't say his name out loud; he didn't think he'd be able to handle it just yet. Plus, he really didn't know who was listening in, and a part of him still wanted to respect Rio's wishes.

"Things ended how they were always going to, I suppose. I just didn't get the hint," Fire said, staring up at nothing.

Vid bit his lip. "I don't pretend to know anything about mating. Slept through that class, remember...but from what I saw, you guys were made for each other."

"We fought all the time. About everything." Fire repeated what Rio had told him once mechanically.

"You were good for each other. Yeah, your tempers ran hot, but that doesn't change that I've never seen you so serious about anything except racing the whole time I've known you. And who says any relationship is rainbows and sunshine twenty-four-seven anyway? It's about sticking through those tough times—"

"It was his decision, okay?" Fire cut off, springing upward. "I was more than willing. I was practically on my knees for it, but there's only so much chasing and waiting I can do before I need to know when to quit."

"Quitting has never been your thing."

"Maybe it should be. You warned me against pushing something so hard it breaks."

"You didn't break it, Fire."

Hadn't he? If he hadn't wanted so much, needed so much, maybe they'd still be together.

"Whatever. The reality is that the ball was always in his court, and he never played it. And now I need to learn to live with it," Fire said, looking away.

"He's still teaching the kids at the Rec Center," Vid said.

Fire breathed through the pain and gave a stilted smile. "I'm glad. He was good at it. He should do something he enjoys."

"You were better as a team."

"I guess he doesn't agree."

Vid frowned, but didn't refute it. "So Coach said he's in on this crazy idea to get you in racing condition in less than two weeks."

Fire smiled. "I don't want to put you in an awkward position. I know your feelings."

"You just want to race?" Vid asked. "No showing off, no crazy tricks... Just one end to the other, possibly in last position and an abysmal time that will stay on your record forever."

"Whatever it takes to get across the finish line."

Vid inhaled deeply and then let it out. "Well, I guess I can get on board with that."

And on board with it he got.

Fire hadn't thought he'd struggle with flying ever again, but he felt like a child. Not only were his muscles screaming from exertion, the aches in his body from Rio's rejection made it all feel like he was moving through water.

He hadn't thought it would be like that. He'd always hoped his knowledge on mating rejections would remain theoretical, but...there he was.

Twitching randomly when a sharper pain stabbed through him. Losing altitude when his wings got too tired because the absence of his mate made him feel heavy. It was excruciating, and Fire wanted it over as much as he wanted to push through.

Endure until he was back to who he was before Rio. Whole. In charge. Without his body being tied to someone who pulled the strings on him without wanting him close.

"Okay," Vid said after a particularly harsh landing. "We're gonna call it a day here."

"But..."

"No." Vid shook his head. "You knew the conditions. You listen to what is said, and you follow our lead."

Fire glared at him, and Vid gave him a congenial smile.

"Hit the shower and head home," Vid said. "We'll pick it up tomorrow."

"Fine," Fire said, grabbing his gear and stalking out of the gym toward the changing rooms.

He showered quickly, wishing the water would wash Rio away from him as well, but he stayed. Glued to him, stuck to his skin. Ever-present.

God, he wanted the pain to stop.

He got dressed, each move feeling like torture, and picked up his bag.

When Fire finally stepped outside, it was dark and cold. The chill in the air made his breaths huff in front of his face, and he snuggled down into his jacket's hood instinctively. The walk across the almost-empty lot to his car seemed like a trek across an arctic plain.

He was debating rematerializing his tired wings as some sort of barrier when he spotted a familiar figure leaning against the hood of his car. Needle-sharp heels were crossed one over the other, claw-like nails tapping on a tablet.

Fuck.

"Anna."

He approached, head throbbing.

"He knows my name," she said in false awe, the glare she gave him not matching the tone in the slightest.

He wasn't in the mood for any of it.

"I just want to get home and get some rest," he told her. "If there's anything pressing on my schedule, just email it to me."

"You were rejected and didn't think to call me?" she said, ignoring his words completely. "I had to hear it from Coach instead of, oh, I don't know, my damn client? Fire, what the fuck?"

He bristled at the reminder and almost snarled at her. "Anna, I'm not in the mood. I don't care about the press. I don't care about publicity. I just want to be left alone to lick my wounds in peace. I don't need a publicist spinning any sort of story about me right now."

"What about a friend helping you through this?" she snapped, and he looked up to see her carefully crafted mask of indifference slip a little. "Fuck you for thinking publicity is all I care about. I've been in this with you for years. I've taken all of your bullshit in stride. And not because the pay is stellar, you asshole. You think I don't care that you're suffering? You think I wouldn't want to help?"

Great. He just kept screwing up left, right, and center.

"Anna..." he started, but she huffed.

"Get in the damn car." She strode over and opened the passenger side, and he didn't dare ask her how she'd unlocked it. "I'm coming with you to yours. We'll have some food, maybe a drink, and you'll tell me everything you've kept a secret from me. Got it?"

He nodded and got in the car, not daring to say another word to her. He took them to his place, the click of her heels at his back sounding like a soundtrack from a horror movie.

He unlocked his apartment and stepped in, having the presence of mind to notice the lights were on before he was crushed between familiar arms, the scent of home and family filling his nostrils.

"Mom..." he breathed out. "How..."

"I called them and told them to come," Anna said, flicking her shoes off by the door and walking in.

"Them?" Fire asked and looked up, eyes misting when he saw his dad, holding his niece in his arms, next to a laptop opened up to a group video call and the rest of his family waiting for him.

"Guys..." he said, voice shaking as his mom pulled him further inside.

"Come on, you," she said. "I brought food, and we'll sit down and chat. I think you need your family around you right now. Your brother will be here soon."

Fire allowed her to guide him into the living room, collapsing between her and his dad and Julie, Anna sitting in an armchair right next to them.

He let their warmth blanket him, the strength of their unconditional love keeping him upright, piecing him back together in ways only a family could.

Not quite whole. But enough to forget for a little while.

CHAPTER NINETEEN

RIO

Following the date night with Fire, Rio's house became a minefield for him. Every word he said was taken out of context. Every sign of hesitation would be seen as him following in his mother's footsteps and abandoning his family. When he tried talking to them, explaining to them that Fire mattered, that he was his mate and no amount of their complaints would change that, they'd shut him off. Ignore him until the pain of being all alone again attacked and he'd try again.

He found himself at the Rec Center over and over and over again. It became an escape.

When the house became too stifling and the marble too bright, he came to the soft padded floors and fluttery wings waiting for him to teach them.

When he missed his dad and how he used to train Rio, he'd come to see the kids and try to find a way to be more like his dad than the rest of his family. He needed to find that little boy who was happy just being at a racing track or the gym. Following his dad's every move and helping him make them even better. He wanted to be that person again.

Someone whose future was brighter than whatever shiny jewel they hung on their wings. He wanted to matter.

He came to the center when he missed him too. And that meant he was there a lot. Because he missed Fire with every fiber of his being. He felt hollow without him—empty.

Like he had finally lost the last good piece of himself. And yet he couldn't bring himself to answer Fire's calls or texts when they came. Or to reach out when they stopped. Not when the only thing he had to offer was still the same mess he'd offered the first time around.

"That's really good, Piper," he told the little girl as she landed softly next to him. "Make sure to touch down with both feet together. We want to avoid getting hurt, okay?"

"Yes, Mr. Rio." She nodded, bright eyes challenging him to give her more, to teach her more. She truly was one of a kind.

All of the children were enthusiastic. Some were decent at flying. Rio enjoyed teaching all of them more than he could have ever imagined. But only Piper was someone Rio saw true potential to be a racer in, and that was saying something. She was determined, persistent, brave, and daring. She didn't mind repeating the same move a million times before she got it, and she always wanted more.

She was irregular at showing up, though. Her dad was always apologetic when she missed practice but never offered an explanation, and Rio never pushed. But he wanted to talk to him at some point. Tell him she truly could have a shot as a junior racer very soon with her skill level and some work. Rio believed in her.

Another kid landed next to him and snapped him out of his thoughts.

"Nice, Maya," Rio said. "Try to start slowing down a little sooner, okay? So you don't land too hard. You have to do it very, very quietly."

Maya nodded and rushed back to the end of the line to wait for her turn again.

"Mr. Rio?" Piper called out to him, and he paused the exercise to go check on her.

"Yes, Piper?"

"Is Fire gonna come see us practice again?" she asked, and Rio truly should have seen it coming. She mentioned him often. She worshipped the ground he walked on.

But the mention of his name felt like a stab through the heart for Rio. He wanted him there too. He wanted to do this with him. They were a good team. Rio had the skill and knowledge to teach theory. To break it down and explain it. Fire had the skill and experience to show the moves in practice. Something Rio just had no desire to do.

They were good together in all the ways that counted and Rio resented himself for being the way he was.

He didn't want to reject Fire. He...he loved him. Wanted him as his mate. Wanted a life with him. But letting go of the last of his blood was hard. Rio didn't want to be alone.

He sighed and pinched the bridge of his nose, observing the last few kids attempting the landing before telling them to grab their things.

The adults picked them up soon after, and Rio went around straightening up the place, heart feeling heavy and hands looking for whatever they could find to occupy himself.

"He's miserable too," Vid said from behind him, and Rio flinched, biting his lip. He straightened a foam obstacle so forcefully it just tipped to the other side and rolled away from him.

"I'm not miserable," he said, glaring after the obstacle.

"Sure you're not." Vid snorted. "You had that same shirt on last time you were here. From what I know of you, that would not be a conscious decision you'd make?"

Rio looked down and tugged the lilac polo he was wearing. He tried to recall the last time he came to the center but found he had no idea what his outfit had been that day.

He was horrified to realize it was quite possible he did repeat an outfit. He snapped his eyes back to Vid, who met him with a smile.

"Miserable," he mouthed in his direction, and Rio groaned, running his hands over his face.

"You are not to mention this to him," Rio said.

"I don't think he cares what you wear," Vid said. "He just wants to see you."

"Well, why doesn't he then?" Rio was unable to stop himself from asking.

"I am not getting involved," Vid said, lifting up his hands. "But from what I understand, he believes the ball's in your court now."

"I despise balls and courts," Rio huffed.

"In any case, I'm heading out," he said. "Thanks for wrapping up and doing the handoff with the parents."

"I didn't mind returning the children to their regular minders."

"Parents, Rio," Vid said. "They're called parents."

"Minders sounds much fancier, though," Rio said.

"Sure..." Vid relented, shuffling in place for a moment.

"Talk or leave," Rio said.

"I just wanted to let you know that the center will be looking for a full-time flying coach. You should apply," Vid said, and Rio stared.

"I have zero qualifications," he said.

"Please," Vid grunted. "You grew up with Bullet. The kids adore you, they've learned so much, and it's a preschool flying practice. You'll be fine."

"Why aren't you doing it?" Rio asked.

Vid looked away for a moment before meeting his eyes again. "My free time is shortening, and I can't make it in regularly enough to keep doing it."

"You getting more clients?"

"No, just…" Vid trailed off, and something about it tipped Rio off.

"He's racing, isn't he?" Rio asked quietly.

Vid nodded, eyes meeting his again. "He is."

"Is he ready for it?" Rio asked, unable to contain the worry. "He's not going to ruin his wing completely, is he?"

"We're doing everything we can to make sure he finishes the race safely," Vid said. "Both Coach and I would like it better if he sat it out, but…he's determined."

"He's a moron," Rio said, and Vid laughed.

"He is," he said. "But you still care for him."

"What…"

"The race is next Saturday," Vid said, heading for the door. "Think about it. And think about the job too, okay? I think you'd be a really good fit. You're already here all the time, doing it for free. Why not do it for a paycheck?"

Now that got Rio's interest. Being financially independent was on his bucket list of things to do in order to become who he wanted to be. Money was one of the bigger things his grandparents held over his head. He wanted to keep his family; of course he did. But he wanted them to want him too. Not own him.

"What's the paycheck like?" he called after Vid, who'd already reached the door.

"Shit," Vid said.

Rio glared. "Shit is still better than nothing."

"That's the spirit," Vid said cheerfully, walking out and slamming the door behind him, leaving Rio with ringing ears and his entire life rearranging in front of his eyes.

He walked out of the center in a daze, trying to compartmentalize so he could focus on one thing at a time. His brain would explode otherwise.

"Uxorious," he heard someone calling and turned to see a familiar grin trained right at him. "You never did find me to figure out a nickname."

"Bellamy?"

"He does remember," he said, nodding and walking closer. He scanned Rio head to toe and frowned. "You look like shit."

Rio recoiled, and his hackles rose. He did not look like shit.

"And yet you came to my party to try and be my mate," he snapped back, and Bellamy laughed.

"Oh, yeah, no, babes," Bellamy said. "I go to those to drink and mock. You're far too skinny and high maintenance for me. I'm the spoiled brat in my relationships. I can't go around mating my competition, now can I?"

Rio stared at him, mouth agape and brain working overtime to find a comeback. He had nothing.

Bellamy's hand reached out to push his jaw up and close his mouth.

"You're so rude," Rio said when his jaw clicked back into place, and Bellamy nodded.

"Generally, yes," he said. "Now what brings you around this area?"

"I could ask you the same thing," Rio said, and Bellamy pointed behind him.

"One of our office buildings is being built just behind the center," he said. "I came to inspect. Your turn!"

Rio wanted to just keep walking, but something compelled him to stay.

"I volunteer with the kids at the Rec Center," he said. "I teach them flying."

Bellamy widened his eyes.

"Never would have pegged you for a hands-on charity guy," he said. "Checks and donations, sure. Volunteer work? Hard no."

"Shows what you know," Rio said.

Bellamy nodded. "Yeah, not much."

Rio blinked at him.

That was right.

Bellamy knew nothing about him. He knew nothing about Rio and Fire, or about their situation. And he wasn't close enough to Rio to have his side just because they were friends the way Kalie did. His conversations with her turned into her agreeing with his moves, and as wonderful as her support had been, he needed an unbiased opinion.

"Are you free for lunch maybe?" Rio asked. "If you lend me your ear for a bit, I'll help you with that nickname situation."

"Well, when you put it like that, how can I say no?" Bellamy said, and Rio nodded, a sigh of relief passing his lips. He needed someone to listen.

"There is a little bistro just down the street," Rio said, familiar with the surroundings after spending so much time there in the past weeks.

"Sounds great," Bellamy said, lapsing into silence as they walked together.

Rio appreciated his ability to read the room and not talk when Rio wasn't ready to talk yet. He had to get his thoughts in order first. He had to figure out how to say what needed to be said to get an objective opinion.

They walked into the bistro and got seated within seconds, a waitress approaching to take their orders and give them both a glass of water.

Rio chugged his and set it back down, twining his fingers on top of the table and taking a deep breath. "Okay, ready."

Bellamy motioned with his hand. "The stage is yours, and I'm all ears."

"How much do you know about my family?" Rio asked.

"My grandmother knows a lot, but I usually tune her out when she starts the gossip." Bellamy shrugged. "She's too boring, and I'm far too young to die from it."

"Right, well... My grandparents raised me after my father died. They're my mother's parents, and she never really wanted kids, so she was never a part of my life."

"Sucks," Bellamy said, and Rio liked the lack of fake condolences.

"It does," he said. "But what sucks the most is that my grandparents never really wanted a grandson. They wanted a totem of their kindness and someone to carry on the Charmichael name."

"Which you have done admirably, truly," Bellamy said deprecatingly.

"I excelled, as usual," Rio said, lip curling. "Until I did exactly what my mother did."

"You went and had a baby you didn't want?" Bellamy asked, this time completely serious.

"I found a mate that isn't to their standards."

"Ah," Bellamy said. "The ultimate betrayal. He's either poor and therefore not worthy, or newly rich and therefore not worthy. So which one?"

"Neither," Rio said. "He's a racer."

"Shit," Bellamy said, and Rio nodded. "So your dad was a racer?"

"He was," Rio said, looking down. "One of the best ones out there. My mother was with him in secret until she realized she was used to a more lavish life than a racer could give her. Even one as good as my dad. So the moment I was born, she left me with my dad and flounced off to live her life. I've never met her."

"And now..." Bellamy prompted, and Rio slumped down in his seat.

"I, apparently, am her son through and through," Rio said, disgust lacing his words. His worst nightmare coming true. "I kept my mate a secret, made him feel unwanted, made it look like I care about money more than I do him."

"Wait, you left him?" Bellamy asked, and Rio flinched.

"No, not really," Rio said, shame and guilt settling in the pit of his stomach. "I told him to let me talk to them and that I'd call him later."

"Don't tell me you just never called," Bellamy groaned, thumping his head on the table, and Rio frowned.

"I needed time to figure out what to do and how to do it," he said, his own excuses sounding lame to him.

"And how's that going?" Bellamy asked.

"Like shit," Rio said. "My grandparents aren't the best people in the world, but...they're all I have. If they cut their own daughter off for making a choice they didn't like...they won't hesitate for a second to do it to me. And then I'm alone..."

Rio lapsed into silence, knowing what he was saying was making very little sense. To anyone normal, their mate would be their first priority. To anyone else, the choice wouldn't even be a choice. They'd give everything up to have their mate with them.

Something was wrong with Rio, for sure. He had no other explanation.

"Look," Bellamy said. "I'll be the last person to give you the whole 'money can't buy happiness' spiel because we both know that's bullshit. Money opens doors and makes life easier."

Rio looked at him from under his lashes. "You're not helping."

"I don't think you need help," Bellamy said, then shrugged. "And even if you did, I'm hardly qualified to give it. But..."

"But?"

"Earlier, when you were talking about your mate and your family, you said *when* I pick him, not *if*," Bellamy said. "That tells me your mind has already been made up."

"What?" Rio asked, running their conversation back in his head. He couldn't remember saying that, but hearing it repeated to him sounded right.

It sounded like a correct way to phrase it.

Fire was his mate.

He was the first person since his dad died who made him feel like he was worth more than the wealth he had tied to his name.

Fire liked Rio for Rio. He had proven that by refusing to use Rio's full name. Detaching him completely from the rich-heir persona and treating him like a person. Like someone worth knowing. Worth having as a mate.

Fire was proud of him. He had introduced him to his family and expected nothing of him but to be himself. He didn't correct him at every turn, didn't demand he behave a certain way. He laughed off his quirks and accepted them as just another part of him.

Rio was never more himself than when he was with Fire.

And he was never freer than when he was with Fire.

He belonged with Fire. He knew that. He had known that since the beginning.

But what became clear was that keeping his family and keeping Fire weren't different things.

His grandparents were never really family to him. Fire was.

He looked up into Bellamy's eyes and found the man smirking.

"Caught on, have you?" he asked, and Rio nodded. "Well, that took no time and almost no effort from me. My favorite way of helping."

"I need to..." Rio said, and Bellamy made a shooing motion with his hand.

"Go, get your life in order," he said. "Lunch is on me."

"Thank you," Rio said, heart hammering in his chest. "Really, Bellamy, I have no idea how to repay you."

"I literally ate lunch while you talked yourself in circles and then came to your senses," he said. "You owe me one thing, though."

"Name it," Rio said. "Anything."

"Tell me, who's your mate?"

Rio snorted. "Fire."

"Hot," Bellamy said approvingly, taking another bite of his food. "Once you have all this mess sorted, I'll allow you to introduce me to some hot racer friends."

"Oh, you'll allow it, will you?"

Bellamy nodded, pointing to the door. "I will. Now go. You're ruining my lunch with all this jittering about."

Rio tore out of the bistro and rushed to his car as fast as he could. His hair was breaking out of the perfect coif he had, and he knew his shoes were not made for running, but he didn't care.

For once, Rio didn't care about being undignified. All he wanted to do was prove to Fire he wasn't a mistake.

He was a good mate to him.

He just had to show him.

CHAPTER TWENTY

FIRE

Fire breathed out shakily as Vid worked behind him on his wings, smoothing out the feathers ready for inspection.

It was rare that someone tried to use performance enhancers on their wings anymore. Too noticeable. But occasionally, someone thought they could get away with oiling their wings for more speed.

Fire cast a glance around the busy room. Each racing stadium was different, but it was common to place racers in larger spaces with areas cordoned off for their respective teams. It built the atmosphere seeing your opponents across the room, and the press liked to drum up excitement by doing a run-through of the staging area before they were forced to leave.

"Okay, we have the qualifying times back," Coach said to his left, walking toward him with a piece of paper in hand. He had Fire's gloves under the other arm and was dressed in Fire's team colors and logo.

"How bad is it?" Fire asked.

Qualifying laps had been yesterday and it had been brutal. It was against Fire's nature not to push, but he didn't want to risk hurting himself for the actual race, so he knew he must have posted a miserable time.

"You're not in the top ten positions, but we guessed that. That means you'll have to watch it when you take off and on the first turn. The back of the pack gets scrappy," Coach said, tucking the paper away and moving forward to put Fire's gloves on for him.

They were black and had his signature flames running up the forefingers and wrapping around the wrists where the straps fastened. The design matched the skintight, insulated racing suit he wore and his racing goggles and boots. The altitude and speeds they raced at could be freezing, so any exposed skin was subject to damage. The Racing Association had ruled years ago about mandatory racing equipment after some people had tried to shed weight by losing as much as they could possibly get away with.

Fire shook his hands out once the gloves were on, feeling like he was donning battle gear. He'd never felt this nervous before a race before, and he knew every eye was going to be on him both as defending champion and because of his injury.

The rejection pains didn't help any either.

He tried to push it all out of his head and focus. His family were waiting out there for him...in a crowd of twenty thousand other people.

Fuck.

"I've never had to give you a pep talk in your life, but you look like you might need one," Coach said, like he was reading his thoughts.

Fire flipped him off, but it was without his usual pizzazz. "I don't need a pep talk."

"Do you need a hug instead?" Vid asked from over his shoulder.

"No!" Vid and Coach shared an amused look, and Fire grunted. "I'm glad you two find this all so funny."

"Not funny. But it is kind of a nice change in pace," Vid said, finishing up and rounding him to stand next to Coach. "Usually I'm chasing you around the pit while you trash talk everyone in sight and boast to every camera."

"I don't boast!" Fire denied. "I state factual information! That asshole Speed boasts."

"Well, he's been doing enough of that," Coach confirmed. "The press were trying to run away from him for once."

"Like I said. A-hole."

"*Racers, line up for inspection*," a female voice over the speakers said, interrupting them and making the whole room fall into stillness. "*Once inspection is done, proceed straight to the ready room. Teams, please wait here and you'll be escorted separately.*"

"Showtime," Vid said, grabbing his goggles for him. "Remember, if you feel any pain, ease off. And if you have to come down—"

"I will. I don't fancy crashing out and having to do this all over again," Fire said, nodding his head.

Vid smiled and offered out a hand. "Good luck."

Fire grasped it and drew Vid into a brief hug before turning to Coach.

"Watch the backdrafts," he murmured. "If you can get into a pocket and coast for a little to rest…"

Fire nodded. "Got it."

"And watch your back. All these racers are going to be gunning for you. Some of them are going to want to put on their résumé that they beat Fire in a race more than actually winning."

Fire clenched his jaw, glancing surreptitiously around the room. "Nice of them."

"It comes with being the best," Coach said. "People want to see you fall down. Don't let them."

Fire swallowed and nodded, walking off to join the others in the line. He ended up between Speed and Zero as they waited for the RA official.

"Sure you wanna race?" Speed asked under his breath, still facing front. "Those times you posted in qualifiers are worse than some of the junior leagues."

Fire rolled his eyes, wishing one of the lightning bolts from Speed's racing suit would manifest and strike the guy in the head.

"How about you concentrate more on your own time? Especially since you could only break top three once I was gone."

"You're washed up," Speed hissed. "Have some pride and bow out gracefully."

"Hm…" Fire tilted his head consideringly. "How about I just kick your ass instead?"

"Quiet," Zero mumbled, just as the official came within hearing range.

Fire had to wonder whose ass Zero was saving, or if it was just a coincidence that Zero's patience with their bickering had run out exactly at that moment. Regardless, no more was said as they were cleared to go, all shuffling into the darkened ready room and putting on the rest of their gear.

Fire rolled his neck around his shoulders and flexed his wings once before pulling on his goggles. He adjusted the tightness, knowing there was nothing he could do about the invisible band around his chest.

C'mon, Fire. It's just a race.

He'd never had to psych himself up before. Flying had come so naturally to him since before he could even remember, and now he was second-guessing every move. Aware of every single twitch of his body.

The gate rolled up slowly, letting in shafts of light and the thunderous roar of the crowds. Claxons and whistles filled the air alongside the cheering, and Fire held his breath as the stadium unfolded in front of him.

Rows upon rows of people were stacked one on top of the other vertically, surrounding the oval racecourse. The grandstand could be seen in the far distance, the podiums already set up and empty against the RA's yellow backdrop.

They walked out one by one, being introduced by the host, cameras panning in to project them onto the massive screens dotted around the stadium.

"And now the returning champion. Make some noise for...Fire!"

It took a second for Fire's legs to work as the crowd erupted. Once he started to walk, he tried to block everything else out. Normally, he played with the camera and his fans, but everything was white noise, his gaze fixed on the single spot where he needed to stand.

He took his place behind the others, finding it strange to be so far back in the pack. He looked around himself, noting the racers who were close, their weaknesses and strengths, as he pulled the cowl of his suit up to cover his lower face.

If he could catch a good updraft on takeoff, it could place him in the middle of the pack. He just needed to watch the backdrafts from the racers in the front like Coach said. Three laps. He needed to maintain position for three laps and then his season would be over.

His thoughts ran around and around as the host went through the usual spiel, his ears tuned for a single sound of a gun, his eyes fixed on the lights, waiting for red to turn to green.

It came in an instant, and then there was movement everywhere.

Fire kicked off the ground first, instinct moving his body like it was old times. His wings weren't able to keep up, though, and he felt the jolt of pain on the first wingbeat. Gritting his teeth through it, Fire pushed upward, knowing that his best shot was to get clear fast. He'd do more damage trying to dodge people.

Other racers began to pass him inevitably on the upward climb, but Fire managed to get to altitude without being lost in the back. The racetrack stretched out before him, the shortest one of the season, looping around the stadium.

He fell into a dive and built up some speed.

The wind tore at the tiny strip of skin between his eyes and nose that his racing suit couldn't cover, and Fire reveled in the feeling of finally *racing*.

Qualifiers had been all about restraint, not coming close to pushing the limits. But Fire felt the immediate strain of his wing as he finally took the training wheels off. It all faded in the euphoria of flying, though. Of being up here again, where he truly belonged, the vast sky stretching out in front of him.

He felt free of shackles, of cares and worries, as he took the first turn, getting jostled but holding the inside line against his competitors.

His eyes didn't move to the board to keep track of his time; they didn't dart back to see who was closing in behind him. They stared straight ahead, fixed on the track and seeing nothing else.

Everything was movement and breaths and his thundering heart in his ears.

And then someone caught someone else on the second lap of the third bend ahead of Fire, two racers colliding painfully, wings tangled as one tried to overtake the other in a risky maneuver on the outside. Another racer ended up crashing into the mess, unable to swerve in time at that velocity.

Fire barely had time to bank to avoid joining them, his own wing clipping into someone else and making it scream out in pain. The racer next to him shoved him away, and Fire hissed but managed to right himself and move past without losing too much speed.

A brief glimpse behind told him that it was Speed and Nimbus that had collided, Ruby being an unfortunate byproduct, but they had all managed to stay airborne.

Fire turned his attention back forward as the commentator and crowds went wild. He could see Zero's massive raven wings far ahead, but the people between Fire and the finish line had just lessened significantly.

The pump of blood he usually got kicked in, and an adrenaline rush had him taking turns faster, beating his wings quicker. It seemed like everyone around him had the same idea, though, and the competition got even fiercer as they rounded the bend into the last lap.

One bend, two, three...

Fire counted them down in his head until he saw the exact moment he could have pushed in the last straight toward the finish line. The racer ahead of him was a few wingbeats away if he could grit his teeth through the pain. He could feel his wings tense up as if preparing for the damage about to come, to give everything to win, anything to win, like always, and Fire...let it go.

Fire saw the racer ahead of him look back in shock before gunning it for the end, and Fire kept at his own pace until he crossed the finish line and touched down to earth once more.

He'd completed the season.

"Fire!" Vid shouted, rushing to him with his coach closing in on the other side. "You did it! You fucking did it!"

Fire was in shock, panting for air. His legs gave out underneath him, sending him to the floor even as more racers landed around them. Vid and Coach sank down onto their knees next to him, grasping him by anything they could get their hands on.

Fire removed his goggles with numb fingers, knowing they had to have bitten lines into his face, looking up at the leader board.

9th place – Fire – 40.002

It was the worst time he'd ever posted in his adult life. It was also the proudest he'd ever been of himself.

Vid had tapered off the celebrating and was already checking over his wings that were spread out in a mess behind him.

"They feel okay?" Vid asked.

Fire nodded. They hurt, of course, and they definitely had earned some time off and TLC, but he could tell he hadn't injured them irreparably. Probably because he'd held back in that last second. He met Coach's knowing eye and the old man smiled at him, clapping him on the shoulder.

"You did good, Fire," he said gruffly. "You did real good."

Fire choked on a happy laugh, an almost-sob caught in his throat as he buried his face in Coach's chest, more than overwhelmed. He couldn't stop shaking, his body finally knowing it could let itself go as the adrenaline tapered off.

"Oh my god..." Vid said faintly, before raising his volume. "*Oh my god!*"

Fire unburied himself to look at him. "What's wrong?"

But Vid wasn't looking at them; his eyes were fixed on the board above their heads. A chorus of gasps and cheers went up around them, and Fire followed Vid's gaze and stopped breathing.

Fire – 3rd place

Fire felt like he was gonna pass out. "*How?*"

Coach grinned, the widest Fire had ever seen him. "You told me at the beginning of all this that you had enough points to win."

"But...I was just talking shit trying to get you to let me train. I wasn't serious!"

"I didn't want to mention it. We weren't going for the podium, and there was no way you could actually win the thing," Coach said. "But I knew if you managed to scrape a high enough position, you might be in with a shot at third, depending on how the rest of the racers placed."

"The crash between Speed, Ruby, and Nimbus," Fire murmured with dawning understanding. They had all been contenders to place, only Ruby and Nimbus hadn't been able to recover, looking at their times. Fire's previous first-place races in the circuit before his DNF had carried him points-wise to that third spot, beating Nimbus by a single point.

It was almost unbelievable.

Speed had managed to scrape into second despite the collision, and Zero was streaks ahead in first, no contenders.

"Somebody punch me, so I know I'm not dreaming," Fire said.

"Don't tempt me with a good time," Vid said, a silly smile on his face from his elation.

"I volunteer," Anna said from where she was standing behind Vid, a smile on her usually pinched-tight face. "Congrats, asshole."

"Thanks," Fire said with a beam.

"Let's get you on your feet," Vid said, taking him under the arm.

They managed to get him upright again, and pretty soon, a camera was shoved into his face. He saw himself on the big screen, his exhaustion plain as day, and the crowd started chanting his name. A grin, bright and full, filled up his face, the pain of everything washing away in that one singular moment.

They were approached by officials soon after to hasten teams to clear the track. They moved slowly, every racer bone-tired, some mired in disappointment and some in happiness. Fire caught sight of Nimbus hopping away with help, and Zero from the corner of his eye showing absolutely no emotion at winning. Speed was the loudest, arguing with an official in a vest about the unfairness of the crash.

Fire had to roll his eyes. Some things stayed the same.

Those that had placed were led into a separate waiting area as they prepared the grandstand. Cameras still followed them at a distance as commentary was made to the crowd and those watching at home.

Fire handed over his gloves and goggles to Coach, slicking his sweaty hair back away from his face, feeling some wayward strands fall forward anyway. "I was supposed to be meeting my family for a consolation dinner right now."

"I'm sure they'll understand, given the circumstances," Vid said, smile never leaving his face.

"They'll be pissed I only got them stand tickets."

"I made arrangements already. They'll be at the grandstand," Coach said.

Fire's brows flew to his hairline. "That's some gambling you did there, old man. I know you knew it was possible, but what if I completely bombed? Those tickets are expensive."

"I hedged my bets."

Fire narrowed his eyes. "Did you put money on me?"

"That would be highly unethical and illegal given my position."

"That isn't a no," Vid said, trading a suspicious look with Fire.

"Racers!" a man said from the doorway, holding an earpiece. "We're ready for you."

Coach moved that way without another word, and Fire huffed a laugh, shaking his head as he followed after.

The grandstand was just as Fire remembered it. Well...grand. It was a huge stage, barriers blocking it from a pit that separated it from the crowd. Guards were placed throughout in case anyone got any funny ideas about hopping or flying over.

Three large podiums of differing heights sat in the dead center of the stage, and as they were called one by one, they settled onto them to face the masses.

Fire spotted his family after some effort, and his heart swelled to see their ecstatic faces. His mom had been crying but obviously trying to hide it, and his dad was yelling like he was competing with his brother, who was doing the same. His little sister Lils had Julie on her hip, who was holding a handmade sign with his name on.

Fire had to blink his eyes to rid them of the sting, zoning in to see the chairman of the RA approaching him with a medal. They did the usual handshake and head nod before he moved on to Speed, whose face was pinched like he was sucking on lemons.

The chairman approached Zero last, carrying the oversized trophy under one frail arm, the other extended for a handshake.

Zero reluctantly shook it, looking like he'd rather be doing anything else. Fire bit down on his laugh, surprised how little it was affecting him being down on the lowest podium on the grandstand. He was still surprised he'd made it *at all*.

The trophy was handed over next, looking actually normal sized when passed into Zero's huge hands, and then the chairman shuffled off, fragile wings following him.

The host approached with a microphone.

"The winner of the seventy-fifth annual Circle Circuit, ladies and gentlemen!" he said, and the crowd let out a roar of cheers and clapping, signs with Zero's name waving around.

A trio of women all approached with oversized champagne bottles and flowers in hand, handing them to each of them. Flashes were going off, and Anna stood to the side, clearly directing the photos of him and which news outlets they would be going to.

"Zero, how do you feel at this moment? After a string of second-place finishes, you finally got your hands on the first-place spot," the host said.

The crowd quieted down for Zero's response.

Zero's dark eyes and placid expression swept over his surroundings before leaning forward to say in a barely there rumble, "I didn't win first place."

There was a stunned silence before the host laughed it off. "No need to be humble. You have the evidence sitting right there in your hands!"

Zero shoved the trophy at the host and went to step off the podium to everyone's shock. Fire's own eyes were bugging out of his head.

"Y-You can't be serious," the host stuttered, barely avoiding being trampled.

"I don't win on technicalities," Zero said gruffly.

"The crash with Speed?" the host asked, baffled. "That was ruled as legal."

"Not that one."

Eyes moved to Fire.

"But it wasn't a technicality," Fire spoke up, brow furrowed. "I injured myself. You won fair and square, Zero."

Zero looked back at him, eyes going to Fire's still-trembling wings. "Next season we'll race again and see who wins."

And with that statement, he walked off the grandstand to a circus of press and questions and his own gapemouthed team, singlehandedly making history as the first person to ever refuse a title.

"Well...well..." The host looked around himself in stupefied confusion. He rushed to the chairman, who looked decidedly unimpressed and was already consulting with other members of the association in a huddle.

Fire cleared his throat and ruffled the back of his windswept hair. "Ahem...this is kinda awkward..."

He could see the ripple of uncertainty moving through the crowd, a hum of whispering as they tried to guess what would happen next.

"By ruling," the host said, repeating what the chairman whispered into his ear. "If the first-place winner forfeits the position, it goes to the next-fastest time!"

Speed blinked, then fist-pumped into the deathly silence. "Hell yeah! I fucking won! I'm the champion! Wooo!"

"Not that fucking guy." Fire rolled his eyes and groaned, leaning around to look in the direction Zero had walked off in. "Zero, come back and take the trophy! You've let an idiot win. Zero!"

Speed snatched the trophy from the host and jumped to the main podium to pose. There was a scattering of cheers from some of his supporters, but mainly, everyone was completely confused.

The host cleared his throat. "Well, uh—hey! That's mine!"

"You were doing a terrible job. Someone needed to take it away from you," an imperious, *beautifully* familiar voice said.

Fire snapped his head around to see Rio standing there, microphone in hand. Fire rubbed his eyes to make sure he wasn't hallucinating. But when he opened them again, it was to Rio shoving Speed off the top podium and taking his place like it was his right.

"Fuck me," Fire heard Anna say. "Nobody fucking tells me anything. I quit. Seriously this time."

He couldn't focus on her. Fire's eyes were starved for the sight of Rio. His long legs, the elegant lines of his body, his straight-tipped nose that invited kisses and his whiskey-brown eyes. Fire's body wanted to move and touch, to kiss and drown. To grab hold and let the pain seep away.

He had to remind himself he couldn't anymore. That Rio had put that space between them. Had taken Fire's heart and left it outside in the cold without a word. It hurt to see him as much as he craved it.

Why the hell was Rio here?

"Hello," Rio said, observing the crowd. "I'm sure you're all waiting with bated breath for whatever that moron wants to say about his fake win, but I have something more important I need to say."

"Hey!" Speed yelled, twin spots of color blooming on his cheeks. "Who the hell do you think you are?"

Fire growled, rejection or not, stepping forward on instinct. "His name's—"

"Rio." Fire's heart lurched at Rio's admittance, and Rio looked over for the first time and met his eyes. "Just...Rio."

Holy fuck.

"And I'm here to say a few things," he said. "To my mate. James."

Fire's heart stuttered in his chest, and the adrenaline that kept his wings stretched gave way to weakness in the face of the one person he wanted the most standing there. The pain he had been feeling since Rio had left ebbed and flowed, as if desperate to disappear but unsure if it could.

He watched Rio as he waited for Fire's reaction to being called out in front of everyone. The wounded part of him wanted to watch him struggle and sweat, but it was drowned out by the instinct to comfort his mate. He nodded to let him know he was listening, the small motion bolstering Rio.

"Okay, first of all," Rio said as the cameras went off madly, focusing on them both as best as they could. "Congratulations on ending your season in third place. With the injury and...everything. I'm really proud of you."

Fire gave him a hesitant smile, bashful now that his mate was the one singing his praises.

"Also, it's good you didn't win first place because that thing—" He pointed to the trophy still clutched in Speed's greedy hands. "—is hideous. I don't know who designs these, but...no. Just no."

And there was the Rio he knew. The diva that just had to voice a complaint about everything and at every point he could. God, Fire felt empty without him. And even though he was standing within reach, he still wasn't his, and it ached.

"Trophy aside," Rio continued, eyes darting to the enraptured crowd before locking back on him. "I owe you an apology."

He looked like he was struggling to get the words out. But they came anyway. Just for Fire.

"I didn't treat you like a mate should," Rio said. "I put other things before you...before us, and I shouldn't have done that. You're not a secret. And I'm not ashamed to be with you. I...I should have made that clear to you. I should have put you first."

Fire wanted to move. Wanted to go to him and hold him and tell him he didn't have to do any of this as long as he was back. They could talk in private, just the two of them. All the things Fire needed to hear from Rio could be just for him.

But he also knew his Rio. And he had to do what he set his mind to. Grand gestures and nuclear options included.

So he took a few tiny steps closer, just enough to let the edge of his wing brush against Rio's legs. To let him know he was there with him.

Rio looked at him, microphone clutched in his hand in front of his mouth, but he wasn't saying a word. The crowd around him was getting restless and fidgety, the press shouting questions at them the longer Rio stayed quiet.

Fire quirked an eyebrow at him.

"You're actually going to make me say it?" Rio asked, looking like he was going to break out in hives if the words touched his lips.

"It's your show, gorgeous," Fire said with a shrug, knowing it would drive Rio up the wall.

Sure enough, he scowled, white-knuckling the microphone.

"I'm sorry," he said finally. "I was wrong, and I'm sorry. I'll be a better mate for you from now on. If you'll have me."

The words barely hit before Fire was scrambling for him, stepping up and pulling him into his arms. He held him close, covering his lips with his own, ears ringing with the sound of the microphone hitting the floor.

It screeched, but Fire didn't care. The only things he could focus on were Rio's fingers in his hair and his tongue pushing into his mouth.

He was back.

He had him back, and he wasn't letting go ever again.

Through the haze of rejection pains dissipating and his mate in his arms again, he heard the crowd roaring. The flashes of cameras penetrated through closed eyelids, and something wet started hitting his skin in droplets.

"What..." Rio started, detaching himself from Fire and looking around.

Fire did the same, laughing at the sight of Coach and Vid spraying champagne over them both while Speed screeched in the distance about all the attention being pulled from him on his big day.

Rio complained about his clothes, the press shot questions at them, and all Fire wanted was to be away from them all.

To take Rio and hide him away.
So that was exactly what he did.

CHAPTER TWENTY-ONE

RIO

He wasn't sure he could breathe.

One moment, he was standing on the podium, holding the microphone and declaring his love for Fire in front of everyone watching, and the next...

Fire pushed him inside a stuffy locker room and pressed him against the closed door, where Rio surrendered fully.

His wings spread around him like a pink cushion, flattened against the door and the wall behind him, the chains on them rattling loudly.

He tilted his head back to let Fire kiss his neck, bite the lobe of his ear, chase the taste of champagne drops off his skin, grip his thighs and hoist him up until he was holding him in his arms.

"James..." Rio breathed, slipping his fingers into Fire's hair and pulling the strands dampened with sweat and alcohol. "Sweaty. Sticky. Ew."

Fire barked out a laugh between kisses.

"Can't believe you're here, princess," Fire said against the skin of Rio's neck, panting and trembling as he held him. "Can't believe I get to have you."

"You do," Rio said. "I'm yours."

Fire unlatched his lips from Rio's neck and looked up, eyes blazing with want and skin flushed from his race. He stared into Rio's eyes, the intensity of it all making Rio squirm. The way Fire looked at him, the way he zeroed in on every little thing on Rio's face would never stop making Rio feel shy.

He wasn't used to being known so well. To being seen not just for the persona he presented to the world.

"Promise," Fire said, after a long moment of silence, and Rio slid his fingers from Fire's messy hair to his cheeks.

"I promise," he whispered, leaning forward to catch his lips in a kiss. "I promise. I'm here to stay. No more running or hiding."

Fire watched him for another moment, and Rio knew he was looking for any trace of insecurity on his face. Any sign that Rio would disappear on him again. It hurt, but he understood. He had fucked up beyond reason. But Fire wouldn't find what he was looking for. He wouldn't find hesitation or doubt. It wasn't there anymore.

He knew Fire realized it too because he let out the most feral growl Rio had ever heard and attacked Rio's lips again. His tongue pushed past to play with his, running over his teeth and mapping out the planes of his mouth. It was all Rio could do to hold on.

Fire's hands left his thighs and traveled up, cupping his ass for a moment before they slid even higher, pushing past the tight waistband of his jeans. Warm, rough fingers found sensitive skin and squeezed tight, one finger straying between his cheeks to brush over his hole.

God, they were still hungry for each other. Still insatiable. Still unable to stop themselves from doing something so intimate in a place everyone could catch them.

Did Rio care?

No.

He couldn't.

He pushed his hips down as best as he could, rolling them slightly to make Fire's touch press harder against the spot where he needed him the most.

"James, please," Rio keened when the tip of Fire's finger slipped inside him, dry and rough against sensitive skin.

"You want this, princess?" Fire asked roughly, lips latching onto the underside of Rio's chin.

"Yes," Rio gasped.

"Here? In public, where everyone can hear us? Anyone could come in and catch us?" Fire said, pulling his hands out and pinning Rio to the door with his body. His hands ran over him, yanking his t-shirt off and unbuttoning his jeans, yanking them down over his ass until the cold air hit the overheated entrance to his body.

"Yes, just do it," Rio said through clenched teeth, nails digging into the smooth leather of Fire's racing uniform.

God he looked amazing in it.

The tight black material clinging to him, the blood-red of his wings matching the flames on his uniform. He looked like a gorgeous demon, and Rio wanted him desperately.

"Please," he added softly, willing to beg, willing to let go completely just to be one with Fire. Just to feel him again. "Missed you. So much."

"I missed you too," Fire said. He leaned away from Rio, unzipping his uniform. "I'll have to put you down."

"NO!" Rio grabbed for his shoulders, absolutely not okay with being put down even for a second.

"I need to take this off, babe," Fire said. "And I need to get lube..."

"Leave the suit on," Rio growled, one hand reaching between them, pushing Fire's zipper down and reaching into his suit. "No lube..."

He found Fire bare, hissing when he realized he didn't have any underwear on. He pulled out his cock, lining it up with his own and tugging.

"You like the suit, gorgeous?" Fire asked with a knowing grin, and Rio nodded, biting his lip as he watched their cocks sliding through the circle of his fist together. Like they belonged. They fit perfectly.

He let go for a moment to do something he never thought he'd do in his life. He brought his palm up and licked it, broad strokes of his tongue making it slick and wet.

He took them back in hand, jerking them both together, throwing his head against the door as Fire muffled his moans in the juncture between Rio's neck and shoulder.

It was filthy and feral and everything Rio knew the two of them would be together. Hot and all-consuming and perfect.

"James," he whined, desperate to come but needing something, missing something. "Please..."

Fire nodded and brought his hand back to Rio's ass, spreading his cheeks and brushing his finger against his entrance again. He circled it a few times, pressing the tip inside, and Rio was gone.

He spilled over his own hand, using the come to speed up the movement. He forced himself to keep his eyes open to look at Fire. Look at his mate as he brought him to the edge and made him feel the highest form of pleasure someone could feel.

Rio was making him tremble like that. Rio was making him groan and hiss and push himself harder into his hand until his hips stuttered, and he bowed his back over Rio, spilling and mixing his come with Rio's. Joining them together once again.

Their breaths echoed around the empty locker room, their bodies pressed together as they struggled to hold themselves up.

"Damn," Fire said, and Rio, while usually a fan of a richer vocabulary, had no choice but to agree.

Fire's arms started shaking with exertion, and he finally put Rio down, not letting go of him even when his feet touched the ground. He held him close, kissing his damp forehead and lids that finally slid closed.

Rio felt his lips traveling over his cheeks, the tip of his nose, and his chin before settling on his lips, fluttering and gentle. Slow, now that the initial hunger was sated. His own hands ran over Fire's body, fingers finding trembling muscles, and Rio could hear his breath still coming out in puffs.

But it wasn't until Fire's knees buckled from under him and he stumbled that he pulled away from the kiss.

"Fire?" he asked, gripping his shoulders to support him and pushing him back to look into his face. "Are you okay?"

"Just tired," Fire said, giving a wan smile. "The race was brutal."

He wasn't looking Rio in the eye, though.

"I think you're lying to me, and I don't like it," Rio said. "You've held me up plenty of times before. Even after training all day. You've never been this tired."

He watched dozens of things flit over Fire's face before it settled on resigned acceptance. "I was in pain the entire race."

"Your wings were hurting?" Rio asked, stomach lurching. "But Vid said they were okay to race, just not to overdo. Did you lie to him too?"

"My wings are okay, Rio," Fire said, squeezing his hips to calm him down. "It's just... Look...before I tell you everything, I need you to know I was completely safe, we had a plan in place for any eventuality, and nothing bad was about to happen to me. Can you trust that?"

"You're scaring me," Rio said, looking at his mate.

"I raced with rejection pains," Fire said finally, and Rio felt like he'd been slapped in the face.

"But...I didn't... I never..." He looked up at Fire with wide eyes, everything inside him screaming in fear and protest.

Images of his dad groaning as he prepared for his last race, memories of him tumbling from the air and landing on his wings. Echoes of doctors telling him he wouldn't be waking up. All because he'd raced with rejection pains. His brain was flooded in moments, and he felt himself breaking down.

"I could have lost you," he said, gripping Fire's suit in his fists and pulling him close. "I didn't reject you. I'd never do that... Fire, please. I didn't know. I didn't know you felt rejected. I'm sorry. I'm so sorry."

"Rio." Fire hushed him, gripping his cheeks and thumbing his tears away. "Listen to me. I told you I was okay. Coach and Vid both knew, and we had a plan in place. I was ready to finish the race last. I just needed to finish it. I needed that for myself."

"But..."

"I don't blame you, and I forgive you," Fire said. "I'm here, and I'm safe, and I'll never put myself in danger and risk losing everything I care for. I promise."

"I don't reject you," Rio whispered against his chest, pushing the words into his skin, hoping they'd stay etched in there for good. "You're my mate."

"And the pain is gone now," Fire said. "I'm very tired, though, so...shower?"

Rio nodded, sniffling softly, feeling like he looked worse than he ever had. There was come drying on his stomach, champagne and sweat sticking to his skin, and he was sure his eyes were red and his nose was runny.

"Yes, please," he said, allowing Fire to lead him to the locker room showers as he tried to calm himself down. He felt like he'd been put in a washing machine of emotions, the only thing grounding him being Rio's hand firmly in his.

Fire dematerialized his wings and shed his uniform, unpeeling the fabric from his sweaty skin slowly. He reached into the shower and turned the water on. The warm steam filled the small space around them in seconds and Fire turned to him expectantly.

"Gonna wear your jeans in the shower too?"

Rio snapped out of his thoughts, looking down and realizing he really had no better option. He pulled his jeans off and folded them on a bench in front of the shower. He reached back and unclasped his wing chains, pulling them off and draping them over the bench to avoid them tangling.

Completely naked, he folded his wings in and retook Fire's hand, letting him pull him under the stream of hot water.

"Feels good," he groaned, leaning his back against Fire's chest, feeling his hands roam all over him, washing the sweat and the dried come off of him.

"All this time and I've never seen your tattoos before," Fire said, leaning back and tracing them with the tips of his fingers.

Rio felt nervous suddenly, waiting for Fire's comment on them. They were swirly and soft, much like his physical wings. The lines weren't crisp and clear like Fire's. They blurred in with his skin, making them look lighter than the usual tattoo. Would Fire...

"They're gorgeous," Fire said, dropping his head to kiss the top of the tattoo. Rio melted against him.

He turned in his arms and fused their lips together, forgetting about everything else in the world. Nothing existed but him and his mate. Together. To think he'd almost lost it all.

Silence and steam blanketed them, and Rio never wanted to come out of their little cocoon.

"Do you want to talk about it?" Fire broke the silence after all, as water cascaded down their bodies. Rio pressed harder into his chest, catching the warm drops on his lips as he kissed his shoulder.

"No, not really," he said, shaking his head, but he knew he should probably share with someone.

"You make for a very cute liar, you know?" Fire said, holding him close, and Rio scowled up at him.

"I am not cute," he complained, flicking Fire's chest. He reached behind him to grab Fire's very generic bodywash from a little shelf. "And this is a tragedy in a plastic bottle. I can hear your skin crying."

"It smells nice," Fire said, and Rio popped the bottle open, sniffing the top of it before scrunching his nose.

"It smells like someone explained what a lemon was to a robot and told him to create something lemon-scented," Rio said, squeezing some of the bodywash into his hands and reaching for Fire.

He needed to ground himself with the feeling of his skin under his fingers. He soaped up his chest, running his hands up and down until Fire's tan skin was covered in tiny, pale yellow bubbles. He drew shapes into it, focusing a bit too hard on reaching every inch of skin in front of him.

It helped his mind settle.

"I told them I was not giving you up," Rio said, pushing on Fire's shoulder to make him turn around. He started the same meticulous routine there as well. "I told them their manipulation wouldn't work. I wasn't my mother. I wasn't picking wealth or fun over family. I was picking my mate over everything else."

He felt the muscles under Fire's skin shift and tremble at his words. He smoothed his hands over them gently, reveling in the contact after being without it for so long.

"I take it it didn't go over too well?" Fire asked, and Rio slid his hands down to Fire's waist, wrapping them around him and leaning against Fire's back.

"It went exactly how I imagined it would," he said. "They threatened to cut me off, threatened to never contact me again, to never allow me to step foot inside their house again. To leave me without family..."

"Rio—"

"The thing is," Rio cut him off. "I don't care."

"That's another lie, princess," Fire said, and Rio sighed, resting his forehead between Fire's shoulder blades.

"Fine, it is," Rio said. "I do care. They were the only family I had for years. I wanted to have both if I could, but they made it impossible. They wouldn't budge and I left without them accepting it. So they'll most likely make good on their threats. Come next week, I doubt I'll be the Charmichael heir anymore. I'll need to find somewhere else to live, some way to make money....but..."

He trailed off, feeling like voicing his thoughts out loud would just make him too vulnerable. But it was Fire. If he was to be vulnerable in front of anyone, wouldn't Fire be the obvious choice for it?

"But?" Fire prompted, and Rio let go of his waist, walking around him to look into his eyes.

"But they're not the only family I have anymore," Rio said. "I have you now. You're my family."

"I am, princess," Fire said, lifting his hand up to caress his cheek. "I will always be here for you. No strings attached, no conditions. Just you and me."

"Always?" Rio asked, and Fire nodded.

"Always," he said. "I love you, Rio."

Rio's heart stuttered in his chest. The first time anyone had ever told him they loved him since his dad passed away. The first time he'd heard the words as an adult.

And they meant so much. They carried so much in them.

A promise of a future they'd build together. A promise of a lifetime of being protected and supported and challenged and driven up the wall by the best, most infuriating, most amazing person he had ever met. A lifetime of loving and being loved in return. Like Fire said, without any stipulations or expectations. Loved just because. Loving just because.

He blinked away a tear that threatened to spill. He looked up at Fire, rose on his tiptoes, and wrapped himself around his naked body. His arms went around his neck, and his fingers snuck back into Fire's hair. Their eyes met, and Rio felt truly seen, maybe for the first time in his life.

He had never felt more confident than in that moment.

"I love you too," he said, giggling when Fire picked him up and spun him around in the confined space, his slippery body sliding out of his arms a little bit as he clung to him.

Fire set him down again, raining kisses on his face wherever he could until they were both breathless and spent. He cradled him to his chest and held the back of Rio's head as he leaned into his neck and just breathed him in. The water still ran. The steam in the shower kept them hidden.

"Princess?" Fire called when the water already turned lukewarm.

"Hm?" Rio hummed from where his face was buried in Fire's neck.

"Remember how you promised you were mine and you weren't going anywhere?"

"It happened like ten minutes ago," Rio said, and Fire pinched his side, making him yelp.

"Did you mean it?" he asked, and Rio looked up, scrunching his brow.

"Why?" he asked, suspicious.

"Did you?" Fire asked, and Rio glared.

"To be determined. What did you do?" he asked, and Fire smiled.

"I ate chips out of your bowl," he said, shaking his head when Rio puffed up. "In my defense, you were gone, and I was very, very angry."

"You ate chips..." Rio bit through his teeth, feeling a flush run to his cheeks and his hackles rising.

"You promised," Fire reminded him. "You love me, remember?"
"CHIPS!" Rio screeched, and Fire kissed the tip of his nose.
"No takebacks, though," Fire said. "Mine."

EPILOGUE

"There aren't actual fleas here, are there?" Rio asked, nose scrunched up under his sunglasses.

He was staring at a huge arch in the middle of the street, leading into something that looked like it came straight out of his worst nightmares.

Booth after booth and table after table lined the street behind the arch, filled with an assortment of objects so incredibly random Rio couldn't find rhyme or reason to it if he tried.

"What the hell?" he asked, and Harriet chuckled.

"It's a flea market, darling," Harriet said.

"Yes, I can see the sign," he said. "Why is it outside? And why is everything jumbled up like that? What brands are in there? Also you never responded about the fleas. I'm very anti-flea."

He heard Fire laughing behind him, and he turned around to glare at him. He didn't stop laughing, so Rio figured his sunglasses somewhat ruined the effect.

"It's not funny," he sniped, and Fire shook his head.

"No, you're right," he said. "It's fucking hilarious."

"Language," Harriet said.

"English, Mom," Fire said, and she smacked his shoulder.

"Don't sass me," she said. "This is a big moment for Rio, and he needs our support."

"He is going to buy secondhand goods, not defend the world from alien invasion," Fire said, and Rio whipped off his sunglasses, glaring at them both now in full force.

"Secondhand?" he said. "This stuff was owned by someone else? Like...used by someone else? And now you want me to buy it? For my nest?"

He had no idea where they got the notion that Rio, of all people, would be okay with buying used stuff. Had they met him before?

"They have cute things," Harriet said, and Rio shook his head.

"Absolutely not," he said, turning on his heel and marching toward the car.

He got a few steps in before Harriet hooked her hand under one of his and Fire did the same on the other side.

"You'll be fine, princess," Fire said as they pulled him backward through the arch. "Nobody ever died from buying secondhand."

"I might," Rio said, tempted to let his heels drag across the floor to make things harder on them. But they were his good shoes, and he didn't want them ruined.

"I'll protect you," Fire said, and Rio scoffed.

"No, you won't," Rio said, and Fire turned his head to kiss his cheek.

"I promise, if any fleas come your way, I'll fend them off," Fire said, and Rio actually dug his heels in this time.

"So there are fleas?" he asked, and Harriet reached around him to smack Fire on the back of his head.

"Stop making it worse," she said. "No, Rio. There are no fleas. In fact, a lot of good things can be found at places like this. Like designer, vintage items people don't want anymore."

"Why would someone not want a vintage designer piece?" Rio asked, wiggling around until he was turned the right way again.

"Sometimes they need the money so they sell them. Sometimes they don't know they have a treasure on their hands," she said.

"And sometimes, they just don't care and want to get rid of their stuff."

"So where are these things then?" he asked, and she smiled.

"That's part of the charm," she said. "You don't know until you find one."

That sounded like a challenge to Rio if he'd ever heard one. He stormed off to the first booth and he scanned the items on it. Nothing stood out to him, but there were countless other booths and tables in front of them.

With a determination only a person on a mission could have, Rio dragged them both around from one booth to the next, picking up items, inspecting them, talking to salespeople and having more fun than he could remember having in a long while. It turned out, if you knew how, you could get the salespeople to change the price to a lower one and save money. Which was a really good thing now that Rio was using his own paycheck to buy things.

His grandparents still hadn't reached out and accepted him back into their family, but they'd also remained quiet about him being disowned. So there was still hope, Rio thought.

Harriet left them at a halfway point, tired and hungry. Rio gave her an absentminded hug and left her to say her goodbyes to Fire as he wandered over to inspect a carved wooden chest that looked very pretty to him.

Before he knew it, the sun started to set, and the vendors started packing their booths up.

Rio was pulled out of his frenzy by an empty table he hadn't even had the chance to look over. He turned to Fire with a pout.

"They're gone!" he said, and Fire nodded.

"Yeah, gorgeous," he said. "You can't expect them to spend the night here."

"But I didn't find any vintage things," Rio said. "Maybe they were at these tables."

"Maybe," Fire said. "Or maybe someone else got to them first."

"But that's not fair," Rio said, and Fire snorted.

"Flea markets aren't fair," he said. "But you did get a lot of other things."

"What?" Rio asked, and Fire lifted several overflowing bags into the air.

Rio had no clue where those came from.

"What are those?" he asked.

"Stuff you picked for your nest," Fire said, and Rio stared at him.

"I didn't get anything for my nest, James," he said, and Fire threw his head back.

"Yes, you did, Uxorious," he said.

"Don't call me that," Rio said, reaching for one of the bags and digging through to find several small pillows, the little chest he saw, a few candles, and a throw blanket in the most amazing color combination imaginable.

He dug through another and found a framed photo of a beautiful sunset, some porcelain knickknacks, and a stuffed animal with buttons for eyes. It was hideous. Rio loved it.

A canvas bag hanging off of Fire's shoulder held a small stained-glass lamp, a matching framed mirror, and a silver brush and comb set that came in a beautifully ornate metal box.

Invigorated by the findings, he inspected all of the bags and found more stuff he absolutely didn't remember buying at any point, but every last one of them spoke to him somehow.

Every item was uniquely stunning and pretty and grabbed his attention. Every last one was shiny and sparkly and colorful in a way Rio had always reacted to, but he'd had to survive in muted pastels and beiges.

He could already imagine his nest decorated with everything they'd got. Fire had let Rio run wild online, and he'd found a set of armchairs he liked and a dresser that cost too much to hold random stuff Rio wanted in his nest, but Fire didn't say a word.

He'd just hauled everything in with Vid and Zero's help, set it up the way Rio wanted, and then left him to it.

He didn't ask for a key to his nest. Instead, he stayed true to his word and allowed Rio to have a spot that belonged just to him. Looked exactly like Rio wanted it to.

"This is amazing," Rio said after he had rummaged through the last bag Fire held and looked up to find Fire watching him with a smile on his face. "What?"

"Nothing," Fire said, picking the bags back up. "Just happy to see you happy."

Rio felt his cheeks flush at the words, but he stuck his nose up and squared his shoulders. He would not be reduced to a simpering mess by a sweet mate. He was better than that.

He strode past Fire, who leaned in as he was walking by.

"Love you, princess," he whispered, and Rio's resolve crumbled.

He spun on his heel, catching Fire's cheeks between his palms and leaning in to kiss him as hard as he could.

In the middle of the street.

In the middle of the bustle of people ready to head home to their own families.

Rio wrapped himself around his mate, his family, not caring about who might be seeing them.

Because Rio was a lot of things.

But he was never ashamed to flaunt his riches in front of people.

And Fire was the biggest treasure he had ever had.

The Inescapable series continues with Vid's story.
Turn the page for a sneak peek...

BOND

Vid was going to be arrested for murder by the end of the day.

He ran his hand over his bleached hair and tugged at the new piercing in the top of his ear. It still stung, and he was hoping it would distract him from what was right in front of him.

And what was in front of him was an annoying, whiny baby shaped like an adult racer.

Speed was strapped into wing stretchers, a small machine that helped loosen them up before training and, in theory, didn't hurt at all. The movements were slow and natural, extending the joints and helping flexibility and mobility of the wings for airtime.

Vid had been doing his job for years now. He had used stretchers before every single training session with his racers. Nobody had ever complained about them being painful.

And…to be fair, Speed wasn't complaining either. He was freaking yelling at the top of his lungs.

"Vid! Vid, how much longer?" he called out, wiggling in his seat and trying to pull himself out of the machine. "This fucking hurts, and it's been going on forever."

"It's been three minutes," Vid deadpanned as he approached, rolling his eyes so hard he was pretty sure he saw his own brain matter.

He sat down on a bench press opposite the machine and put his elbows on his knees, letting one arm hang down between them and using the other to prop his cheek up on a fist.

"Well, how much longer?" Speed asked, blue eyes glaring at him.

"Until you complete the full extension for a full set."

"What does it look like I'm doing?"

Vid eyed his silver wings boredly. "Not extending."

"Like fuc—"

"I'll count them out for you," Vid interrupted with a faux smile. "Ready? One..."

Speed growled and extended his wings out and in quickly. The point was to hold for a second before retracting slowly, and Speed knew it. He'd used the machine before, but obviously he was used to cutting corners. Vid sighed. People hiring him just to ignore his expertise really irked him.

"One..." he counted again.

"I just did one!" Speed thundered.

"One," he repeated, meeting his ire steadily with an impassive gaze.

Speed did the same thing one more time, and Vid just about threw the towel in, feeling a massive headache beginning to bloom.

"Listen, Speed," he said, pinching his nose. "I don't know what your routine is with your regular sports therapist. I'm sure they're a lovely person with the patience of a saint. I do my job a bit differently, it seems. I want my clients to get the best out of the exercises I put them through. They're not just there as a pseudo warm-up you whine about to get to the part you wanna do."

"I hear Fire complain all the time," Speed scoffed, and Vid snorted at the mention of his name.

"Point," Vid said. "However, he does what I tell him to do. Properly."

Speed glared at him, taking the bait exactly the way Vid intended him to.

"I can do anything he can," he said. "Set the timer."

"'Course you can, buddy," Vid said condescendingly, doing as he was told.

Coach owed him takeout for the rest of his life after roping him into taking over for Speed's therapist, who was away on honeymoon for two weeks.

Two weeks.

And it was only day one.

Vid walked away after he saw Speed was actually taking it seriously to set up an obstacle course and clear some room for Speed to run it a few times with his coach. It wasn't his job at all, but at that point, he was willing to retile the bathrooms just to be away from Speed.

The obstacles he saw Speed's coach use all required careful calculation, some precision maneuvering, and tactics to get around without losing altitude or decelerating too much. There was a reason his coach had chosen those exact ones.

And there was a reason the man was nicknamed Speed and not, like…

Accuracy.

Or Brains.

Vid wasn't saying the man was empty-headed, but if you lit a candle next to his ear, his eyes would glow.

He finished the setup just as Speed's coach walked in, coming straight over. He was a man in his late fifties and just as loud as Speed was. Much less obnoxious, though.

"Vid, my boy," the man boomed, coming close and slamming his gigantic palm on Vid's shoulder, nearly making him buckle. "Thanks for setting up."

"No problem," Vid said, flexing the abused area.

"Decided to come on board full time yet?" the coach asked, and Vid shook his head at the millionth iteration of the same question.

Speed wanted Vid to come work for him full time to spite Fire. Conflict of interest prevented Vid from working with both racers. Which would mean leaving Fire. And that wasn't something Vid was ever going to do. Not after what Fire had done for him when Vid was fresh out of school and trying to make a name for himself.

"Sorry." He shrugged. "Too scared of Rio to quit on Fire."

The coach laughed, familiar with Fire's mate. The majority of the current generation's coaches used to race alongside Bullet. They remembered Rio as a stubborn child, and they all stayed well away from adult Rio when he was angry now that he was hanging around the scene again. Vid found it hilarious. And understandable.

"Gotcha," the coach said, nodding his head toward Speed. "He give you any trouble?"

"Just the usual." Vid shrugged.

"Bitching and moaning?"

"Yup."

"I swear to god he's a good kid," the coach said. "If only he came with a mute button, we'd be golden."

Vid laughed just as the stretcher beeped. He walked over to unstrap Speed, who flailed dramatically and cradled his wings around his body, running his fingers over the feathers.

"I never want to do that again," he said, pointing a finger at Coach. "You tell him."

"Sure, kid." The coach nodded. "I'll give it to him in writing. Now fly two laps to warm up properly and hit the course."

"What course?" Speed asked, and Vid pointed to the course he had set up for him.

Speed looked at it and groaned. "Not the maneuvering. I hate it. Can we just—"

"And with that," Vid interrupted, "I have reached my daily limit of complaints. Do try again tomorrow, when the counter is reset."

"See ya tomorrow, kid," the coach said.

Vid gave him a small salute before picking up his stuff and leaving him to deal with his overgrown toddler in whatever way he saw fit. Vid was done.

He greeted a few coworkers on his way out and then made his way to his car. He put his stuff in the trunk and had just flopped into his seat when his phone rang.

"Hello?" Vid picked up the call as soon as he started his car, Rio's voice drifting from the car's speakers.

"*Fire would like to know if you're free to grab drinks with him after training?*" Rio asked.

Vid snorted, pulling out of the parking lot. "And Vid would like to know why Fire can't call him himself."

"*He is currently busy boasting...I mean, showing the kids how to do a vertical spin in the air so he is unable*," Rio said, and sure enough, the sound of kids giggling could be heard in the background.

"Of course he is," Vid said, glancing at the clock. He was running a bit late for his final appointment but had no real plans for the rest of his day other than heading home and vegging out in front of the TV. "Tell Fire we can go grab drinks, sure. My last client is a short home visit close to the Center, so I'll meet him in the parking lot after."

"*We have two groups today, so we'll be done at six*," Rio said.

"Are you coming with?" he asked. The dynamic between Fire and his mate was like free entertainment.

"*I have other plans for the evening*," Rio said, and Vid laughed at the posh voice.

"Well then," he said, stopping at a red light. "Have fun."

"*You as well*," Rio said, hanging up before Vid could say anything else.

The light turned green and Vid turned left, directly into the worst traffic jam he had seen in his entire life.

"Oh, fuck me sideways," he said, opening his window and craning his neck out to try and see what was happening. He saw absolutely nothing but rows and rows of cars stuck behind each other in a long line of misery.

Great.

He'd be late for his appointment.

Almost forty minutes later, he parked the car right in front of the Rec Center, figuring that was safer than hoping for a spot in front of his client's building.

He grabbed his bag and stormed out, locking his car over his shoulder as he sped across the lot. His sneakers hit the gravelly floor of the parking lot, sending him sliding a little as he tried to pick up even more speed.

He had informed his client he'd be running late, but he hated looking unprofessional in any way. Vid had to maintain the best record and reputation he could.

Wrapped up in his own cloud of worry, he didn't exactly watch where he was going other than making sure he was moving in the correct direction.

In his defense, when seeing another person in a clear rush, other people should be watching where they were going. But they weren't.

So he collided with something tall and solid. His bag went flying and his phone jumped several times against his fingers before he managed to get a good enough grip on it to make sure it wouldn't smash.

"Shit," he said, bending down to grab his bag, but someone beat him to it.

Long, thick fingers wrapped around the leather strap and pulled it up, offering it to Vid in the slowest, most mind-numbing way known to mankind.

He was in a hurry, dammit.

"Thank you," Vid said, looking up and coming face to face with a guy that looked around his age.

Thoughts of running late dimmed a little because the guy was really hot. Stupidly so, Vid thought.

He was around the same height Vid was, shoulders broader and thighs thicker than his own. He had dark, messy hair flying every which way and steely gray eyes, sunken into his face a little bit. The pale skin around them was tinted dark, and he looked tired.

Beautiful, still. But tired.

Speaking of tired. It rhymed with fired.

Which was what Vid would be if he didn't stop ogling hot strangers he nearly flattened to the ground.

He gripped the strap of his bag and gave it a tug, the man's fingers slipping away from it as Vid hoisted it up his shoulder.

"Sorry for slamming into you," he said. "You okay?"

The man stared at him without a single word, intensely focused on Vid's face, gray eyes scanning every inch of him.

Vid frowned.

"Um...dude..." He waved a hand in front of the man's face, trying to get his attention. "I asked if you're okay?"

He raised his tone a little bit, and that seemed to kick the man into action.

His lips split into a really wide, quite stunning smile, and his hands came up to grasp Vid's upper arms.

Weird choice of action.

"I'm Mateo," the man said, and Vid frowned.

"Okaaay," he said slowly. "Mateo...I'm very sorry I slammed into you. Like I said, I wasn't watching where I was going."

"That's okay," Mateo said, and Vid really wasn't sure what was up with the breathy voice and the glassy eyes. Surely, he hadn't rattled the man into a concussion. "I'm so glad you did."

"You are?" Vid asked.

What the hell? Kinks really did come in all shapes and sizes, didn't they? Dude liked being mauled over in parking lots. Go figure.

"I couldn't think of anything better," Mateo said, and Vid stared at him for a few long, very long moments before deciding shit was getting a smidge weird for him.

"Right," Vid said. "Well in that case, glad I could make your day. Now if you'll excuse me, I'm really late."

"You can't leave," Mateo said, eyes wide and looking at him as if he'd done something to hurt him.

"Well, no, not when you're holding on to me," Vid said. "So if you don't mind..."

He gave his shoulders a little shimmy.

Mateo frowned, chest rising and falling with rapid breaths and face turning even paler than it had been seconds ago.

Vid could feel his fingers trembling where he was still holding on to him, and he frowned.

"Dude, seriously, are you okay?" he asked again, and Mateo gave him a little shake.

"You don't feel it?" he asked.

Vid widened his eyes at him. "Feel what?"

Mateo didn't explain, looking like he couldn't. He simply stared at him like he wasn't really seeing him, hands loosening their grip and eventually falling back to his sides.

Vid bit his lip, torn between making sure the guy was okay and the ever-pressing clock ticking down on him. In the end it wasn't like he had a choice. He couldn't afford to fuck up his client base.

"Sorry, man. I really got to go," Vid said, skirting around him and then sprinting toward his destination.

One last look over his shoulder before he turned the corner showed Mateo still standing exactly where he had left him, and he felt an answering stir in his heart that was quickly buried.

Also by A. M. Rose

Standalone
Returning Home
mybook.to/Returninghome
Faces
mybook.to/Faces

Daydream, Colorado series
Blindspot
mybook.to/Blindspot

Heartwood
mybook.to/HeartwoodAMRose

Whirlwind
mybook.to/WhirlwindAMRose

Spectral
mybook.to/Spectral

Daydream, Colorado short stories
Daydream (prequel)
mybook.to/Daydream

Mischief
mybook.to/Mischief

Inescapable series
End (Prequel)
bit.ly/InescapableEnd
Storm
mybook.to/InescapableStorm
Dream
mybook.to/InescapableDream
Still (short)
mybook.to/StillShort

Made in the USA
Las Vegas, NV
03 February 2025